The Silken Empress

Robyn Bee

Book Cover by ZeD, Miblart

ISBN 978-1-0689295-0-2

To my own Empress, without whom this story wouldn't exist.

Note

The Silken Empress is a work of fiction. This book is not meant to be an accurate representation of history, though, many of the characters, places, and events in this book are a matter of historical record. I freely admit to modifying that record for my own narrative ends, while at the same time, doing my best to maintain a certain level of historical authenticity.

Any historical inaccuracies within this book (deliberate or not) were made by me, in service to the story I wished to tell.

Chapter One

An Empress's Guard

"Tell God that He made a mistake, dear Father, when He gave me only three holes for pleasure."

I turned those words over in my head, shifting in my seat. I could still remember the moment I'd first heard them, one of the last afternoons I'd spent working in my mother's shop.

The woman who'd borne me was a tough, tight-lipped seamstress who could heave a bolt of silk over her shoulder with one hand and slap a lesson into me with the other.

She was not given to outbursts, though I swear she'd near died of apoplexy that day. "*Failed women,*" she'd spat. "*What's our world come to that the words of whores and painted actresses carry any weight? Remember yourself when you encounter such creatures, my little lion. Hold onto what you know, and make your father and me proud.*"

Guilt twisted my stomach, but I shoved the feeling away. I pushed myself to my feet and made my way to the nearest window. Stretching out before me was Constantinople, the golden capital of the Byzantine Empire and center of the Roman world. I breathed in the scent of nearly half a million people, my eyes wandering out past the Hippodrome's track to take in the city's glittering domes and columned grandeur. There was no place quite like it in all the world. And even now, more than two weeks after my arrival, I often lost my way in its crooked streets.

"Get back to your seat," a voice said.

There was a pair of armored guards in the room with me. I turned to find one of them glaring at me from where he stood before a large, richly carved wooden door.

I scowled, but obeyed, spending the next few moments trying to find a comfortable position in the chair. I quickly gave up, my leg bouncing with restless energy.

In all fairness, my discomfort wasn't the fault of the furniture. This was, without a doubt, the finest chair I'd ever sat in. Its cushion was thick, held up by four intricately carved legs of scented wood. The rest of the small antechamber was just as luxurious. Everywhere I looked, I saw gold and marble and fine pottery. Even the metal that armored the two *Excubitors* was inlaid with gold.

"You're the runner, right?" the guard said. "The soldier who won the Emperor's foot race?"

I tried not to dwell too much on the memory of that race. I love to run, but that race had been brutal. The heat had been intense, though we were still early into summer. I'd run for almost an entire day, racing against the thousand others who had decided to compete.

"I am."

"You can't be much of a soldier, then, if all you can do is run." He bared his teeth, and his partner beside him snickered. I glared at the Imperial guardsman, biting back a retort. The man's chest was broad beneath his armor. He was handsome, with the sort of bright teeth and smooth skin that only a life of wealth could provide.

"Watch how you look at me, plebeian," he sneered. "You don't belong here."

I looked away. This guy might be a prissy little pick, but he was right. I shouldn't be here. I was *stratiotai*, an infantryman, as my father and his father had been. My place was in the legion's shield wall, my sandals stained with the dirt of kingdoms that dared raise their blades against Rome.

What in God's name was I doing in the Emperor's own palace?

Time passed, and I squirmed in this damnable seat as my thoughts drifted back to my mother. I could picture her face and knew exactly what she'd say to her only child in so exalted a place.

"*... three holes for pleasure.*"

She'd remind me of those words, would command me to take myself from here and close myself off to whatever else that failed woman had to say.

My mother didn't care that this woman would eventually be crowned *Augusta*. It didn't matter that she'd risen from the flea-riddled pallets of the city's meanest brothel to command the wealth of half the world. This was a woman on whose shoulders rested the fate of millions. She was the co-ruler of the Mediterranean's mightiest empire, a woman whose beauty and ruthless intelligence were already being woven into legend.

She was Theodora, Empress of Rome.

But no, my mother would care for none of that. She'd hate the fact that I'd been called to meet her.

Finally, the guarded door opened on silent hinges.

I leaped to my feet, stiffening into a salute as a woman emerged. It wasn't the Empress, though as her hobnailed boots rang against the stone floor, I realized that she was unlike any woman I'd ever seen.

"Leontius?" she asked.

This woman wore a breastplate, greaves, and an armored skirt. She carried a heavy, iron-rimmed shield, and a short sword and dagger were strapped to the belt at her waist. The whole of it looked polished and well cared for, made of functional steel that had none of the *Excubitor's* ceremonial brilliance.

This was a *stratiotai's* kit, standard issue amongst the Emperor's legions. It was the twin of the one I'd worn nearly every day since my sixteenth birthday, right down to the helmet she held in the crook of her arm.

"Yes, sir!" I trumpeted, holding my salute as I would for any legion *centenarius*.

The woman's cheeks flushed, and behind her, the guards didn't even try to hide their snickers. I knew why they laughed, of course: it was taking all my self-control not to gape like the world's biggest fish.

Women weren't soldiers. They couldn't be soldiers.

This was a belief woven into the very fabric of our Empire. A woman's place was with her husband, tending to his home, shop, or farm.

"*From crib to hearth to crib to grave*," my mother would say, pinching my cheek. A good woman could be happy nowhere else.

Yet, this woman frowning at me through dark-green eyes fit nowhere within that carefully shaped mold. And though my mind roiled with questions, stuttering disbelief, and my mother's condescending rant, I shoved it all aside to be dealt with later.

I was *stratiotai*, and to see the future, one first had to live through the present.

"I'm Helena, of the Empress's Guard," the woman said. "You will follow me into her highness's quarters."

"Women guarding women," the mouthy *Excubitor* drawled. "You're joining an illustrious order, runner."

The guardswoman, Helena, clenched her teeth. She said nothing more, however, spinning on her heel and marching back through the door. I trotted after her a moment later, biting my tongue over the thousand questions that had popped into my head.

We were in a narrow, spear-straight corridor made of stone with narrow windows. I could see another door at the far end, maybe a few dozen paces away.

"The Empress's wing of the palace starts here," Helena said after a few silent moments. "This is the only entrance."

"Yes, sir," I answered.

She whirled on me, eyes flashing. "Is my gender not clear to you?"

"No, sir!" I cursed inwardly, stepping back. "Sorry, sir! Ma'am!"

"Then what's your fucking problem?"

I felt my heart plummet. Winning the Emperor's foot race was the honor of a lifetime. It gave me the opportunity to step off of the battlefields that were the lot of a *stratiotai* and to serve in the palace instead.

And here I was, insulting the Empress's guard and ruining that chance.

"Nothing," I said. "I just don't know what else to call a superior officer."

She blinked, taken aback. Then, her eyes narrowed, and she searched my face for several long moments. I don't know what she found there, but she seemed to take in the rest of me for the first time. She scrutinized me with an intensity that made me flush. Her eyes drifted down from my bearded face, taking in the light tunica and sandals I wore and tracing the muscles of my limbs. I saw her notice my scars, her eyes returning to linger on my face.

"Helena," she said, at last. "If the Empress approves of you, you'll just call me by name."

"Very well, sir."

She scowled. "Were you even listening?"

"Of course, sir. And as soon as I'm officially sworn into the Empress's Guard I'll be sure to use the proper protocol, sir."

Helena's expression turned to one of disbelief. Then, she laughed. It was a deep, full-bellied sound that thrummed through my chest and seemed to surprise her as much as it did me.

I felt my cheeks burn brighter.

After years in the legion camps, I wasn't too used to being in the company of women whose time I hadn't paid for. That feeling of awkwardness wasn't helped by the strangeness of this situation, and the fact that Helena was intensely beautiful.

Her skin was a warm bronze, touched by the light of the summer sun. Her hair, held back at her forehead by a band of cloth, was a copper-colored wave that tumbled past her shoulders. But Helena's most striking feature was her eyes; they were expressive and dyed a shade of green that I couldn't quite place.

"Fair enough," she said. "And you're right, winning the foot race only gives you the chance for an interview. The Empress has the final say." She paused a beat, then added. "Congratulations, by the way. I was in the Hippodrome when you came in for your final lap."

I straightened. "Thank you, sir."

I opened my mouth to speak again but closed it after an instant's hesitation. Helena smirked, taking pity on my obvious uncertainty.

"You have a question, don't you?"

"No, sir."

"Come on, spit it out."

"Sorry, sir, I just thought that it was the Emperor who chose his *Excubitors*."

"You're right in that," she said. "But we're not *Excubitors*. They're responsible for the Emperor and the whole of the Imperial Palace. Our duties are to the Empress and to her alone. That clear?"

"Yes, sir!" I said, though, of course, her answer had just raised a hundred more questions in me. "Clear as the giant's foot."

I cringed at the slip of my tongue. But to my relief, the air did not regain its earlier tension. Instead, Helena turned to continue down the hallway with a chuckle.

"You're full of surprises."

"Sorry, sir!" I said. "It's an expression from my home. God as my witness, I meant no offense."

"Your home," she said. "Rhodes, right?"

"I—" I blinked. "Yes, sir."

She grinned over her shoulder, an expression that made my heart quicken. "I'm from Lindos, on the eastern side of the island."

"Yes, sir. I know it."

I shoved that information into the same corner of my mind as my mother's voice. I had family in Lindos and had visited it as a boy. To find out that we may have once crossed paths was too much to take in.

"I'm from Rhodos," I said, instead. "The city. Though I haven't been back since I joined the legion."

"It's been a long time for me as well."

We were at the far door now, Helena's hand on an ornate handle. She hesitated a moment.

"A word of advice," she said. "The Empress will not be what you expect. Obey her, and remember that while you're in that room, you're as responsible for her life as I am."

Without giving me a chance to respond, the armored woman threw open the door and we entered Empress Theodora's private chambers.

Chapter Two

An Oath to the Empress

We entered what appeared to be a sort of salon. It was large and airy, kept cool by an open balcony and several wide windows. The sounds of the city drifted in with the breeze, along with the briny scent of the sea and harbor. The smell was noticeable, but not sharp, muted as it was a few smoldering sticks of incense.

The walls were stone, the ceiling resting on a half-dozen decorated columns. The stone was decorated with tapestries, art, and golden-hued icons. Beautifully carved wooden chairs, couches, and divans were spread throughout the space.

And lounging on one such divan, a book held delicately in one hand, was the Empress Theodora.

"Highness," Helena said. "This is Leontius."

"*Augusta*!" I said, dropping to my knees and lowering my gaze. "It's an honor!"

"Is it, now?" she said in a voice tinged with laughter. "Stand up, soldier. Let me get a good look at you."

I obeyed, keeping my eyes downcast.

"How do you expect to guard me if you're always looking at the floor?"

Heat crawled up my neck. I stammered an apology and hurriedly lifted my gaze to her. And for a moment, I swear that I couldn't breathe.

I had heard Theodora described a thousand different ways, had heard a hundred different versions of how she'd come to be named *Augusta*. Born in faraway Cyprus, she'd come to Constantinople as a child. Her father had trained bears for the circus, and when he'd died, her family had been doomed to the worst sort of poverty. As she grew, she'd survived as many a young woman had: by trading her body for a roof and something to eat.

Theodora had worked at a brothel, and later as an actress, which many said were the same profession. Today, Constantinople's taverns were full of men who claimed to have known her. They'd wax lyrical about the times they'd had her body, for one night or many. Others would reminisce about her time on stage, their eyes far away as they recounted watching her dance clothed in nothing but a long, red ribbon.

Yet, none of those stories could prepare me for the sight of her.

She was young, not far into her third decade. She wore a long, wine-colored *stola,* the kind of dress that my mother had often made for Rhodos' wealthiest ladies.

The Empress set her book down and stood in one smooth motion. Then, she glided towards me on bare feet, silent, save for the whisper of fabric.

Her dress was made from the thinnest sort of silk, the material clinging to a figure that retained its dancer's curves and strength. Dark, intelligent eyes considered me from above a long neck that swept up gracefully from her chest, a golden chain disappearing down into the space between her breasts.

My eyes lingered for a moment as I wondered what else was hidden there, safe and out of sight.

How warm the gold must be, I thought, cradled against her.

The Empress smirked, and I wrenched my eyes back to the floor, mortified. My face was a bonfire of burning horror. What in God's name was I doing? She could have me killed! She—

"I did not say that you could look away, soldier."

I swallowed and lifted my gaze back up to hers with some difficulty.

Her eyes were wrinkled in a smile. Her skin was smooth, a warm brown, only a few shades lighter than the thick, wavy tresses that cascaded past her shoulders.

"*Stratiotai*, Leontius," she said, stopping to examine me carefully.

The sound of my name passing through her lips made me shiver. "*Au—Augusta*?"

"Am I making you uncomfortable?"

I croaked something, coughed, and then tried again. "No, *Augusta*."

"Good," she said. "Because I am impressed with you, soldier. And that is without taking into account your victory in my husband's race. You fought in Persia, did you not?"

"Ah, yes, *Augusta*, in General Belisarius's army."

"Indeed," she said. "You shared in his great victory at Dara, and in his subsequent defeat at Callinicum mere months ago."

"Yes, *Augusta*."

I did not want to remember those battles against the Sassanid Persians, neither the baking sun and trenches of Dara nor the way their cavalry had swept through us at Callinicum.

She made a small sound in her throat, starting to circle me with slow, measured steps.

"I've spoken to many of your fellow soldiers since the legions have trickled back to the capital. You are well regarded by your comrades."

I ducked my head. "Thank you, *Augusta*."

"A thoughtful man, they all say, one who is serious about his duty. You had few friends amongst your cohort, yet all respected you," the Empress continued. She was past my shoulder now, out of sight. "You enlisted at sixteen years of age. You've served a decade already, and I believe that you would have served another decade if you'd not caught my husband's attention."

I nodded, ignoring the twist in my stomach.

"In short," she said, "an exemplary man."

She completed her circle, once again stopping before me. She considered me for a final few moments, her head tilted to the side.

"He's quite handsome, is he not?"

I coughed hard enough that I had to blink tears from my eyes. Both women laughed.

"I suppose so," Helena said.

"Lean," the Empress said. "A runner, obviously. Well-muscled, though his shoulders are a little too small. I'm not sure about the beard either, though the jaw beneath looks strong."

"It's just a dusting of whiskers, Highness. I don't think it suits him badly."

"Yes, well, you've always liked them rather savage, Helena. Your Rhodian blood, no doubt."

"He's Rhodian too, Highness," the guardswoman said with a smile.

"Figures. I suspect that he will be as uncivilized as you are, then."

The Empress's own smile lightened her words. My palms sweated beneath the attention of these two beautiful women and I tried not to squirm like a virgin in a whorehouse.

"Now," the Empress said. "Lie down. On your back."

The command confused me. But she was my Empress, and so I obeyed. The stone was cool through the linen of my *tunica*.

She smiled down at me. "Your obedience is commendable, soldier. And fear not, you're down there for a reason."

She moved until she stood beside my waist. Her large, dark eyes twinkled as she kept her gaze on my face. Inexplicably, I felt my cheeks redden and I looked away.

"Look at me," she snapped.

My eyes, wide with sudden panic, flew back to her face. Her smile was gone, replaced by a downward twist of her lips.

"Emp— *Augusta*," I stammered, frozen, like a rabbit beneath the eagle's shadow. "Forgive me. Please, I didn't—"

Her smile returned to replace her frown, softening her features and providing a better companion to the sparkle that had never left her eyes.

"Shh," she said. "There's nothing to forgive. I need your eyes to be on me at all times. This is very important."

"I—of course, Empress."

"Good," she said. "You're to guard my life, soldier. I need to be able to trust you. And so, we're going to have a little test."

She lifted one leg, stepping over me so that she straddled my midsection. My body stiffened, but I didn't dare look from her face.

"Very good." She stretched the words into a long exhale, the ending low and breathy. "You'll do very well, I think. Keep your eyes open, soldier, whatever happens."

I nodded, swallowing past my dry throat. There was a heat to her gaze now, a smolder within her that made her skin glow. Her lips were parted, air escaping in slow measured breaths.

"Then, let's begin."

She took one step up my body, and then another. Her movements were smooth and deliberate in their slowness. She flowed forward until

I lost her eyes, the hem of her *stola* sliding over my face so that I was trapped beneath the tent of cloth.

Then, my Empress stopped. I forgot to blink. My heart began to pound, loud enough that I almost didn't hear her speak.

"Are your eyes open, soldier?"

I swallowed, choking out an affirmative.

"Very good," she almost purred. "Now, tell me, what do you see?"

Theodora's bare legs rose above me on either side. Her skin was smooth, darker in the red shadow of her dress. Her flesh curved around the muscles of her calves and thighs, two winding trees whose canopies melded together high above.

My breath hitched.

The shadows were deeper where her legs wove into each other, though there was light enough that I saw the shape of her. No wrap or slip of cloth obstructed my eyes, and my gaze found the curve of her buttocks.

Starting from where her ass disappeared up into the darkness, my gaze ran down along the shadowy crevice between her cheeks and legs, eyes straining for any tantalizing detail within that shifting darkness.

Once I came upon her center, I could go no further. It trapped me, the sight of her. Mesmerized me with its lush, shadow-veiled arches and looping seams.

When I finally spoke, it was with a voice heavy with awe. "I see ... everything."

The Empress made a small sound of pleasure, shifting the muscles of her legs.

"Good," she said, a breath I could barely hear. "Keep your eyes wide, my soldier."

Then, her legs moved. They folded at the knees, two mighty trees cracking at their center, bringing their canopies down to meet the ground beneath.

I didn't breathe, didn't shift, blink, or even think. I was still that rabbit, unable to flee from beneath the glory of the descending eagle.

With her descent, the shadows fled, revealing every curve, every ripe fold and detail of her sex. She stopped a mere finger's breadth above my face, holding herself there and letting my eyes drink in the sight of her.

I let out something like a whimper. At my side, my hands curled into shriveled fists. I was burning, scalded by her nearness and the furnace heat of her flesh.

There was the soft curl of her dark pubic hair, trimmed short and sculpted into an inverted pyramid. That arrow forced my gaze down into the lush smoothness that waited below. Folds of soft pink peeked out from her seam of oiled flesh. Her sex was a silken wonder, a gate to a warm paradise only a chosen few would be admitted. I yearned for it, longed to slip between those lips and lose myself within her.

"Breathe," the Empress murmured. "I want to feel your breath on me."

I obeyed, venting the fire in my chest through my parted lips. My breath swirled around her. She made another small sound, her skin prickling. "Very good."

I inhaled, then released another stream of air to caress her.

"Very, very good," she breathed. "Now, in through your nose. Deeply, my soldier. Bring my scent into you."

Once again, I obeyed, pulling the furnace-hot air into my lungs.

I groaned, flooded with the complex smell of her. It was sweetness and sex and perfumed oil, a scent that was powerfully, intoxicatingly, head-swimmingly feminine. My world blurred. Everything was too hot. My breathing became erratic, my chest heaving as ragged chunks of air were torn from me. I was afire with her, my heart smashing against my ribs.

Then, I heard the Empress let out a soft gasp. Her muscles twitched, and I watched her soft folds quiver, letting slip a faint, glittering trickle of moisture. My breath, my heart, my entire being stilled. All of me focused on that single drop, watching it slide lower and lower; every shiver of her body helping it along its meandering path down her soft folds.

My throat was dry as sun-scorched rock, my tongue thick with a sudden, raging thirst. A taste. I was desperate for a taste. I wanted to drink from her, to bring that soothing wetness into me.

What felt like an eternity later, I sensed more than saw her shift backward. The movement pulled the center of her away from my eyes so that I stared up through the cloth of her dress towards the ceiling of her chamber. And the knife that glinted there.

I reacted before any sort of thought entered my head. I pushed off the floor and threw myself in a roll, catching the Empress with my rising arms and pulling her away from the plunging dagger. My elbows slammed painfully against the stone, but I didn't let myself fall, cradling the Empress beneath me and shielding her with my body.

She screamed while I struggled to free myself from the folds of her dress. A few chaotic heartbeats later, I was on my feet, blindly spreading my arms wide in a desperate attempt to catch the killer's blade.

But nothing happened. I heard no sigh of metal parting flesh and felt no cold blade break my skin. And, as I stood there blinking frantically, the Empress's screams turned into a stream of delighted laughter.

It wasn't some masked assassin that I faced, but Helena. The armored guardswoman was grinning beneath her auburn curls, sheathing a dagger.

"Well done," she said, taking a step to move past me.

I moved to block her. My eyes were wild, my heartbeat still frantic. I was tense, my blood afire with the need to fight or ... something. Was Helena a killer? I couldn't think, couldn't understand what in God's name had just happened.

Her eyes narrowed. "Move."

"Let her through, my brave soldier," the Empress said from behind me. "Helena was part of my test."

"Sorry, sir," I said, falling back into mindless military discipline. I let her step past me this time, turning with her to help the Empress to her feet.

"Are you hurt, Highness?" Helena asked.

"No, no." Theodora waved her off, moving towards a nearby table and taking a small sip of wine from a waiting cup. "Though, that was rather bracing."

"What about you?" Helena asked, turning to me.

"I don't ... I don't think so, but I ..." I cleared my throat. "I'm fine, sir. Thank you."

"Sir?" The Empress said, coming back towards us. "What's this now?"

I was surprised by the spots of pink that colored the guardswoman's cheeks. "I tried to get him to use my name, but you know how stubborn legion men are about this stuff."

"Is that right?" The Empress considered me for a few moments. "You're still a little lost."

"I—Yes, *Augusta*. I'm sorry."

She smiled, looking at me with surprising warmth. She reached up to touch my cheek.

"Don't be afraid, my Leontius. Your trial is over. You did exactly what you were supposed to." She let her hand fall, and my cheek felt cold at the loss of her touch. "As my guard, you will be with me always. You will see a lot of things that might shock you. A lot of things that will ... make it hard to focus. I needed to make sure that no matter what you see or what you do, you'll still be able to do your job." Her eyes twinkled. "This won't be the last time you see my pussy, soldier."

I choked, and the Empress laughed.

"You kept your head," she continued. Then, her smile turned wicked. "I might be disappointed by that if I couldn't see the ... *small* effect I had on you."

Her eyes flicked downward, and I suddenly became aware of the fire raging between my legs. I was hard as a mountain, the tip of me pushing painfully at the cloth of my *tunica*. I was horrified, especially upon realizing that the *very* visible bulge between my legs was pointing directly at the Empress.

"*Augusta*!" I cried, crashing down onto my knees. I desperately wanted to shift my stubborn cock back into place, but I would sooner cut it off than reach down and adjust it here. "Forgive me! Please! I mean no disrespect. I—"

The Empress howled with laughter, an ugly, snorting peal that blotched her skin and caused tears to run down her cheeks. "The terror! Your face! Look at you—!"

Words failed her, and she motioned to Helena for support. And I watched with slack-jawed amazement as the Empress of Rome, the most powerful woman in the world, laughed about my erection.

"I'm sorry!" she gasped when she finally mastered herself. "It's just that I've seen men trampled in the Hippodrome with more serenity on their faces."

"Truly," Helena grinned, her eyes alight.

"Don't you start, Lena," the Empress bubbled. It was a few moments before she could speak again. "And don't worry, there's nothing to forgive. No woman wishes there to be no reaction at all."

My knees ached against the stone floor, but I ignored them. What in God's name was this place?

Then, Theodora stepped up to me and transformed. Her face lost all traces of mirth, her back straightened, and I saw a glint of steel in her eyes. She was regal. A ruler. An Empress.

"Will you swear yourself to me, Leontius?" she asked, gazing down at me. "Will you grant me your body and life? Will you serve me, forsaking all thoughts of self until death or the moment that I should release you from this oath? Will you swear to all of this on almighty God?"

And though my thoughts were addled, my body and mind a mass of fire and chaos and confusion, I did not hesitate. This woman had captured me, and I did not look away as I spoke.

"I swear it, in God's name and my own. I am yours, *Augusta*."

She pulled on the golden chain around her neck, a golden cross emerging from between her breasts. She leaned down, holding the crucifix to my lips. "With this kiss, you seal your oath to God," she said.

I pressed my lips against the cross, the soft metal warm from the heat of her body.

The Empress straightened, tucking it away. Then, she smiled, and bit down on the corner of her lower lip.

She slid right before me, reaching down to pull the spiderweb-light folds of her dress up to her waist. My breath caught, heat rushing into my face as I found myself once again face-to-face with her luscious sex.

I swallowed. It was even more wondrous in the naked light of the sun.

She slowly lifted one bare leg, resting her thigh on my shoulder and opening herself to me. "And with this kiss," she breathed, "you seal your oath to me."

She flexed the muscle of her raised leg, pulling me into her soft, sweet-smelling center.

Theodora gasped, a low sound of delight, when my face touched her. I was overwhelmed, my thoughts seared away. I couldn't move, but my Empress had no such trouble. I felt her fingers weave themselves into the curls of my hair, pressing my face to her and holding me in place while she began to rock her hips. She ground herself against my nose, sliding back and forth, the motion made easy by the wetness that flowed from her.

I couldn't breathe, smothered by her scent, engulfed by her parted folds of flesh. I could taste the sweetness of her on my lips.

"A kiss," the Empress said with a breathy laugh. She made a sound from deep in her throat, grinding herself harder onto my face. "I need a kiss, my soldier. Kiss me."

I managed to purse my lips, some of her taste seeping into me.

"No. No. Stop teasing me."

She pulled my face away, tilting my head up so that I could look at her face. Her eyes and her skin were burning, red heat suffusing them. Her breath came quickly through parted lips.

"Your tongue," she said. "Kiss me with your tongue."

She brought the hem of her dress up to her mouth, holding it in her teeth, and so freeing a hand to move down between her legs. Then, she splayed her fingers, unfurling herself before me. The whole of her gleamed with moisture, the petals of a flower drenched in the morning's dew.

"Right here." She murmured through the cloth. "Kiss me."

The air exploded out of me, my chest gasping. I was freed from my mindless paralysis, her command, and the sight of her finally allowing me to obey. She pulled my nose back into the soft curls of her pubic hair, and my tongue flicked out.

Her taste exploded through me. An indescribable sweetness, a delicious hint of sourness, and a lush ripeness all blended into a heady mix that was as wonderfully feminine as it was uniquely hers.

"Ah," she sighed, pulling me deeper. "Very good."

I'd thought to be like the serpent, tasting her with quick, clever flicks of my tongue. But that wasn't enough. Instead, I found myself running my tongue over her silken folds in long strokes. I lapped at her wetness like a dog, desperate to taste every part of her.

"Very good," she moaned, rolling her hips. "Oh, my soldier. That's very good." Her fingers were tight in my hair, and I couldn't move even had I wanted to. My tongue explored further, plumbing her depths, drowning in her nectar.

"Ah!" Theodora gasped. "Yes! Right—" Then, her body locked tight. She crushed me into her quivering softness for one, two, and then three heartbeats.

She relaxed, her frame unclenching. She let out a low, pleased sound, sliding her leg from my shoulder and leaving my face coated in her liquid arousal.

"And with that kiss, your oath is sealed," she said, letting her dress fall into place. "Now rise, my Leontius. Rise and take your place as guardian of my body."

And thus began my first day as Empress Theodora's bodyguard.

Chapter Three

The Empress Takes a Bath

"The Empress's chambers are the only place that we can leave her unguarded, though never if she has a visitor. Our rooms are right here, see? We're close, in case she ever needs us."

Helena was giving me a tour of the Empress's private section of the Imperial Palace. She was listing some of my new duties as she named each room we stepped through. And there were many, for the Empress had an entire wing set aside for her use.

I tried to focus, to shove what had just happened into a corner of my mind. But it was too much, the memory too vivid. I had a few lucid moments throughout that afternoon, but always, my thoughts returned to Theodora.

I could still feel the heat from her, could still see her unfurl her moisture-drenched sex. I recalled how she'd slid herself against me, her folds silky, slick with her own wetness. I swallowed past my dry tongue, remembering how I'd nearly drowned in the taste of her.

And then, I'd feel a shift between my legs, heat would rise through me, and my thoughts would drift from my ears in a cloud of steam. I'd wander after Helena in a haze until something pulled me out of it.

It was only once we left the Empress's wing entirely, and a different pair of *Excubitors* shut the ornate door behind us, that I was finally yanked out of my daze for good.

I froze mid-step, my body suddenly corpse-stiff. Horror washed over me and then my entire frame shook.

"Ah," Helena said with a grin. "I was wondering how long it would take. Come on."

"The Emperor," I choked.

"Yes, yes," she said, pulling me away from the watching *Excubitors* and out of earshot. "I thought that you'd have worked this out sooner."

I collapsed onto a convenient bench, blinking rapidly as Helena lowered herself down next to me.

"I saw her—I licked her—" I could barely speak. "The Emperor's going to have me flayed."

"He won't," Helena said.

"Of course he will!" I nearly screamed. "You saw what I did! He probably already knows."

"You're right about that second part," Helena said. "He knows. The Empress loves that little test."

I let my head fall into my hands. "Then, I'm already dead."

"Stop being dramatic," Helena said. She leaned back against the wall, her armored shoulder brushing mine. "Didn't you hear me? You're not the first man to ... give her a kiss."

I peered over at her. "What?"

"She worked in a brothel, man. Just like—" She cleared her throat, speaking hurriedly. "The Emperor knew all of that when he married her. And just wait until she throws one of her parties."

I couldn't even comprehend what Helena was saying. The words she spoke made sense, but I just couldn't grasp the meaning of them. It was like she'd just told me the sky was green.

"The Empress and her husband adore each other," Helena continued. "They've been married for years yet still dote on one another. I don't think I've seen two people more in love."

I groaned, slumping back, my stomach sinking even deeper than before. He'd have me flayed first, then he'd tie my skinless body to his chariot and drag me through the sands of the Hippodrome.

"Stop that," Helena said. "Let me finish. They adore each other, and that will never change. But the Empress is a lot more ... sexual than her husband. The Emperor knows and even encourages her to pursue her passions. He'll even join in when he feels like it."

No amount of ingrained military discipline could have kept me from gaping at that. This wasn't how men and women, wives and husbands, were supposed to act. Life was supposed to be simple.

"One day, you'll marry a good woman from a good family. You'll love and be true to each other. She'll care for your house and bear your children and you'll be oh-so-happy, my little lion."

Happiness was a formula to my mother, a set of steps to be taken along a pre-determined path. It was simple, and yet, to stray meant the doom of misery and failure. None of this made sense.

I shifted and felt Helena's iron-clad shoulder once again against my own. I hadn't forgotten that she was another abnormality. Women weren't soldiers. And yet, here she was, bearing a *stratiotai's* kit as naturally as any veteran.

This palace ... nothing about my life so far had prepared me for this. I felt myself becoming untethered. I was lost, completely overwhelmed by this new, alien, universe. I needed to ground myself, and so, I reached for what was familiar: the scent of steel and sweat, the creak and jingle of armor, and the solid presence of another soldier beside me; all of these things spoke to me of the legion camps.

And right now, these things came from Helena.

She was a woman, and while my mother's voice insisted that she had no business wearing that armor, the rest of me simply accepted it and moved on.

"Sorry, sir," I said, letting out a breath.

"Good," she said, pulling me to my feet. "And no more 'sirs.' Protocol, remember?"

"Right ..." I said, wondering at my sudden discomfort.

"Helena," she said. "Say it."

She was watching me, a small smile curling her lips. She was tall, I suddenly realized, her eyes a bare handbreadth below my own. Her bronzed cheeks were pink with the summer's heat, and she was near enough that I caught the scent of her auburn hair.

"Helena," I said.

Heat bloomed in my cheeks, but I found myself unable to look away from her eyes. They drew me in, their green hue sparking something within me. In my head, I had a vision of a cypress, a tree growing wild and strong through sand and rock.

She grinned, and I saw that same tree sway in a storm, its needles shifting and dancing. "And I'll call you Leo. Although, I haven't seen much of the lion in you."

I snorted, shaking my head.

"Come on," she said, turning away with her grin still in place. "Let's go get you fitted for your armor."

"Alright," I said, moving after her. "When am I going to meet the rest of her guard?"

"We're it, Leo. So I hope that you're ready to work!"

☧

The sun was low in the sky, the heat of the summer air fading with it.

The Emperor was hosting a banquet at his palace that evening. He'd invited dozens of men and women of note: generals, senators, ambassadors, priests, and merchants. It would be a grand night.

But before it truly began, the Empress wanted a bath.

Helena and I had accompanied her down to her private bathing chamber, an ornately tiled room with a large pool set into the floor at its center.

The pool was large, a dozen paces wide, its bottom tiled in a patternless mosaic of varying shades of blue. The bath was entered by three wide steps, the water growing deeper the further in one went. There were seats all along the pool's edge, sculpted for comfort.

The Empress lay on a long, shaped bench. She was submerged to the neck, her eyes closed. The water was hot, letting out a cloud floral scented steam. Her long, walnut-colored tresses were piled high atop her head, pinned to stay out of the water.

I stood by the room's only door, my hand resting on the hilt of the short sword belted to my waist. I wiped the sweat from my forehead, grateful now that my armor wouldn't be ready until morning. Even in just my *tunica*, it was uncomfortable in the billowing clouds of oil-scented steam.

Although, with a glance towards Helena, I decided not to complain. She was still in her full kit, sweat having long since plastered her auburn hair to her skull. She was seated at a small wooden desk not far from the Empress's bath. And though her skin was flushed a deep red, her voice didn't waver as she read from a stack of reports.

"The Patriarch begs an audience. He intercedes on behalf of his flock."

The Empress snorted and didn't even bother to open her eyes. "On behalf of his flock? Is that what he's calling this? The rapacious old fool wants money to plate Hagia Sofia's altar in gold. I'll see him next week."

Helena took up a ready quill, quickly scribbling down a few words before she kept reading. "The weaver's guild complains about the price of wool."

The Empress raised her arm to make a shooing gesture, sending the perfumed water swirling in a series of ripples. "Skip it."

"The Governor of Crete wishes—"

"Pass," the Empress said. "Is there anything I need to know at this moment?"

Helena fell silent for a few moments, flipping through reports. "The Sassanid delegates should be here in about a month."

I started at that. I knew that the Emperor had sued for peace after our defeat at Callinicum, but I didn't know that things had progressed far enough for the Persian king to have sent envoys.

"They're making good time," Theodora remarked. "Have the servants start tidying up the northern wing for them. Anything else?"

"Alexius sent another message."

The Empress groaned, finally deigning to open her eyes to glare at the other woman. "There's one from the Greens too, I guess?"

"Yes, Highness."

Theodora lifted a hand from the water to massage the bridge of her nose. "My husband grants the Blues too much leniency. Alexius is a viper. And Diocles of the Greens isn't any better."

I'd never spent much time in the capital before now, but even I knew those two names. They were the leaders of the two largest party factions of the city. Those factions were filled with groups of the Empire's richest men: senators, merchants, priests, and lords. Though they held no official power, their influence could not be underestimated.

The people of the city loved them. Each faction employed hundreds of men and women, sponsoring charioteers for the sands of the Hippodrome. They put on plays, games, and other grand spectacles to dazzle and amaze. They ran businesses and owned entire streets of houses and tenements. In fact, 'gang' might be a better word to describe them.

The Blues and Greens had carved out wide territories for themselves in Constantinople's streets, making it dangerous to wear certain colors in certain places. And on the race days that the mob so loved, whole neighborhoods of their supporters emptied to fill the hundred thousand seats of the Hippodrome.

"Are they complaining about the crimes of the other? Or do they want a tax break?"

"Both, I believe, Highness. They're each using next week's chariot race as an excuse."

"God deliver me from the short-sightedness of vain and greedy men," the Empress said. "My husband and I are trying to do good for this Empire. I'll ease their taxes as they pledge more of their wealth to its growth."

Helena's quill started to scratch, but the Empress interrupted her with a sigh. "Don't write that down. I'm sure they'll have people here for my husband's banquet, so I'll tell them myself. More artfully, I suppose."

"Very well, Highness. Next, we have—"

"No! No more, Helena. Give me a moment."

Theodora shifted against the bath's shaped seat, the motion causing her breasts to bob above the surface of the water. I caught a glimpse of the chain nestled between them, the soapy water rippling to reveal a hint of her dark nipples.

I ripped my gaze away, spinning to face the door. Heat rushed up the back of my neck, a fire that had nothing to do with the steaming air of the baths.

"Careful, my Leontius," the Empress said. "You might lose your head if you keep twisting that quickly."

"Yes, *Augusta*," I managed. "Apologies."

I heard the splash and shift of water, followed by the faint sound of Theodora's laughter.

"Put the message scrolls away, Helena," she said. "I need to clear my head before this dinner."

"Very well, Highness," the other woman answered.

"Turn around, Leontius," the Empress said.

"I—Ahem. I'd like to keep an eye on the door, *Augusta*. For intruders."

"This propriety of yours is already getting rather tiresome, my Leontius," Theodora remarked. "Helena was never this prudish."

Helena snorted. "I'd already seen your tits more times than I could count, Highness."

"I suppose that's true." I heard the smirk in her voice. Water trickled and swirled. "Besides, with breasts like yours, mine don't seem too impressive."

"Oh, yours are perfect, Highness," Helena said, her voice teasing. "Just look at the effect they've had."

The water shifted again, louder this time, a cascade of drops splattering into the steaming bath. "Yes, well, I find it frustrating. Do you think he'd look if pulled you in as well?"

"Perhaps," I could hear the laughter in Helena's voice. "I think his restraint is rather nice. It's refreshing, isn't it?"

Another trickle of water. "You Rhodians are a strange people. Leontius, turn around."

I started at the sound of my name. I sucked in a mouthful of air. I'd been holding my breath, I realized, strangely intent on capturing every word spoken between the two women.

"Empress, I—"

"I will not keep speaking to your back," Theodora cut in. "Turn around. I am decent."

I turned and my entire being stilled, my heart seeming to freeze in the space between beats. My mind stuttered, unable to move past one single thought: naked.

Theodora was completely naked.

She was perched up on the bath's tiled edge, leaning back onto her palms with one foot trailing in the water while the other was planted flat on the floor beside her. She was open to me.

Her skin, glowed a deep gold in the lantern light, scented oil clinging to every curve and slope of her body.

"Now isn't this better?" she said with a languid smile. "Come closer, my soldier."

Her voice, and the sparkling ember in the darkness of her eyes, jolted me into action. I took a step closer, then another, advancing until I stood directly across the pool from my Empress.

"Good," she purred. "Keep your eyes on me, now."

As if I could do anything else. I was entranced, falling into the burnished depth of her oil-slick flesh. Fire burned beneath my skin, and I longed for a quenching taste of the water that flowed down her.

I followed one such rivulet with my eyes, tracing its path down the curve of her neck and onto the soft sloping valley of her chest.

Her breasts were smooth, firm, and with the same dancer's tightness as the rest of her. Two nipples, round and colored a deep rose, stood high in the naked air. Water beaded upon them both, the gathered drops quivering with every breath she took.

My blood roared in my ears as I fixed upon that long, golden chain that spilled down from her neck. One side of it flowed through the smooth space between her breasts, shaping itself to her slopes and curves. The other half of the chain lay draped across one breast, the soft, golden links of metal held back by the delicate protrusion of her rosewood nipple. I longed to brush it away, to hear Theodora gasp as the warm links of gold slipped over the stiffness of her nipple, and to watch it slide down her oiled flesh. Then, the Empress stretched herself back, and I watched that chain move exactly as I had imagined.

"God," she breathed. "Do you see it, Lena? The need."

"I see it," the other woman answered. There was an edge to her voice that I hadn't heard before. "Look at that hunger."

The Empress made a sound in her throat, her fingers trailing down the links of her golden chain. I followed her hand watching as it brushed past the heavy cross that lay upon her taut, angled stomach. My eyes traveled lower, past her navel, coming to rest on that silken, glistening seam between her open legs.

"The sweetest sort of hunger," Theodora said. Her fingers slid past the matted, oiled curls of her dark pubic hair, slipping between the soft, oil-slick folds of her sex. "Do you remember our morning, my soldier? Do you remember the taste of me?"

"Yes," I choked.

Her fingers slid over every inch of her silken slit. She brought her leg out of the pool, planting that foot flat upon the tiled floor as well, spreading herself wide before me once more.

"Would you like another taste?" Her fingers had begun to move in a slow circle, massaging the upper folds of her seam. I saw the heat rise beneath her skin and heard the pace of her breath quicken.

"Yes," I groaned. God help me, but I would drink from her every day if I could.

"Take out your cock," she said.

That heat burned within her eyes, her breath emerging through parted lips. Her gaze was fixed on the bulge aching between my legs

I pulled my *tunica* up, and it was the work of a moment to free my erect nakedness from the loincloth beneath.

"God," my Empress moaned, her fingers working faster. "Take it in your hand. Stroke it. I want to see."

I obeyed, my eyes locked upon her body. My manhood was a bar of molten lead in my hand, the skin tight, every ridge searing into my palm. I worked my hand along it, slowly.

The Empress made a sound that was something between a purr and a moan. Her body tightened as she curled a finger into herself. She slid another to join it in her silken-wetness, pushing the fingers in and out of her. "Come here," she said.

But I didn't. Something held me back, that last shred of myself that hadn't yet been consumed by the inferno I felt rising in me. Theodora wasn't my wife; she wasn't a prostitute. She was my Empress, and I was just a soldier. I couldn't.

"Hurry," she begged. "I want to taste you."

"*Augusta*." The word grated out of my throat. "I—I can't."

"You want to. I see it, my Leontius."

My cock was still in my hand, her own fingers urgently pumping in and out of herself.

"I can't," I repeated, cursing myself as the greatest sort of fool.

Her fingers slowed, though the heat in her eyes and beneath her skin did not fade. "I could make you. I could order you to fuck me, to bury yourself in the tightness of my pussy." She pulled her fingers from herself, holding them up so I could see the wetness that dripped from them. "See how ready I am for you, my soldier," she breathed. "See how easily you would slide into me?"

"*Augusta—*" My will was drifting away, consumed like the rest of me by the heat of her eyes and her golden flesh. She was right. I wanted to; God but I wanted to. So, why didn't I?

I was shifting my weight, about to take the first step towards her, when she let out a long breath. "But you aren't yet ready." She tilted her head. "Should I take him anyway, Lena?"

"Uh, I—" Helena coughed. "Maybe not, Highness."

Theodora sighed. "Bring me my golden spear, then."

Helena stood from her desk, but I hardly noticed. I was still stroking myself, backing away from the edge over which I'd been about to fall. My hand slowed and I thought about stopping and retreating from the edge of the pool. The look in the Empress's eyes, however, told me that both were bad ideas.

"Oh, my soldier," she said, bringing her fingers back down to her silken folds. "You will come to me in time, and you will taste all the sweeter for it. But for now, make sure to keep your eyes on me."

"Y—yes, *Augusta*."

Then, Helena arrived with a ... golden cock?

I blinked, taking a second look. But the more I looked at it, from the rounded swell of its bulbous tip to the end of its burnished shaft, the more I became sure of what I was seeing.

"Do you like it?" the Empress asked. "It was a gift from my husband." She took her moisture-slicked fingers from between her legs, trailing them up the golden shaft to the blunted tip. She rubbed her wetness onto it, coating the golden cock in her liquid arousal until it gleamed. Soon, her hand traveled easily along the slickened member as she stroked it in the same way I touched my own.

Its base was strangely shaped, though I learned of its purpose a few moments later when the Empress rose to her feet and took a bare two steps back from the pool's edge. She screwed the cock into a spot marked by a tight ring of golden tiles, turning it until I heard a click.

"A golden spear," she said, standing naked above the erect, golden member. "For when I have nothing else to impale myself with."

She lowered herself to her knees, straddling it. Her breasts quivered, nipples reaching towards me, begging to be touched, to be tasted.

She bit her lip. "Don't look away, my Leontius."

Then, she brought her hips down until the tip of the golden cock teased open the first of her soft folds. She held herself there, muscled legs flexing, as still as she had been when suspended over me that morning.

Fire tore through me. My manhood twitched in my hand, reaching towards her across the pool.

Theodora laughed, low in her throat. She rolled her hips, teasing herself and spreading more of her silken wetness over the whole of that eternally stiff, golden head. "I, too, remember our morning well, my soldier," she said. "The feel of your breath against me. The way I ran myself over the ridges of your face."

She let out a breathy little moan, twitching lower, taking a finger-breadth and more into her. Her hips never stopped moving as she impaled herself with slow, tortuous gyrations. "The way your tongue came into me, so desperate for a taste."

She watched me stroke my molten hardness, her flesh red with furnace heat.

I watched her in turn, my throat dry and flesh ablaze. My eyes stung, but even when I remembered to blink, the rhythmic circles of her naked hips followed me into the darkness.

"Faster," she breathed.

I obeyed, pumping up and down. I *ached* with need, with hunger. My manhood stabbed into the air, spear-straight and desperate to reach out past the limit of its growth.

"Oh God," Theodora panted, a shiver running up her naked flesh. "Oh God!"

Her hips shifted, this time swallowing a finger-length of her golden spear. She completely engulfed the bulbous head now, her pussy clinging to the burnished shaft as she slid herself even lower. Her hips moved differently, though no less rhythmically. The strong muscles of her thighs flexed as her body climbed up and down.

"How does it feel?" She said.

The Empress brought one hand down to where her legs parted, caressing herself as she slid further onto the golden cock. Her other hand went to her chest, to where her breasts jerked and quivered with the motion of her hips. Her fingers gripped that heavy golden cross, keeping it from rebounding against her. "Is it hot? Does it burn?"

"Yes, *Augusta*," I croaked.

That metal cock disappeared deeper into her with every shift. She moved faster, her breath ragged, desperate to take it fully into herself. And when she did, sinking her oil-matted pubis to the tiled floor, she froze. For a moment, her body stiffened and her back arched. She moaned, pulling the sound from deep with her, her body wracked by shivers. I stroked myself faster. I couldn't look away. I flexed, twisted, and pulled on myself, drawing heat to my already burning, blazing cock.

Theodora's stomach rippled as her hips ground against the base of her golden spear. She leaned forward, supporting herself with one hand on the floor while the other hand brought the golden cross to her tits, rubbing the metal against her taut nipples. Then, the muscles of her legs shifted, and she started to bounce.

"Oh fuck," the Empress mewled, riding her golden cock. "Don't stop, my soldier. Oh God, oh God!" She moved even faster, impaling herself again and again.

God, she was so wet. I could hear the squelch of her liquid arousal around the golden member within her, and I yearned to quench myself in her ready moisture

Her movements were fever-quick now, her breasts rebounding in a way that seemed to defy nature. I was almost at my limit, the heat wild within me. We matched each other's rhythm, breathing in the sight of one another.

"Come for me," Theodora begged, her lust-glazed eyes fixed on my cock. "Please. I'm almost there."

That did it for me, the final part of me that might have held back evaporated. I let the fire rage through me unchecked, feeling it reach the tip of me. I pointed my cock towards the Empress and exploded. I pumped thick ropes of milky fluid into the air over the pool, my eyes glued to Theodora.

She gasped when she saw my climax, hammering herself to the floor once, twice, three times. Then, her eyes screwed shut as convulsions ripped through her. She cried out, arching her head and body back.

I don't know why, but my gaze went to her hand, the one that still gripped the cross at her chest. That golden symbol of God. I watched her orgasm, and a thought flashed through me like lightning: Theodora believed.

That cross was not worn as some gesture of heretical mockery. It, and her body, were symbols of her faith. She made love and shared herself with others as an act of worship. Her every moan, a prayer, her every cry, an exultation to her creator. The font between her legs, the sweetest sort of holy water.

And in her religion, it was no sin to revel in what God had given her.

"Ah, my soldier," Theodora panted. "You are a worthy distraction."

☧

Afterward, the Empress cleaned the sweat from herself with a soft linen towel. She circled back to where I stood near the steps of the pool, trailing her fingers along my forearm as she returned to the water.

She took a few moments to scrub at her skin while I retreated to the door, her face curled in an expression of satisfaction.

After we traveled back to her quarters, Helena and I stayed in her salon while she disappeared with an army of maids to get dressed.

I stood numbly at Helena's side, my guts twisting around as if I'd taken a knife. I heard my mother's voice in my head, and I hated myself, both for what I'd done and for what I hadn't let myself do. She was my

Empress, yet I couldn't get the sight of her naked body devouring that golden spear out of my thoughts.

"You surprised me again, you know," Helena said into the silence.

Her voice drew me back into the real world. I tilted my head to find her eyes on me.

"In the baths," she clarified. "Your restraint."

Right. She'd been there. She'd seen me, my nakedness ... I dropped my gaze, cheeks burning.

"Don't worry," she laughed. "I've seen many others, and been a lot closer to a fair bit of them. Although, yours was nice ... " She trailed off, her voice teasing.

"Restraint?" I said, looking for a way out of this. "What restraint?"

"You know what I mean," Helena answered. "The Empress practically begged you for more. Most men, and many women I've met, wouldn't have hesitated to jump in. But you didn't, even though you wanted to. I can't really figure out why."

I let out a long breath, breathing back in through my nose. I caught the whiff of oiled steel and was talking before I knew it. "Honestly? I don't even know. But she's the *Empress* for God's sake, not some camp follower. And she's married. I know the world is different here but ... I don't know. It just felt wrong, I guess."

"I told you that neither she nor the Emperor care about that," Helena said. "Their marriage isn't built on fidelity."

"I know. But a good woman isn't supposed to be like that."

"And just how is a good woman supposed to be?"

It was a sign of how lost I was in my own confusion that I missed the flint in her voice and the sudden stiffness of her frame. I just kept talking, staring at my outstretched hands. "I don't know that anymore either. My mother always said that good, happy women were ... " I let out another long breath and shook my head. "Not like this. Not so ... I don't know. But it doesn't matter." I looked back at her with a shaky grin. "Anyway, it's not for me to tell lords and nobles how to live."

Silence fell between us for a time. I listened to the commotion of the Empress's preparations, and it was Helena who eventually spoke again. "And what about me? Am I a good, proper woman?"

“No,” I said, meeting the challenge in her gaze. I let my lip quirk into a wry smile. “But Helena, you might just be the sanest person here.”

Her lips parted in a wide smile, and her cypress eyes brightened just a little. She laughed, and I felt an altogether different sort of warmth rise through me.

Chapter Four

The Empress's Guard Train

My little lion.

Your letter has been an answer from God. I feared for you when I heard about the army's defeat at the hands of those barbaric Persians. But God is good, and I knew that He would not let you fall to those heathens.

I do not know when, or where, this letter will find you, but just know that I love you and that your dedication to your career fills me with pride.

Your father would be proud too, seeing you continue along in his footsteps.

I let out a breath, leaning back from my little desk. This was the last letter I'd received from my mother. I'd found it waiting for me when I'd arrived in Constantinople back at the end of May.

We were near the end of June now, the third morning since I'd sworn my oath to the Empress.

I'd put this off long enough, I told myself. I had papyrus, quill, and inkpot. It was time to write, to tell her that I was safe and working in the capital. She should know that. I could tell her that I'd won the Emperor's foot race and that I'd ... left.

I'd left the legions.

I groaned, rubbing at my eyes. I needed to do this. I needed to tell her. I was *stratiotai* for God's sake; I could write a letter to my fucking mother.

But luckily, there was a knock at my door.

I just about leaped from my desk, opening the door to find Helena standing there.

"Morning!" she said with a wide smile. "You ready?"

"Helena," I said. "Ready? Almost, I ... uh ...?"

I trailed off unable to figure out what I wanted to say. Helena stood in my doorway without her armor—without much of anything really.

She wore only a strip of cloth over the swell of her breasts and a loincloth wrapped snuggly around the curve of her hips that did little more than swaddle her center. Her stomach was naked between those meager garments, and I could see her muscles flex with every breath she took. Her body was lean, her bare shoulders and arms more powerful than the Empress's.

My gaze followed down the endless, sculpted smoothness of her legs, my eyes tracing every swell and divot. I lingered for a time at the strip of cloth looped around one thigh, wondering at its purpose before I arrived at her sandaled feet.

"Like what you see?" I could hear the smirk in her voice, and I looked up to find her cypress eyes alight beneath the free-falling curls of her copper hair.

"Yes," I instantly replied, the word springing out of me without bothering to stop by my brain.

She snorted, a faint flush of color creeping up her naked skin. "Come on, you're settled in now. We're going for a run."

"A run ... ?" My eyes flicked back down to the shape of her thighs. Then, my mind finally lurched back into motion, and heat seared up my body. I tore my eyes from her. "A run! Yes, sorry. I'll be ready."

My eyes flailed about for a place to rest. Helena laughed, and I took that as permission to settle back on her grinning face. Helena had mentioned the day before that, unless a situation prevented it, the mornings were for us to train. I'd expected her here, but not like this.

"Sorry," I said. "You ... took me by surprise."

"I can see that," she said. "Now, take off your *tunica*. We need to go before it gets too hot."

"Ah, right," I said. "You're sure the Empress doesn't need us?"

Helena shook her head. "She doesn't need us today. She'll be in the senate chamber most of the time, and while normally we'd be there with her, she wanted to give us the day to work together. The Excubitors will guard her until we're done."

I nodded. "Give me a moment."

"I'll meet you down in the Hippodrome, then."

She turned, moving away and giving me a view of her back. My gaze slid down the smooth arch of her spine to the curved firmness of her hips. Her loincloth was tight, looping around her waist and between her legs. It left much of her rounded behind visible, each hump jiggling faintly as she walked.

I was mesmerized by the sway of her hips and the rhythmic bouncing of those cheeks, by the curve of her back and the muscles shifting beneath the flesh of her naked thighs. But most of all, by the way her ass completely devoured the strip of cloth down its center.

I heard her make a small sound and looked up to find her peeking back at me from over one shoulder. I flushed and saw her lips curl into another smile. She turned her attention forward once more, reaching down to remove the loop from around her thigh and using it to tie back her hair.

Then, Helena disappeared around a corner with a final snap of her hips.

I stared at that corner for a few moments after she'd gone. I'd grown almost used to the sight of her in her armor during these past couple of days. The protective steel masked the shape of her body, and so—despite the beauty of her features—I'd somehow convinced myself that Helena wasn't a woman.

But now that the sight of her swaying, curving waist was locked tightly in my mind, I could no longer deny her femininity. I knew that I would never forget this first glimpse of her.

Or the way her eyes had danced when she'd smiled.

☧

Constantinople's Hippodrome was one of the great wonders of the world.

It was huge, the U-shaped track built directly into the western wall of the Imperial Palace. From the Imperial Box, Justinian and the hundred thousand others who could squeeze themselves into the surrounding grandstands could watch the thunder of the chariot races that were the center of life within the capital.

The seats were empty now. Yet, I remembered the way the sands had shaken with each one of the crowd's roars and cheers at the end of my own race.

Helena and I started to run after a few minutes of stretching. We ran the circuit of the charioteers, doing lap after lap around the low, obelisk-framed wall that divided the track in two. She was a good runner—better than good. Her breathing was steady, her long legs devouring mile after mile of the sandy track.

We ran in silence mostly, each of us focused on the air in our lungs, the sun on our naked backs, and the sand beneath our feet. It felt good to run again. My head was emptying itself of everything but the motion of my body. Slowly, as one hour slipped past, and then two, I felt that calm settle deeper into me.

My thoughts, my confusion, and my doubts from the past few days all started to flow away. Running was something I knew, something I loved. I anchored myself to the joy it brought me, and how good it was to run in the company of someone who seemed to love it too. By the time we stopped, I actually felt like myself again.

In the hours since we'd arrived, a unit of *Excubitors* had started drilling nearby. They attacked wooden posts with heavy training swords; another group fell in and out of formation beneath the heavy batons of their officers. I watched them while we rested, noting the emphasis on marching and formation drills, rather than on actual combat. It wasn't what I was used to, but it would serve.

"Let's go train with them," I said. "I haven't practiced in weeks."

Helena, her skin flushed a healthy pink from the long run, didn't meet my gaze. "Ah, you go. I'll just run some more, I think."

I frowned. "Come on, we need the practice. Let's get those guys at the posts to do some actual sparring."

She shook her head. "I can't. Just go, Leo. I'll do a few more laps before I go back in."

"Helena," I said. "We're the Empress's Guard. We can train with them whether they like it or not."

Her face twisted. "Oh, they very much don't like to train with a woman."

My frown deepened. "That doesn't matter. You guard the Empress. They have to train with you."

"You'd think so, right?" She made a bitter sound. "Oh, they're all happy to stare at me when I run, but as soon as I approach them with a training sword in my hand, everyone suddenly finds somewhere else they need to be. I just do what I can with the wooden posts."

I was getting angry. "That's nothing."

"It's the best I can do."

"It's not enough."

Her eyes flashed, but I turned away and started towards the closest rack of training swords. "I'll train you myself, then."

She caught me before I'd taken my third step. Her hand closed around my arm, whirling me around to face the anger in her wild, cypress-green eyes.

"Fuck you," she hissed. "I don't need your pity."

"Pity?" I wrenched my arm from her grip. "This isn't about fucking pity. You're Empress Theodora's bodyguard. We swore to keep her safe. How the fuck are you going to do that if you can't fight?"

"I'm not a coward," she said. "I won't run."

I snorted. "So, what? Any idiot can take a knife to the gut. But what happens to our Empress after that?"

She didn't back away from me, but neither did she speak.

So I did. "You're my shield-mate, Helena. We stand beside each other. While we fight, your shield stays locked onto mine." I slapped my hand loudly against my forearm, my voice rising. "We're Romans. We make a wall out of our shields and bodies. We let our enemies break themselves upon it, and we grind through them."

I was angry. I was angry at her for not trying. I was angry at the self-important guards who refused to teach her. And I was angry at myself, that I hadn't noticed any of this sooner. "We sell our lives as dearly as possible." I was roaring now, my voice hoarse. "That's our fucking duty. You and all these shit-brained *Excubitors* may have forgotten, but I haven't. And I'm not going to die because my shield-mate doesn't know what the fuck she's doing."

I grabbed her arm and spun her around, kicking her towards the rack of wooden swords and shields. "So, go get us some gear. We're starting now."

Helena hesitated a moment, her back stiff and trembling. My fists were clenched, ready to meet her rage with my own. I'd be damned before I let her put her pride in the way of her duty.

But she didn't, surprising me by starting towards the nearest rack within another heartbeat.

"Don't forget the shields!" I shouted after her. Then, I let out a long breath, trying to unclench my muscles. I tried to let go of my anger, knowing she'd done her best. It wasn't her fault.

I noticed some of the *Excubitors* throwing me furious looks. They'd clearly heard me shout. I glared right back. No, it wasn't her fault. It was theirs.

One of them started to come towards me, a sneer painted onto his face. I was surprised to see that I recognized him. It was the mouthy one from my first day here.

He was pretty without his helmet. Bare-chested as the rest of us, his muscles gleamed with oil. He swung his wooden sword in lazy arcs while he walked, his shield low enough that it nearly dragged through the sand.

"Runner," he said in a refined accent. "What are you and that woman doing here?"

I felt my hackles rise. I knew my place now, and I wasn't going to let some tarted-up parade ground soldier speak to me like I was some fucking dog. Even if he probably was some senator's son.

"We're the Empress's guard, boy," I snapped. "Piss off."

The idiot's face darkened. "Watch your mouth. This place is for soldiers, not women and cowards."

"Fuck off. I won't tell you again."

But I knew he wouldn't back down. He'd come this far, in full view of his entire unit. He couldn't let me win. And so, when his sneer shifted into a snarl and he swung his wooden blade toward me, I was ready.

I caught the blade in one fist, ignoring the flare of pain. The mouthy fool's eyes widened. He tugged on his sword, trying to pull it out of my grip, but I swung my other fist into his nose, smearing it across his face. He collapsed to the sand, screaming. The idiot hadn't even raised his shield.

I kicked him in the stomach, wrenched the sword from his grip, and ripped the shield from his other arm. I quickly looped my own limb through the too-loose straps of the shield, cinching them tight with my teeth in time to see one of his friends charging at me.

I rushed to meet him, tucking my shoulder into my shield, and crunched into his body. I hit him like a battering ram. He went down, and I ground my heel into his stomach before facing the rest of his unit.

"Come on!" I roared. I slammed the flat of my sword against the face of my shield. "Who's next!?" I slammed my sword onto my shield again and again. The sound was deafening, though it was nothing compared to what it could be, to the thunder of tens of thousands on the battlefield. "Show me! Show me who you are!"

A few of the other *Excubitors* started towards me. I waited for them to come, slamming my sword into my shield and bellowing my anger into theirs.

But these weren't *stratiotai*. It had been generations since the Emperor's Guard had gone to war. They knew nothing of blood, nothing of death. But I did.

I kept beating my sword against my shield. And for the first time in God knew how long, the walls of the Hippodrome echoed with the crashing drum of the legion at war.

The very heartbeat of Rome.

The advancing guardsmen faltered before ever reaching me. They settled for shouting a few curses and bending down to tend to their friends once I'd backed away.

I let the sound die when Helena returned from the rack of training weapons. I spat on the ground, and felt the sneering fool's blood beneath my fingernails, my anger not yet burned away.

"Leave that extra sword and shield here," I told Helena, turning and striding to an empty corner of the Hippodrome "I've got my own."

The sun was low in the sky when I finally called an end to our training.

We shuffled through the halls of the Imperial Palace, exhausted. My muscles were stretched and quivering; my head hurt and I was sun-scorched and hungry from skipping our midday meal.

Yet, I felt good. Great even.

"Leo," Helena called.

She was a few steps behind me, stopped at a junction with a corridor I didn't recognize.

Guilt flashed through me. She looked worse than I felt; her muscles were taut and shaking beneath her dirt and sweat-crusted flesh. Bruises were already blooming all over her, some scabbing over with dried blood.

"Come this way," she said, turning down the new hallway. "I want to show you something."

"What is it?"

"You'll see," she said, disappearing from view.

I hesitated a moment before forcing my aching body after her. I'd worked her too hard. I hadn't been fair; I'd used her to work through anger that I held more for myself than anyone else.

Going after her now was the least that I could do.

I followed Helena through the twisting palace corridors, surprised by how fast she was moving now. She pulled open a door a few minutes later, gesturing me over before she slipped through. Inside was a room bathed in light.

The golden rays of the setting sun flooded this unused bedroom, washing over the bed and tapestry-covered walls from a columned balcony. Helena was already stepping onto it, tilting her head up to catch the final warmth of the day.

I stepped out with her, coming to where she stood by a stone balustrade. I noted the way her copper hair, sweat-darkened and held back from her face by that loop of cloth, seemed to burn brighter in the fading light.

"This is my favorite spot in the palace," she said, leaning onto her elbows. "Just look at this view."

She was right: the view was spectacular. We faced south-west, looking out over the glittering expanse of the Sea of Marmara. I could see the dark silhouettes of ships coasting through the placid waters. Constantinople was the center of the world, the crossroads between the east and west. I wondered how far some of these ships might have traveled to drift here beneath our eyes.

"I come here whenever I can," Helena said. "I like to watch the fishing ships coming in."

I breathed in the warm, salty air, listening to the cries of the gulls, sailors, and merchants. It was comforting, and reminded me of another time and another place. Here, sheltered by the palace from the sights and sounds of the city, I could almost believe that I was looking at a different stretch of sea.

"It's like home," I murmured.

"I knew that you'd like it," Helena said with a smile in her voice. "My father was a fisherman before we left Lindos. I used to wait for him like this for hours every night."

I smiled as well. "I always liked the markets. All the people talking and laughing. I went every night I could."

She snorted. "What kind of kid wants to go to the market instead of sailing?"

"The kind that needed to hear something other than his mother's constant tales of his father's days as a soldier."

Helena shifted beside me, her eyes still looking out over the sea. "I guess that you were always meant for this life, then."

I didn't answer, my stomach clenching.

"I'd always wanted to be a fisherman," Helena continued. "I used to beg my dad to take me out with him on his boat. But he never did."

I looked over at her. There was so much strength in her, this woman, whose skin seemed cast from liquid gold in the sun's dying light. Her eyes met mine, her smile sad. I didn't speak, for what was there to say?

No matter how right it would feel, women weren't sailors. They didn't go out and fish.

"Did you mean what you said?" she asked me.

"When?"

"In the Hippodrome, before you beat those two *Excubitors*." Her expression was strangely hesitant, open in a way I hadn't seen before. "Do you really see me as a fellow soldier? As your partner?"

"No," I told her.

Her face twisted, eyes falling away. "Then, I'm still just some—"

"Weren't you listening?" I interrupted. "You're my shield-mate, Helena. Partners might stand one behind the other, but shield-mates stand side by side."

Her eyes shone when they lifted back up to mine. She nodded, her expression an unreadable swirl of emotions.

"Then," she said, "I look forward to more training with you. Together."

"Don't," I said. "I'm going to ask the Empress to give us more time in the morning. And if you think that you hurt now ... " I trailed off, smiling at her laughter.

"I guess I'd better go get some rest then," she said, turning away from the balcony. "Coming?"

"Of course."

We walked back through the palace in silence, enjoying the comfort of being at each other's side. And though there was once again blood crusted beneath my fingernails, my step felt lighter than it had for a long time.

Before long, we were back within the Empress's wing. The two *Excubitors* on guard at the entrance glared at me but did not say a word. Evidently, they'd heard about what had happened earlier.

I waved Helena off when we reached her room, taking a single step towards mine before her voice called me back.

She reached both hands up to slide the sweat-soaked cloth from her hair, her gaze on my face. The motion stretched her body, the muscles of her naked shoulders and stomach shifting beneath her skin.

"We stink," she said.

I nodded, my throat suddenly dry. The sour, faintly musky scent of her filled the hallway. It was powerful, no doubt, but it was as feminine as the curve of her hips. And was as uniquely hers as the light in her eyes.

"The Empress lets us use her bath. If you want."

I had to swallow before replying. "I'll go later. I—" I cleared my throat. "I have one more duty to take care of."

She arched one eyebrow but didn't press. "Well, wash up before tomorrow. I'm the one who has to stand next to you, remember?"

I laughed, turning away and heading back into my quarters.

The blank stretch of papyrus and my mother's letter were right where I had left them. I lowered myself to my desk and felt that my lips were still curled into a smile. I shook my head and began to write.

Chapter Five
The Touch of an Empress

I DUCKED, HEARING THE whistle of the wooden sword cutting the air just above my head. I stepped forward in response, ramming my shield into my attacker and sending them stumbling back.

"No big moves," I chided, lowering my shield to look at Helena. "Stab don't slash. There's no room for anything else in the shield wall."

We were on the sands of the Hippodrome, the only ones here on this particular morning. Helena was in her training wraps, her exposed skin flushed with sweat and the heat of the rising dawn. She glowered at me from behind her own shield.

"I couldn't help it," she said. "Your fat head is such a good target."

I grinned. "You'd think that you'd actually be able to hit it, then."

Helena fought to keep the scowl on her face, motes of light brightening her cypress eyes. She readied her sword. "It's going to feel so good to finally hit you."

I chuckled at the challenge in her gaze, feeling my heartbeat rise to meet it. I brought my shield back up and slammed the flat of my wooden sword against its surface. "Come on, then."

Helena came forward more cautiously this time. She stayed behind her shield, her sword licking out in fast, calculated thrusts.

I stayed on the defensive, blocking and falling back. She stayed right with me, not giving me space.

"Good!" I shouted.

Helena bared her teeth in a savage grin, redoubling her efforts. She attacked faster and faster, trying to overwhelm me.

I laughed with the joy of it. Helena was a warrior-born, and in the month and a half since we'd started training together, she'd improved at a pace that I hardly believed possible. We were out on the sands every morning before sunrise, sparring for a handful of hours until we were due at our place within the Empress's quarters.

Her sword was a blur of motion, the air between us filled with grunts, gasps, and the staccato thwack of our clashing armaments.

I kept falling back, the sand hissing with every shift of my sandals. I weathered her assault, biding my time like any wily old *stratiotai*.

Then, tilting my shield in a way that her thrusting sword skittered a bit too far along its face, I saw my moment. I snapped my shield forward, surging into the space I'd created. Helena's shield met mine, but I was on the offensive now, tucking my shoulder in and ramming her back.

She was on the back foot, and I powered after her with my shield held high. I shoved her back again, thrusting my sword low to cut at her thighs and belly. Helana stumbled, lashing out with her sword.

But my shield blasted through the weak blow to crash into her once more. This time, I knocked her down, the wind bursting from her as her back slammed against the packed sand. I ended the fight by stepping forward and pushing the tip of my training sword into her stomach.

"Dead," I said.

Helena groaned, letting herself flop back. She sucked in huge lungfuls of air, the sand and dust sticking to her skin and sweat-matted hair. I stepped back from her, pulling my sword away and planting it in the sand. My own naked chest was streaked with sweat and dust, though my breathing was steadier.

I walked the dozen steps to the nearest of the Hippodrome's walls, scooping up the pair of waterskins we'd left there. When I returned, Helena was sitting up. Her side was in the sand at her side and she watched me approach with a thoughtful expression on her face.

"I wasn't using my shield," she said, catching the waterskin I tossed her. "Not like you were, anyway."

I nodded approvingly; she had a good mind. I slapped the flat of my shield. "You have to remember that this is a weapon too. Don't ignore it."

Helena blew a breath out between her lips, "I know." She freed her arm from the straps of her shield, letting it fall to the sand beside her.

She massaged that shoulder with her free hand. "I just wish it wasn't so fucking heavy."

I lifted my eyebrow, looking down from where I stood above her. "Are you saying I should make you do more push-ups, shield-mate?"

Helena snorted, but I saw another smile try to fight its way through her features. She was still seated in the sand, a bare two steps from me. Her legs were crossed, her knees brushing against the sword and shield discarded on either side of her. She brought her waterskin to her lips as she spoke. "God I can't wait to beat you."

I laughed, bringing my own waterskin up to drink.

Looking into the brightening sky, I knew that we would have to leave soon if we wanted to have time to wash the sweat from our bodies. But I did not feel rushed.

I let my thoughts drift up into the cloudless summer sky. I'd felt ... lighter since settling into life at the palace. Although, perhaps I shouldn't. It was strange, a lot of things were still so new and the people here were nothing like what I'd been expecting or prepared for.

Especially the Empress, I thought.

I flushed, pushing the image of her from my mind. I took another long drink of water, washing the grit from my throat. I felt good, I realized. Right here, in this place, with Helena and the Empress, I felt ... content.

Was that okay?

Then, a small wind blew past me carrying with it the smoke and smell of the city beyond these walls, and my thoughts turned inexplicably to my mother.

In an instant, everything inside me *twisted.*

"Leo," a voice said. It was distant, easy to ignore. "Leo?"

I wondered if my mother had gotten my letter. Was she reading it now, seated at that little table by the kitchen hearth?

I curled around myself. It was like all the guilt that I'd been repressing since my arrival was clawing through my stomach. I was intensely nauseous, sick about the decision I'd made to walk from the legions. I shouldn't have done it.

This wasn't where I was supposed to be.

I blinked, and suddenly I was back in that little house, stepping into the light streaming in from the pair of windows. My mother was indeed at that table, her day's sewing beside her.

She turned to me, and I recognized this as something from my memory. Her smile was wider than I'd ever seen it, stretching cheeks that were still marked from years of hunger. I was sixteen years old, uncomfortable in my shiny, ill-fitting *stratiotai* kit.

It was the day I'd joined the army.

My mother wrapped her arms around me and started to cry. I once again felt the weight of her arms and the way her frame shook with the force of her tears. Though, when she pulled away, I saw that the smile had never left her face.

"*It was all worth it*," she said. "*Everything that God put us through was worth it, my little lion. Look at you, so much like you're father. You're finally ready to walk his path.*"

"Leo!"

I blinked, finding myself in the present once more, my stomach a writhing mass of guilt and doubt. Helena was scowling up at me, and I met her gaze with eyes that were open too wide. She looked into me, within the endless beats of that instant.

And I felt the light of her cypress eyes touch my very core.

Then, I blinked once more, and it was like shutters against the sun's brightness. I ducked my head, at once yearning for, and deathly afraid of the sudden softness of Helena's features.

"Sorry," I said, looking at everything but her. "Were you saying something?"

She hesitated a moment, but when she spoke, I could hear that the scowl had returned. "Yes! I've called your name three different times. Help me up, we need to get going."

My mother's voice was so loud in my head, but still, I stepped forward. I plastered on a smile and grasped Helena's outstretched hand, pulling her to her feet in one smooth motion.

I must have pulled her too hard, however, because instead of just regaining her feet, my shield-mate stumbled into me. I caught her without thinking, feeling one of her arms snaking up and around my back, her hand gripping my shoulder.

“Sorry,” she said, pressing her body into mine. “I tripped.”

“Oh,” I said. “It’s ...”

She was so warm, I thought. Her arm flexed, squeezing me tight. I raised my own arms, while I lowered my chin to her shoulder. Her sand-crusted hair tickled my cheek and her scent was all I could breathe. It was sun-warmed skin, salt, sour sweat, and damp hair. It was light and life, strength, and femininity. It was Helena. And she was so close, so soft, and so *here.*

My arms closed around her. “It’s no problem. It’s no problem at all.”

“Good,” she said. Then, I felt the tip of something dig into my side. “Because you’re dead.”

I pulled back, my hands on Helena’s waist, blinking at the wooden sword she held pushed against my ribs.

Her eyes were dancing when I looked back at her, her smile full and wide. “I was right,” she said. “This feels amazing.”

I gaped, and she burst into laughter. The sound thrummed through me, loud, full-bellied, and tinged with the trickster’s joy. It wrapped around my mother’s voice, smothering it, pushing it away.

Helena’s laughter, her warmth, and her scent eased the knot within me. I smiled, enough that a bit of my own laughter slipped free.

☧

A little more than an hour later found Helena and I back in the Empress’s salon. We were both armored, standing guard by the door that led into the hallway beyond. Theodora swept in from a deeper in her quarters, and within moments, I was surrounded by more delighted laughter.

“So, you were finally defeated, my Leontius,” the Empress said. Her dark eyes were alight. “What a battle it must have been.”

Theodora was standing right before Helena and me, her smile wide and teasing. Her walnut hair was looped into a complicated pattern of tails and tresses, the whole of it pinned and clipped together with gold. The skin of her face, neck, and shoulders glowed with a burnished depth; an added richness that was the result of a long bath and applied oil. Gold glinted around her bare arms and neck, while the rest of her body was robed in a long *stola* of deep purple.

"It was incredible, Highness," Helena grinned. "You should have seen his face!"

Both women laughed once more, and I felt my face heat up. I thought I should be embarrassed, but in truth, I didn't quite know what to make of this situation. My mother still screamed loudly about this new life I'd chosen, about my faithlessness and the sinful, wicked lives of these women.

Yet her voice was distant, held at bay by warm laughter and shining eyes.

"And what expression did you wear after your loss, my soldier?" the Empress asked, facing me with that teasing smile. "Did you blush so brightly?"

I coughed, shifting in my armor. "No, *Augusta*."

"He did when he noticed my chest pressed against his," Helena chirruped. "And that he was grabbing my ass!"

I dropped my eyes, my cheeks ablaze. I expected to hear the Empress's laughter, though it did not come. After a few heartbeats, I flicked my eyes up to find her considering me. Her eyebrows were bent in a frown of scrutiny.

"*Augusta*?" I asked, my voice unsure.

"Were you angry when you lost to her?"

"I—*Augusta*?" I stammered. "Angry? No, I wasn't angry."

"How did you feel, then," Theodora pressed. "In that moment."

"Surprised, mostly. Empress, I don't—"

"She tricked you," the Empress interrupted. "She attacked you while you weren't prepared. You aren't angry that she did not fight you head-on?"

"No, *Augusta*," I said, confused by the abrupt change of tone. I glanced over to Helena for help, finding her instead to be intent on our conversation, observing me with her own heavy scrutiny.

"Why not?" the Empress said, bringing my attention back to her. "She's not as strong, or skilled as you. She cheated."

"*Augusta*? Please, I—"

"Answer the question, soldier."

Gone was the laughter from her face, replaced by the bright, piercing glare of an eagle. A dangerous sort of calm had settled over her, her body relaxed and arms loose by her side.

Confusion roiled through, a storm made stronger by sudden doubt and anxiety. I didn't know what the hell was going on, or how we had come here. I didn't know what to say, though as I let out a long breath, I decided that I could only tell the truth.

"There is no cheating in war, *Augusta*," I began, meeting her eyes. "There are only those who live and those who die. The mind is a weapon to be used, and Helena's is sharp."

I thought about stopping there, but I found more words within me. They flew out of me with ease, filling the air around us.

"So, no, I wasn't angry. Helena is good. I've trained many *stratiotai* during my years in the legion, and she is gifted beyond many. She trains hard every day, and her skill has grown by leaps and bounds."

Without meaning to, my eyes flicked over to Helena. She was watching me, her eyes wide and face open in a way I'd never seen before. Without knowing why, I kept my gaze on her as I continued to speak.

"I'm proud to fight beside her, *Augusta*, proud to call her my shield-mate."

And within the depths of Helena's wide, cypress eyes, I saw something start to grow. It was a small thing, a seed just sprouted, but already the wonder of it tightened my throat.

"Ah, my Leontius," the Empress said. Suddenly she was there, stepping past my shield and into the circle of my arms. I stiffened in alarm, and would have recoiled had I anywhere to go.

Theodora rested one palm against my breastplate, lifting my chin with the other. She smelled of lavender, a subtle aroma that blended with her own body's fragrance and the oil that shone upon her skin. Her eyes were warm when they met mine, her smile small but happy. "You are the best sort of man."

Then, she stretched up and kissed my cheek. Her lips were soft, and I found that tears were now flooding my eyes.

"Ah," I said, my voice hoarse and eyes blinking rapidly. "Ahem—Thank you, *Augusta*."

"You're very welcome," she said, finally stepping away from me with a much wider smile. "Now, open the door for me, my soldier. The Sassanid King Kavadh's delegates are due within the hour, and I must be there to greet them beside my husband."

"Of course, *Augusta*," I said, rushing to obey. In so doing, I caught sight of Helena's face. Her cheeks were bright with two spots of pink, and her lips were curled into a smile that seared itself into my mind.

I had no time to decipher its meaning that day, busy guarding the Empress through interminable speeches and ceremonies, though it came back to me as I lay down to sleep.

Helena's smile ... I'd like to see it again, I thought.

Though, as the lonely darkness wrapped around me, I watched that smile morph and twist into my mother's watery grin. I tossed and turned through the long night, wondering if my mother wept even now, tortured by the news that her son had forsaken her.

Chapter Six

To Love as an Empress

"Stand up straight," I hissed.

At my side, Helena snorted. "There's no one else here, Leo."

"I don't care!"

"I'm not taking orders from someone who smells like yesterday's catch."

"What?" I said. "I bathed yesterday."

I glanced to find Helena grinning at me, the light dancing in her cypress eyes. I had to resist the urge to surreptitiously sniff beneath my arms. She was just teasing me. Probably.

"In any case," I continued, trying to regain my momentum. "You never know who's watching. Straighten up."

Helena and I were in the Empress's salon, at our place on either side of the main door while Theodora's maids helped her dress. I shifted in my armor, checking to make sure that my shield was strapped on tightly and that my sword was sheathed in its place.

I was excited about today. It had been a week since the arrival of the Persian delegation, and this was the first day that we weren't headed right for the council chamber.

It was the day of the most anticipated chariot race of the summer. We were to go to the Hippodrome, and from here, I could hear the muted roar of the thousands already gathered.

"Are you saying that I'm the one who stinks?"

Helena's was still slouched against the wall. She'd raised an eyebrow, an expression of mock indignation on her face. As usual, she'd ignored everything I said. But I found that it didn't bother me. Much.

I grinned. "I guess so."

She reached up to swat at my head, the back of her breastplate scraping the stone. “Don’t be an ass. You can’t tell a lady that she stinks.”

“Stink is too weak a word for this.”

She laughed, and I felt my grin stretch wider. We continued back and forth for a few more minutes. As time went by, however, my armpits started to prickle. What sort of stench lurked there? I didn’t want to offend the Empress. We’d trained as usual these past few mornings, and though I wasn’t always good about washing immediately after, I didn’t wait *too* long.

Usually.

“Oh, Leo,” Helena said. “You make this too easy.”

“You should be watching for danger,” I said, dooming myself when I added: “I don’t stink.”

Her eyes danced. Again. “Check for yourself.”

“I’m not going to sniff at my armpits in the Empress’s salon.”

“Alright then,” she said with a shrug. “I’m sure that the Empress is too polite to say anything if she notices a smell.”

God dammit.

I chewed my lip, glancing about the empty room. Fuck. After another heartbeat of hesitation, I lifted my arm as much as I could in my armor and lowered my nose.

“My Leontius,” Empress Theodora said, choosing that moment to enter. “What are you doing?” She glided into the room, her walnut tresses piled elegantly atop of her head. Pale sandals were strapped to her feet and she wore a dress of dark-blue silk that did little to hide her dancer’s body.

“*Augusta*! I—Nothing! I wasn’t—” I clicked my mouth shut. My cheeks burned as I snapped back to attention, my shield out and back straight.

“I told him that he reeked, Highness,” Helena said with a grin. “He didn’t believe me.”

“Is that so?”

I saw her eyes flick between us, something flashing across her features. It was too quick for me to see.

In any case, I forgot all about it when a few moments later she slipped into the space between my body and the shield I held before me. I froze, staring ahead, as surprised by her sudden nearness as I had been the week before.

The Empress's scent flooded my mind; that blend of lavender, oil, and the sharpness of her body's natural aroma. The cool fabric of her *stola* slid across my bare thigh, her naked back warm where it brushed against my inner forearm. She leaned against my chest, shaping her body to mine.

I opened my mouth, but no sound emerged.

Then, she brought her face down to my armored collar, and sniffed. "Hmm, when was the last time you bathed, my soldier?"

I was mortified, my skin afire. "*Augusta*! I'm so sorry! I didn't realize, I—"

"Hush now," she said. I could hear Helena's muffled laughter. "I didn't say that it was unpleasant." She inhaled once again, making a pleased little sound with her throat. "Come here, Lena. You'll like this."

"Oh, yeah?" Helena said, pushing herself off of the wall.

The armored woman's voice was suddenly a notch deeper, strangely languid. She stepped into me, folding herself onto my other side with remarkable smoothness. She ducked her bare head beside the Empress, tucking herself into the crook of my neck, her coppery hair tickling my jaw. Her scent overpowered Theodora's: a swirl of oil, iron, and the feminine sourness of her sweat. My head swam with her, my heart hammering into my chest as she breathed deeply.

"Hmmm, you're right, Highness. That is rather nice."

"You're doing a hundred extra push-ups tomorrow," I somehow managed to say.

Both women laughed, their breath raising the flesh on my neck. The Empress tilted her head up to press her lips against my cheek. "I knew there was some life in you, my Leontius."

Both women stepped away, leaving me alone with my burning flesh. I looked from the Empress to Helena, finding my shield-mate's face as flushed as my own. She smiled at me, and I saw something shift beneath her cypress eyes.

Then, there was a knock at the door.

I immediately leaped away from the two women, petrified that someone might see. Helena pulled open the door while I tried to calm my racing heart.

It was the Emperor, bright-eyed, his beard streaked with gray. I'd seen him often this past week, the negotiations with the Sassanids proceeding with grinding slowness.

I hurriedly took another few steps to the side, praying that he wouldn't notice my burning face. I needn't have worried. When he swept into the room, Justinian had eyes only for his wife's delighted smile.

"My Theodora," he said, pulling her to him. "You are an angel gracing us from heaven."

She laughed, leaning her body away from his to caress his face and stare into his eyes. "You old flatterer. We've been apart too long."

Emperor Justinian, first of his name, smiled down at his Empress. "Indeed we have my dearest." He leaned down and kissed her. She threw her arms around his neck, kissing him as if they hadn't just seen each other that very morning.

I watched them from the corner of my eye, wondering what it would be like to be so obviously in love. To be so happy with the person that you'd sworn to God you'd stay with.

"*One day, you'll marry a good woman from a good family. You'll love and be true to each other. She'll care for your house and bear your children and you'll be oh so happy, my little lion.*"

That was part of the path my mother had set for me. It was proper. But looking at the Empress and her husband, I couldn't help but wonder if this unnamed woman from my future would truly love me. Could I ever be this happy?

Inexplicably, I found my eyes drawn to Helena.

She was smiling towards the Empress, her expression warm. Then, her eyes found mine, a question swirling within.

I looked away, a familiar guilt tearing at my stomach.

Chapter Seven

The Empress's Best Friend

We left for the Hippodrome not long after, Helena and I marching behind the couple, who walked arm in arm.

We listened to the Imperial pair worry about the crowd's mood. There had been some restlessness caused by the newly implemented war tax. This event was meant to help pacify and distract the capital's people.

The Imperial Box, when we finally arrived, thronged with many of the Empire's most prominent citizens. It was large, its many descending rows of seats protected by a wide awning. The heat of the early afternoon was brutal, though the stretched-out cloth did wonders to shelter us.

Dozens of well-dressed men and women milled about the wide, flattened area just before the door. They shouted to each other over the dull roar of the packed Hippodrome, picking over tables of fruit, olives, wine, and honeyed treats granted to them by the Emperor's generosity.

Guests moved to greet the Imperial couple. There was the well-groomed Persian ambassador and his entourage. I saw senators, nobles, and bishops; each man and woman better dressed than the last. I recognized many from the interminable council meetings that the Empress attended every day. And though I knew their faces, most of their names still escaped me. I even noticed Alexius and Diocles. The two merchant lords of the Blue and Green factions stood on opposing ends of the Imperial Box. They glared at each other, surrounded by their own gangs of sycophants.

"Belisarius!" The Empress said. "I'm so happy you're here."

Belisarius, the commander of the Roman armies and the highest-ranked general within the Empire, had arrived at the palace the day before.

I'd served beneath him in Anatolia and needed no help recognizing the powerfully built man. He was of an age similar to the Empress, his hair was black and he sported a thick beard trimmed into servility. His skin was dark, roasted from our campaign beneath the hot, Anatolian sun.

He kissed Theodora's cheek, turning to shake the Emperor's hand next.

I kept my back spear-straight. He wouldn't recognize me, of course. I'd only ever been another nameless *stratiotai* beneath his command. Yet still, I searched for a spark of recognition within his eyes as they swept over me. I'd served under him for a long time. And though I wasn't surprised, I couldn't help but feel a little swell of disappointment when his face remained blank.

He did nod a greeting to Helena, however, before the Emperor pulled him aside to speak.

"Ah, Theodora," another voice said. A woman moved towards us. She was blonde, her eyes dark, a smile curving the edge of her full lips.

"Antonina!"

The woman, Antonina, was stunningly beautiful.

She was pale, with the creamy sort of pallor of one who rarely venture out beneath the sun. She was a bit taller than the Empress, her body fuller. The sheer, yellow fabric of her dress did little to hide the lushness of her curving hips and strained against her two, massive breasts.

She swayed towards Theodora, the skin of her milky white legs and thighs flashing through the long slits on either side of her *stola*. There was just a single flap of fabric hanging between those shapely limbs, the only thing protecting what little of her remained hidden.

The two women embraced, chattering amicably while Helena and I shifted back a step. We stood stiffly to attention, two immovable rocks amidst the flow of humanity that surrounded us. There were a few other guards scattered throughout the box, *Excubitors* all, mostly standing by the rear wall.

"Who's that?" I asked Helena, my voice low.

"Antonina," she hissed. "Belisarius's wife, and the Empress's best friend. Be careful with her."

The comment surprised me. But before I could whisper another question, both women had turned towards us.

"Ah, it seems like you've gotten a new guard, Dora," Antonina said. Her voice was rich, tinged with the same fullness of her curves.

And her smile: there was a strange quirk to the corner of it—one that tempted and tantalized, like the sweetest sort of indulgence.

Heat crawled up my neck. I averted my gaze, but not before noticing the golden chain around her neck. It appeared the twin of the one Theodora wore, the links swallowed by the rounded fullness of her chest.

"He's handsome, is he not?" the Empress said. "He's that runner from the foot race we held at the beginning of summer."

"Of course," Antonina said, her eyes wandering over me. "I remember hearing about that. A soldier from my husband's army. How has he served?"

Theodora's lips curled into a smile. "I have no complaints."

"Ah," Antonina answered, her voice languid. "And tell me, how does he taste?"

My eyes bulged. I coughed, trying to keep the terror off of my face. My eyes flicked over to where the general still spoke to the Emperor. The two men were right there! What would they do to me if they heard?

The Empress sighed theatrically. "I'm afraid I don't know, Nina. My Leontius here has proven ... set in his ways."

The blonde woman raised an eyebrow. "That's not like you, Dora." Her eyes returned to me, tracing the shape of my face, the set of my shoulders, and the muscles of my arms. "I admit that I'm intrigued."

"Yes," the Empress said, her smile on me. "My Leontius is quite unique."

With that, the two women drifted away, leaving me with a belly full of this newest stress. They went to their seats, joined by Belisarius and the rest of the gathered citizenry. Helena and I drifted to the rear of the box, standing with our backs to the palace's wall.

It wasn't long before the Emperor ascended a nearby set of stairs. It brought him up to a speaking platform within full view of the assembled crowds.

He spoke to the waiting horde, his voice carried along by a series of loud-voiced callers. He bade them welcome, offering his hopes for the day, informing them of the wars abroad and the negotiations for peace that were underway. After he had spoken for fifteen minutes or so, he signaled for the show to begin.

Trumpets blared and the crowd roared. Their thunder shook the very air. Down on the sands, a flood of jugglers, dancers, and acrobats tumbled out, dressed in either blue or green. Each performed to their utmost, all trying to outdo the others and capture the eyes of the crowd and the attention of their faction lords.

Helena and I did not speak much. My shield-mate did not slouch either, her gaze set forward. The attention of the world was upon us, and none would find fault with the way their Empress was protected.

A mere ten minutes had passed when I saw Antonina, who'd been seated next to the Empress, stand and come towards us.

"Here we go," Helena muttered.

The blonde-haired woman ignored her, meeting my eyes with that edged smile. "Leontius, is it not? You're to escort me to my chambers."

"Ah," I said, my heart suddenly beating faster. "Your chambers, mistress?"

"Yes," she said, her lips curling wider. "I'm afraid that I underestimated the heat of the day." She absentmindedly hooked a finger into her straining neckline and pulled. "It's too hot. I need to get into something more ... comfortable."

I coughed, managing to swallow past my now dry throat. "Apologies mistress. I cannot leave the Empress."

"Oh, come now," she said. She leaned forward slightly, revealing more of the milky flesh of her breasts. "I might collapse. I really need to get out of these clothes."

I nearly choked. I managed to shift my gaze to the side, my eyes flicking over to where the Emperor sat speaking with Antonina's husband. Belisarius was one of the most powerful men in the Empire, as famous for his temper as he was for his skill on the battlefield.

His back was to us now, but I needed no help imagining the fury that would paint his face if he found me alone in his wife's chambers. He might even have me crucified. The punishment had been abolished nearly two hundred years ago, but perhaps my death would bring it back into vogue.

"I apologize again, mistress," I managed. "I cannot leave."

Annoyance flashed across Antonina's expression, wiping her smile away for an instant before it returned again. "Your dedication to your Empress is admirable, soldier. But my chambers aren't far. And I assure you, we will not be long."

"I'll take you there, Antonina," Helena cut in. "Leo would probably only get lost."

I nodded energetically.

The woman's gaze flicked disdainfully over to where Helena stood. "Thank you, Helena, but no. I need a real guard."

"I promise that you'll be safe with me."

A little smirk twisted Antonina's lips. "Lena, please. You were always better on your knees than with that sword."

Helena flinched. Her eyes flicked to me before she lowered them. Her lips tightened, and she didn't speak again.

"Shall we, then?" Antonina said, her gaze returning to me.

My face hardened, angry now. "No."

She lost her smile. "Your Empress has granted you to me for this, soldier. You will do what I desire."

I opened my mouth to tell her exactly where she could shove her desires, but Helena spoke over me. "You'd better go, Leo." Her voice was tight. "The Empress is watching us. I'll keep her safe."

When I glanced over, I did indeed find Theodora's dark eyes on me. She smiled, nodding her head and turning away.

I grit my teeth, wishing I had a choice.

I followed Antonina out of the Hippodrome. She didn't speak to me as we moved through the wings of the Imperial Palace.

My anger left quickly, to be replaced by fear. I was alone, following the general's wife to her private chambers. But, as the minutes passed, I found that my fear started to fade as well. It was hard to stay terrified, guided as I was by the rhythmic sway of Antonina's hips.

The pale flesh of her thighs and the rounded curves of her behind were clear beneath the yellow of her twice-slit dress. I was hypnotized by the way her muscles shifted; held captive by the way her ass *bounced*. Her body played with the earth's pull, the weight of each heavy cheek adding to the snap of her hips. We eventually arrived at a carved wooden door within an empty hallway. Antonina placed her hand on the handle.

"Come in with me."

"I'll guard the door from here, mistress."

I expected her to be angry—would have welcomed it, even. Instead, she just smiled.

"Ah, Leontius," she said in that low, rich voice. She swayed towards me, forcing me back until my breastplate scraped the wall opposite her door. "You served beneath my husband, correct?"

I nodded, my heart pounding. I stiffened when I suddenly felt the warmth of her hand on my arm.

"Shh," she said. Her hand touched my shield arm, her fingers finding the straps that bound the armor to my body. "Don't worry. He adores me, you know. My Belisarius."

I didn't know what to do. I was trapped, frozen by her nearness. The fog of her scent was filling me, a spiced, rich sort of sweetness blended with a flowery perfume.

"He's very protective."

My shield suddenly clattered to the floor, and I nearly jumped from my skin. Antonina laughed from deep within her throat. She leaned into me, her palms pressed against my breastplate.

"There's no need to be afraid," she breathed. "Not if you give me what I want."

"Mistress?" I croaked.

"You'll give me what I want," she said, "or my husband will hear that you attacked me."

I inhaled sharply. "What? Mistress, I—"

"Shh." That spark had turned to flames behind her eyes. Her palm rose to cup my cheek. "You're mine."

And I was. There was no way out of this. I was completely at her mercy—at the mercy of whatever word she brought back to her husband. We were alone in this part of the palace.

And of the two of us, it wouldn't be my word he'd believe.

"You will give me what I want," she repeated, curling her fingers to scrape along the stubble of my jaw.

I shivered, despite myself, my arms limp at my sides. Her lips curled further, and she pressed herself completely against me. Her fingers trailed down to the tip of my chin, holding it between her thumb and forefinger.

With a slight bit of pressure, she pulled my head down, guiding my eyes down to where her chest pushed up against my breastplate.

My eyes were swallowed by the soft, creamy curves of her flesh. My heart thundered in my chest. The way her body pushed into mine turned the slopes of her already-large breasts into a vast landscape that rose higher than I would have believed possible. The golden links of her chain had disappeared from my sight, devoured by twin dunes that cascaded into one another.

I swallowed, suddenly aching to explore the darkness of her curves, guided by nothing but the heat and perfumed softness of her skin.

She made a small sound of pleasure. "You see?"

I shivered, her breath raising bumps along my flesh. My fingers curled inward as she made another small sound, something between a purr and a laugh.

"I am generous, Leontius."

Then, she pressed her lips into my neck, searing me with their heat.

My breath was ragged, the muscles of my body clenched tightly. The space between us was too hot; it burned with the heat from her eyes and our reddened flesh. I felt myself tighten further, shriveling into myself until I suddenly felt a spot of cool, blessed relief: her tongue had emerged from between her lips, soothing my flesh with its liquid coolness. A low groan escaped my lips, my body loosening.

"I want to taste you, soldier." She continued to kiss my neck, moving higher. "I want to taste everything the Empress has not."

She pulled her lips away, their absence yanking another groan from deep within me. My arms rose of their own accord, poised to either push her away or crush her to me. Our eyes met, and I saw it: the endless, burning hunger within her. A dragon's appetite, one that could never truly be sated.

"I will have what I want."

Then, she pressed her lips to mine, consuming me.

For a moment, I didn't react. I was the lamb in the grip of that same mythical dragon. It reminded me of when I knelt before the Empress, though this was not the same. There was no benevolence to Antonina. I was at her mercy, and there was nothing I could do to escape her. I would be swallowed by her, used to feed the fire within her.

I was trapped. No laws, no rules of marriage, propriety, or human goodness would protect me. I'd be killed if I fought this.

So, why not enjoy it?

That knowledge awoke something within me. The heat of her selfish lust burned through the twisted knot in my stomach, freeing me from the snarl that kept me frozen in place. And there, revealed within the depths of me, was a lion's hunger.

I wanted her.

My hands clamped around her waist and I jerked her to me, parting my lips and opening myself to her. Her tongue flicked into me, and mine rose to curl around it. I kissed her back, pushing against her. She gave way, my tongue following hers back into the sweetness of her mouth. We parted with a gasp, her eyes bright, our breathing frayed.

"Let's take from each other then, soldier of my husband."

I growled, kissing her again, our tongues slipping around each other. My hand rose to where her chest pressed into mine. She purred into me, angling herself so the heavy fullness of one breast fell into my palm. I caressed her through her silken dress, working my fingers around every curve.

Antonina pulled away from me again, her bottom lip wedged between her teeth. She took my hand in hers, guiding it up to one of her bare shoulders. My fingers worked themselves beneath the strap, sliding it across the burning smoothness of her shoulder.

"Hurry," she panted.

But I took my time, pulling the silk down, teasing more of her free with every heartbeat. I followed the emerging links of that golden chain, the warm metal hugging the milky curves of her chest. Finally, just as I was deciding to rip the dress away, a single breast burst free. My breath caught, and I exhaled a moment later with a groan of raw *need*. My eyes drank in the sight of her lush, creamy fullness. Her nipple was small in the vastness of her flesh, pert and pink, and starting to stiffen in the naked air.

She threw herself back onto me, mashing her lips onto mine. I matched her fervor, squeezing and exploring her naked breast and pinching her ripe, taut nipple. She moaned into me, her tongue frantic, tasting every inch of me as our breath tore into each other.

Then, I felt her hands slip beneath my armored skirt. I growled, pushing my hips into her body. Our lips parted for an instant, this time for a breathy laugh of satisfaction to escape her. My lips found hers once more, and her fingers began to work themselves over the loincloth-covered stiffness of my cock.

When next we parted, she bent her legs into a low crouch. Her eyes burned into mine, her fingernails trailing down the steel of my breastplate and pinging against the metal—a sound I barely heard over the roaring of my blood. Her face was level with my crotch, one hand massaging my still-covered manhood. Her eyes burned into mine, her teeth bared in a draconic smile.

I grinned my own predatory smile, feeling my hunger rage within me. I would take from her, sating myself with her body.

I undid my armored skirt, letting it fall to the floor. Then, I dug my fingers into the wrap around my waist and wrenched it away. My cock sprang free, rising, tall, and eager before her, the pale flesh of it afire with need. Every ridge, every curve, and every vein pushed against the tightly stretched skin.

"Hmm," she said. "Good."

She wrapped her palm around my manhood, working it up and down. The motion was slow at first, her hand luxuriating in the fire that raged beneath my skin. I felt myself growing even harder, my cock reaching out to close the space between us.

Antonina leaned in closer, her face flushed. "Oh, fuck," she moaned. "That stink. God, I love how it stinks."

She pumped my burning erection, her tongue slipping from between parted lips. I reached down and tugged on her dress, freeing her other breast to hang beside its sister. But she hardly seemed to notice. She inhaled the sour stench of my cock, her free hand slipping beneath the silken flap of cloth between her legs. She stroked herself in rhythmic circles, her breath coming in ragged little bursts.

Then, she tasted me.

She started at my base, her tongue gliding to the tip of me in one long, languid stroke. Once there, she rolled the skin back to expose my pink, bulbous head. She breathed me in, her fingers digging into the slit between her legs.

"Take it," I growled, weaving my fingers into her mass of blonde hair.

Her eyes were slits of heat and hunger, her lips curled into a smirk. "Then, give it to me."

She opened her mouth, letting her tongue spill out. She welcomed me within her, and I groaned as I slid between her ready lips.

I didn't shove it to the back of her throat, merely poked my tip into her and let her work the cool, lushness of her tongue around it in languid swirls. I pushed in deeper, and she released a moan that thrummed up the entire length of my cock. Her throat flexed as strings of saliva started to trickle down her chin to hang over her naked tits. She began to bob her skull, taking more of me with every slow motion. It wasn't long before she'd taken all of me.

I was at the back of her throat, her lips wrapped around my base, and the rest of me squashed in with her teeth and flexing tongue. Hot air blasted from my chest. I groaned, my muscles clenching. I pulled on her skull with both hands, grinding her nose into my pubic hair and quenching myself within the tight wetness of her mouth. I held her there for several heartbeats, my eyes fluttering and my body curling around her. Antonina's throat spasmed, and I loosened my grip on her.

She came off my cock with a ragged gasp.

Her tongue spilled from between her lips, releasing a flood of fluid and spit that splashed down to soak her heaving chest. Within moments, her tits shone with wetness, thoroughly coated by the rivulets that flowed down her rounded slopes.

"Fuck," she panted, her eyes glazed.

With the hand that wasn't still clawing at her pussy, Antonina wrapped her very long, golden, saliva-slickened chain around my cock so that the heavy cross dangled beneath my twitching member. Her fingers closed around the warm links, stroking me with the warm metal.

She'd chained us together, ensuring neither would escape the other's hunger.

"More," she said, her voice crackling. "I want it all."

She opened her mouth, and I didn't hesitate to thrust myself back into her. I twisted my fingers deep into her hair, slamming my cock into the back of her throat. A growl tore itself from my throat, a furnace-hot rumble that matched Antonina's moan. In the next heartbeat, she closed her eyes and surrendered herself to me. I held her skull in place, thrusting into her mouth again and again. I pounded into the wet heat of her throat, her teeth brushing against the ridged length of my cock.

I closed my eyes, my entire awareness on the tight, liquid confines of her hot mouth. Everything was burning. I was desperate, shriveling with the need to vent the inferno that was raging hotter and hotter within me. It took a mere minute before I jammed myself into her one final time and exploded.

I groaned, muscles locked, my entire body quivering with every throbbing pulse of my release. Antonina didn't try to pull herself away. Instead, both of her hands flew up to my thighs, digging her nails into me and anchoring herself there while she devoured me.

The Empress's best friend took everything I gave her, her throat flexing, draining every last drop from me. I let out an explosive breath, letting go of her hair as a few final tremors ran through me.

Antonina slowly slid herself back off my cock, making a sound low in her throat. She slipped the chain out from around me, the muscles beneath the naked flesh of her thighs shifting as she rose back to her full height.

"Leontius," she purred. "I guess there really is a lion within you. You've earned my silence."

Her eyes still burned, though it was now but the flicker of embers rather than the blaze it had been. Her lips quirked into a satisfied smile, and I saw that not one drop of what I'd given her had escaped her hunger. She pressed her gleaming chest against mine and kissed me. Her breath was hot, sour with the taste of what I'd pumped into her. "For now," she added when we separated.

I gazed at her, slack-jawed, sweat sheathing my body. My thoughts started to swirl into motion as I watched her glance down at her spit-coated breasts.

"Hmmm, look at all this," she laughed. "Now, I really do need to get out of this dress. Guard this door for me, soldier."

She crossed the hall to her chamber door without bothering to pull her *stola* back up over her naked chest. She disappeared a moment later.

I was left alone in the, thankfully, still empty corridor. As my heartbeat slowed and my breath evened, my mother's haranguing voice returned.

"*These women are vile,*" she said. "*There is no goodness here, no happiness to be found around such filth. You have to run,*" she told me, "*to return to the path your father and I set you on.*"

But the sound was faint, weak without the twisting guilt. I didn't move. My eyes were on the floor, gazing into a small puddle of liquid that had dripped onto the stone from the slit between Antonina's legs.

Then, I looked at my hand, at the old, old blood beneath my fingernails. There was a decade of it there, blood that I could never really wash away.

Perhaps it wasn't good, this thing I'd done with another man's wife. I didn't know. But surely this was a better liquid to spill than the blood in another's veins. This certainly had brought less pain into the world. And as I waited for Antonina to emerge, hearing the roar from the Hippodrome grow louder, I wondered if that even mattered.

Chapter Eight

What the Empress Desires

This place.

Just when I thought that I was getting a handle on it, something would knock me free of the base I'd anchored myself to.

Antonina, the wife of the Empire's greatest general, had just taken me with her mouth. She'd spit on her marriage vows, risking her future, happiness, and respectability. And for what? A whim? A silly streak of competitiveness with her best friend?

She was perverse. She should be ashamed, not strutting away with bared breasts and lips curled in a satisfied simper.

I let out a breath, shifting within the empty corridor, Antonina's door at my back. If she was wicked, what then was I, who felt neither shame nor guilt at my own part in the act we'd just committed?

My mother's voice, still there, in the back of my head, certainly believed I should feel ashamed. Where was her little lion, she asked through a veil of tears, who'd once so diligently walked the path she'd laid out for him?

I didn't know. I looked down at my hands once again. I thought they looked clean. Well, not clean, but cleaner than when I'd checked a few minutes ago. Was some of that blood flaking away?

The sound of footsteps made me raise my head. I stiffened to attention, flicking my eyes about the space to make sure that everything was in order. It wouldn't do for Belisarius to arrive to find me with my manhood out, my flesh still gleaming with his wife's saliva.

To my great relief, it wasn't the general that appeared down the hallway, but the Empress and Helena.

Theodora moved towards me, graceful as the dancer she'd never ceased to be. She smiled, the corners of her dark eyes wrinkling in the way to which I'd grown accustomed.

"Vigilant as always, my Leontius?"

"*Augusta*," I answered, keeping my back straight.

Without conscious thought, my eyes slid past the Empress's shoulder. Helena was there. My eyes found hers, and I belatedly realized that I might not like what I saw in her. It felt like a fist had just clenched my heart. Did she know? Did she know what I'd just done, I wondered, searching her smile.

She did. And for a moment, I thought I might shatter.

Helena knew, and the shifting green of her cypress eyes begged my forgiveness. She'd known what Antonina had wanted and she had failed to put herself between us. I saw relief in the folds of her face, a careful uncertainty in the shape of her lips.

Something cracked within me. Helena didn't hate me. She knew, and she was still here, glad to see me. I felt my throat squeeze itself shut. Of course, there was nothing to forgive her for, my eyes said. My shield-mate was here, and that was what mattered.

"You've cared well for my dear Antonina, I trust?" the Empress said, pulling my attention back to her. Her smile had changed. There was an extra curve to it now, a hint of knowing in her eyes that made me flush. Of course, I'd never be able to hide this from her.

"Yes, *Augusta*." The words came out a little hoarsely, so I cleared my throat. "She is safe within her chambers."

"Good," Theodora answered. "Well, my Leontius, you had better let me in. Nina tends to lose track of time when fabric is involved."

I nodded, reaching back to open the door. The Empress brushed past me, trailing her fingers along my outstretched arm. Helena moved to follow, but Theodora stopped her with a few words. "Stay here, Helena. I won't be long."

Helena hesitated a moment. Something seemed to flash between them, and she nodded, stepping back and letting me shut the door. She placed herself on the door's other side, stiffening to attention beside me.

I let out a breath, feeling the knot within me loosen.

"You stink worse than before."

I choked on my exhalation, and Helena burst into laughter. I'd sucked a bunch of spit back into my throat. I hacked and coughed, my eyes watering, as her laugh deepened into that thrumming, full-bellied sound that made my stomach tingle.

She was bent over, leaning her behind against the stone wall for support. She laughed, and even through the haze of my tears, I could see the way her eyes danced.

"Not funny," I croaked.

She howled, tears starting to stream from her own eyes. "Stop! Stop!"

I glared, and she wasn't able to speak again for another minute.

"Turn around," she gasped between fits of laughter. "Stop—don't look at me!"

I grumbled and spent another minute staring at nothing while she composed herself.

"Are you done?" I asked, turning around.

"Yes," she said, through another bubble of laughter. She cleared her throat. "Yes. I'm sorry."

I nodded, although I felt my lip quirk into a small smile. "Why did you leave the box? Did we miss the race?"

Helena shook her head. "It hasn't started yet. You were gone a long time, and the Empress started to wonder. I think she wanted to catch you doing something ..." She trailed off, and heat rushed back to my face. I looked away. There it was, I thought, the shame.

"Leo," she said. "I'm sorry. I knew what she wanted, and I tried, but I—"

I shook my head, staring ahead. "Stop. Helena, please. You did what you could, and then you fell back and did your duty. Just as any soldier should."

"Yes, but—" She bit off her own words.

My eyes flicked back to her. She was chewing on her lip, concern still writ large across her features. I couldn't help but smile, feeling the final pieces of what had broken within me being washed away. "It's not like I was fighting a battle or anything."

She snorted. "With Nina, it might as well be. She's not known for being gentle."

I sighed. "Yeah, well, I hope that her husband is when he rips my balls off. I have this theory that I might soon be the first man crucified in centuries."

She didn't laugh like I thought she would. Beneath her coppery curls, her expression remained worried. "Are you ok, Leo?"

"I think so," I smiled, resisting the urge to look at my hands.

"Was she that good, then?"

"It's not that," I said. "Although, yes, I can't deny that."

I met her eyes. Her expression had hardened, her cheeks were flushed and angry, and her jaw was set. This time, she was the one to look away.

"Great. Well, don't worry, you can go see her whenever you want."

"I don't want to."

My eyes unfocused while I tried to order my thoughts. "I don't like that kind of ... experience. There was nothing behind it. I don't really know how to explain it." I hesitated a moment before I continued. "It was like eating just because you're hungry, taking no joy from the food. Sure, it fills you up, and sometimes that's exactly what you need. But, I don't know. There can be so much more to something like that. And that's what I want."

My eyes focused back on Helena. I smiled ruefully. "Does that make sense?"

She nodded. Her cheeks were still red, but there was something else shifting within the swaying cypress of her eyes. My heart started to beat faster. A warmth rose through me, a much softer heat than Antonina's burning, draconic hunger.

Though, it had been that fire that had pushed me further along this new path that I'd chosen. And now that I was moving once more, I didn't want to stop.

"It's just that ... I think I like it here." I stood up straighter once the words had been said as if they'd been a weight on my shoulders. "My life isn't where it's supposed to be, and I'm becoming someone other than who I was. But, I think that it's good. At least, some of it is. Being here with you, with the Empress, it's so different than anything I was ever supposed to know. But, I think ... I think that I'm actually starting to be happy, even though I maybe shouldn't."

I hesitated, unable to look away from her. Her eyes were so soft. There was no hatred there, no disdain. Neither was there any of the cringing disgust that my mother's voice assured me would be there. Instead, I saw only understanding.

"Is that ok?" I asked.

A breeze blew within her, shifting the green of her eyes. It showed me something else, the edge of that thing growing within the depths of her. I didn't yet know what it was, but it took my breath away.

"Yes," she said. "I think it's alright."

She smiled, and that warmth spread all the way down to my toes. I opened my mouth to say something else but was interrupted by Antonina's voice calling loudly from through the door. "Open the door! We're ready."

I grumbled and turned to push the door open. Helena turned away as well, hiding what remained of her smile.

Antonina had changed into a long, ivory-colored dress. It was looser than the other one had been, though her chest still threatened to erupt from her neckline.

"Thank you, soldier," Antonina said, with a smile. She'd re-arranged her hair and had wiped her face and breasts clean. She'd washed away all evidence of our ... encounter, save for the slight redness that still glowed beneath her milky flesh.

Her expression soured when she caught sight of Helena.

"Antonina," my shield-mate said, inclining her head.

"I see that you've managed to keep from disemboweling yourself with that sword of yours," the other woman said. "I'm impressed, I admit."

"It shouldn't be a surprise," Helena said. "There's a long history of women skilled in the use of weapons. Your talent with the ... spear, for example."

The blonde woman's eyes flashed. "Indeed, it is a worthy weapon. I enjoy the use of it. You would be better with it than that blade, I think."

"Perhaps. Though, is it not dangerous? I hear that you are often, ahem, *skewered* while you spar."

Antonina surprised me by barking out a laugh. "You seem to have found your teeth again, little Lena. Come, you can escort me back."

Helena nodded, flashing me a quick look before she followed behind the blonde. I stared after them in shock. What the hell had just happened?

"Those two have known each other a long time," I heard the Empress say. "Their friendship has always been a little ... contentious."

I turned to find Theodora standing in the still-open doorway. She smiled when my eyes found hers, laying a hand on my outstretched arm. "Would you escort me back, my Leontius?"

"Of course, *Augusta.*"

I let the door close behind her, raising my arm slightly so she could hold onto it as we walked. She raised an eyebrow but remained silent

Soon, we were trailing a distance behind where Antonina and Helena still exchanged cutting remarks. Something seemed to have come over Helena, some new feeling that didn't let her simply fade into the background.

The Empress's arm shifted to loop around mine, gripping my bicep. "I worry about her sometimes."

"*Augusta*?"

"Helena. I believe that she enjoys this life—at least, some aspects of it. Though, it has never been what she really wanted. It was hard for her ... before." Her eyes were on the pair ahead of us, watching as they rounded a corner.

"In a way, Helena was the strongest of the three of us. She was able to hang on to more of herself than Nina and I were, despite her being the youngest." She squeezed my arm, the gesture involuntary. "Her stubbornness makes her strong, but there's a brittleness to it too. That rigidity has cost her at times, though perhaps that is changing as well."

"*Augusta*?" I asked again, confused.

She laughed softly. "Don't mind me, Leontius. I like to let my thoughts air from time to time."

We walked in silence for a few more steps before she added, "She likes honeyed figs, you know. And honeyed olives. Anything with honey really, but the figs are her favorite."

I was running out of ways to express my confusion. So, I just remained silent. I was further surprised when the Empress pulled me to a stop. I glanced down at her as she leaned into me and pressed her silk-covered breasts into my arm. My eyes widened, my body stiffening. Her lips parted, and she pulled herself up on my arm until her breath tickled my ear. Gooseflesh erupted over my neck.

"Don't you forget, my soldier," Theodora murmured. "I will have my taste. Nina has told me too much of it for me to give it up now."

I shivered, and she made a small, pleased sound in her throat. She pressed her lips against my cheek and leaned away. The smile didn't leave her lips until we reached the Imperial Box.

Chapter Nine

Chariots Race for the Empress

The Hippodrome: a monument of pale stone adorned with golden statues. It was at the center of Constantinople, at the heart of an empire whose borders had once stretched to the very end of the world.

The Empress and I stepped into the Imperial Box just as four charioteers emerged onto the track below. There would be nearly a dozen races today. The Blues, Greens, and various other factions of wealthy men and women had sponsored dozens of charioteers and their teams. It was this first race, however, that was the most anticipated.

The mob was screaming, pounding on drums, and waving strips of blue or green cloth into the air. The line where they met was as sharp as any horizon, a rippling field of green touching a sky of pulsating blue.

Their champions had taken to the sands.

Maleinos and Velanis: elite charioteers and the veterans of a hundred races. Maleinos, his hair streaked with gray, waved toward where the Blue supporters chanted his name. Velanis, a younger man with an easy smile, did the same for the Greens. Both of their chariots were painted in the colors of their factions, and Maleinos even led a team of horses with coats so dark they appeared almost blue in the light of the August sun.

I didn't recognize the other two men; their chariots were painted in colors whose meaning I did not know. They did not appear intimidated by the Hippodrome's crowds; experienced racers, then.

The four teams were moving slowly around the track, completing this first lap at a walk. I got a good look at them as they passed. Roman chariots were small and light, an open basket of wood that was designed for speed rather than war. A single driver stood within, leashed to the four horses that were his team.

"*Nika*!" I heard voices call. "*Nika*!"

The word was faint, nearly lost amidst the rest of the cacophony. But as the charioteers' lap came to its halfway point, I heard it again. And then again, growing louder and louder as more of the crowd joined in.

"*Nika! Nika! Nika!*"

It was an old word, a call to unify. It meant taking victory from your rivals. It had been used by armies once, a word hammered on by generals in their speeches. The legions had loved that word and had once chanted it to the rhythm of their crashing feet.

For *nika* was to conquer.

The Empress's grip shifted, and I escorted through a scattering mass of senators, bishops, and merchant lords. Theodora smiled at me in thanks, lowering herself down between her husband and Antonina. I returned to the rear of the box beside Helena. The charioteers were coming to the end of their slow lap.

The crowd's thunder intensified. "*Nika*!" They chanted, ripping the air with their flags. "*Nika! Nika!*" The sound was the rhythmic hammer of the surf. It was wave after wave—a pounding storm of frenzied excitement.

The mob roiled, like currents ebbing and flowing, rising and falling. It was a sea of humanity with waves gathering only to crash and swirl into one another. That ocean seethed and boiled, raged, and calmed. And like the sea that surrounded my island home, I wondered what would happen if that tide ever rose. Would we float away? Or would it drown us all?

I shook myself, forcing some steel into my spine. I'd been to the races before, I knew what the crowds of the Hippodrome were like. Though, admittedly, I'd always been just another drop in that ocean. Now ...

I snuck a glance towards Helena. She stood to attention, alert, though comfortable beneath the shade of the sheltering awning. I remembered our conversation, the flicker of that wonder I'd seen growing at the center of her.

Honeyed figs? I thought.

Below us, the charioteers were lining up to begin the race. Through the corner of my eye, I saw Maleinos of the Blues wrapping the reins of his horses around both forearms, his body taut. Velanis of the Greens did the same, though he was loose enough to keep bobbing his head towards the crowd.

Sensing my gaze, Helena tilted her head towards me. Her eyes were questioning. I smiled, mouthing words through the crowd's roar: "Seven *nummi* on Green."

Helena's eyes glittered, and I arched my eyebrow in a silent question. Seven *nummi* was the daily wage of a soldier in the Empire's legions. Those small bronze coins were used to buy what comforts could be found in a traveling legion camp.

She nodded, and I felt my grin widen. I watched the racers prepare with more attention. I liked the way Velanis looked; the younger man was more relaxed than any of the others.

Then, with a nod from the Emperor and the peal of a trumpet, the race began.

Sand flew as sixteen sets of hooves tore forward. The charioteers shouted, whipping their reins, their muscles bunching as they leaned their bodies into their vehicles. The mob roared, drowning the racers in their exaltation.

Maleinos of the Blues was quick to take the inside track. The canny old charioteer fended off the others with sharp maneuvers of his chariot. His team was eager, the horses straining against their harnesses. The muscles of their legs were thick beneath their glossy coats.

Velanis slid into the second position, to one side of the dust plume kicked up by the blue team. He was a few horse-lengths back, crouching low.

The lot of them ripped around the first curve, the horses blurring past in a rolling mass of thunder. I watched in awe, hardly able to blink as they careened back towards the finish line. The iron and bronze of their wheels and buckles sparkled in the sun, making them look like glittering Persian *djinni* in the growing cloud of dust.

"*Nika*!" The crowd chanted. "*Nika! Nika!*"

Maleinos rumbled across the finish line, the first of seven laps completed. Helena turned towards me. Her grin was wild, eyes alight with the arena's thunder. I returned her grin, my chest thudding with the same sort of excitement. If the Hippodrome was indeed Constantinople's heart, then the pounding of hooves and the roaring of the mob was its heartbeat. And the charioteers were its blood.

The crowd screamed as Velanis narrowly avoided a collision. He slipped back into third place, giving way to the man who had nearly crashed into him. This third charioteer was aggressive, lunging forward to where the Blue driver still held the lead.

My eyes flicked back to the Green driver. The muscles on his arms and shoulders bulged beneath the winding leather of his reins. He pulled his horses towards the track's center, urging them to greater speed. My grin widened. He was biding his time, slowly putting himself into a position to pass. The horses seemed tireless, charging around turn after turn as the number of remaining laps ticked downward.

I felt something shove into my arm. I looked over, finding one of Helena's hands closed around my forearm. Her auburn hair was dancing in the wind of the passing chariots, and the skin of her cheeks flushed.

She leaned towards me, shouting in my ear, "Last lap!"

I laughed as she waggled her eyebrows.

Her Blue was still in the lead, having kept his place along the track's interior by blocking his rival's every move. The unknown charioteer was still the nearest to him, having finally managed to get his team of horses parallel to the wheels of Maleinos's chariot.

Velanis was further out, closing in from the direction of the wall. He'd put on a burst of speed as they'd finished the sixth lap, managing to line his horses with those of Maleinos. The Green began to close in on the final straight away. Along with the third charioteer, they made a sort of inverted triangle. Velanis angled his team in towards Maleinos, trying to slip his nose ahead of the Blue right before the final curve.

I felt myself bounce up and down, Helena's grip tightening on my arm. He was doing it! Velanis was pulling ahead! Maleinos would have to pull back! Or they'd—

And that's when it happened.

Seeing his chance at victory slipping away, the third charioteer, trapped between the Blue and the Green, pulled back on his reins. I'm not sure what he was thinking. Perhaps he was hoping to slip out from behind Velanis to try to race around them on the outside. In any case, it didn't work.

He pulled his team to the side too quickly, his horses clipping the edge of Velanis's chariot. The Green was thrown to the side, and his swaying body yanked his own team sharply towards the track's center—directly into Maleinos.

Horses screamed and wood splintered as the two chariots smashed into each other. The Blue vehicle crashed into the dividing wall, skipping off of it and throwing its driver high. Horses and chariots rolled, Velanis disappearing into the tumbling wreckage. Behind them, the third chariot was too close. The shattered pieces of the other vehicles speared into his team, tripping them and sending them crashing to the sand with bone-cracking force.

The fourth racer, who'd lagged behind the entire race, was far enough away to avoid the wreckage. He steered his team around the debris. His gaze flashed backward, but he didn't stop.

The blood roared in my ears. Helena's grip on me didn't loosen.

Everyone rose to their feet.

In the Imperial Box, bishops pushed past senators, crowding the railing's edge, searching the obscuring dust for any sign of their fallen champions.

Slowly, the dust started to clear.

I don't remember who shouted first, or who was the first to point their finger. But soon, as the dust cloud broke apart, we all saw them. Maleinos and Velanis; both men lying still.

The crowd's roar turned into a wordless groan, fading into quiet disbelief as neither charioteer rose from the puddles of blood that were spreading below each of them. The men were dead, a sight that was not uncommon on these sands.

My breath was coming faster, for though the men and mob were silent, the horses were not. The horses' bodies had been broken by the crash. Their legs were shattered, jagged spears of bone ripping through once glossy coats. They thrashed and kicked, their lifeblood pumping from their torn limbs.

And they screamed. God, how those horses screamed. Their high-pitched, dying shrieks of agony filled the Hippodrome. My fingernails dug into my palms, adding my own blood to that which was already beneath them.

This was the chorus of war, the sound that followed victory or defeat. It brought me back to the fields of Callinicum. I remembered the charge of our cavalry against the Sassanids, how we'd broken each other on the spears of our armies.

The third charioteer was still alive. Beneath the eyes of thousands, he pushed himself to his knees. He crawled over to where one of his horses bucked and screamed, digging bloody trenches in the sand. The man had a knife at his belt. He drew it and gave the poor animal the only mercy he could. His frame shook with sobs, though he did not hesitate in moving to where another of his team lay.

At the track's end, the sole remaining charioteer crossed the finish line. He did not celebrate, did not raise his arms or pump his fists in triumph. He led his team towards the arena's exit with his head bowed.

The crowd's silence twisted into anger.

Chapter Ten
The Empress's Reforms

The mob started to hiss and murmur, the sea starting to boil. Someone threw a clay jug; dozens and dozens more were tossed after it within a breath.

"Fuck," Helena said, her hand finally slipping from my arm.

Her voice, her scent, and the lingering warmth of her touch brought me back from my memories of war. I glanced over, met her eyes, and felt myself loosen. I let out a shaky breath. "Yeah."

Fights were starting to break out along the line of fans. Blues blamed Greens for the death of their champion, and Greens blamed anyone but their own Velanis.

"Think that will get out of hand?" Helena asked.

I shifted my shoulders into a shrug.

The few fights were already breaking up, devolving back into insults and shaking fists. The deluge of thrown garbage slowed. The Hippodrome's master sent out a flood of slaves to clear the wreckage. The mob seemed to settle down into a calm that I did not trust.

"I don't know," I said. "I don't think anyone's quite drunk enough yet. For now."

Helena snorted, shifting her weight. "That's probably true."

Within the Imperial Box, among Constantinople's great and good, the mood was subdued. Most of them had gotten up while the slaves worked, mingling and speaking to each other with worried faces and shaking heads. The air simmered with the same anxious, confused anger felt by the crowds of citizens.

The Persian delegates looked on with barely concealed disgust. I saw many wipe their hands on their long robes as if dirtied by what they had just witnessed.

Alexius of the Blues and Diocles of the Greens, meanwhile, were in each other's faces. They wailed about their lost fortunes, screaming their accusations into the other's throats. *Excubitors* were closing in, watching to make sure that nobody came to blows in the Emperor's presence.

"Let's go to the Empress," Helena said. "I don't like this."

I grunted, approving of her caution.

Theodora was with her husband, speaking with a group that included Belisarius and Antonina, as well as a man dressed in the robes of a priest. "You're going to have to speak," the Empress was telling Justinian. "Announce the next race. Speak about this loss. Show them that their Emperor is with them."

Justinian let out a breath, scratching at his beard. "I suppose you're right. Damned shamed about Maleinos, too."

"Empathize with them, my love," Theodora continued. "Show the Blues you feel this loss as they do. Although, you must make sure that the Greens feel included as well. We cannot afford to favor one over the other at this moment."

Beside them, the general nodded. Antonina hung off his arm, whispering something into his ear. Belisarius spoke a few moments later. "I will send some of my soldiers to patrol the streets."

The Emperor shook his head. "That won't be necessary."

"Listen to him, my love," Theodora said. "The general knows his business. There will be fires tonight."

"Fires? Come now, Theodora. The people have settled down."

"Indeed, they have, *Augustus*," another voice added. "You are wise to say so."

A man approached us. He was older, though his dark hair remained mostly free of gray. His face was handsome, confident, and he was dressed in the finery of a senator. An armored *Excubitor* trailed behind him. This man was younger, his eyes ringed with fading purple bruises.

The younger man's gaze fell on me and I bristled at the naked hostility I saw there. I recognized him a heartbeat later. He was the pretty, loud-mouthed idiot whose face I'd smashed in for insulting Helena and me. I hadn't seen him for more than a month, and I couldn't say that I was happy to see him now.

"Senator Hypatius," the Empress said. Her tone had dropped into one of cold civility. "A pleasure."

"*Augusta*," the senator answered, bowing low. "As always, your beauty makes my tongue feel awkward."

"Is that why you don't agree with my words, senator? Because I can assure you, the people will not forget this. And when the races conclude and the city's wine houses start to overflow ..."

"Of course, you are correct," Hypatius said. His voice was smooth and practiced in a way that only a trained orator's could be. "They will not forget. But, your Imperial Majesties, you must understand that the people are angry."

Antonina rolled her eyes, and I saw the Empress fight to not do the same. Senator Hypatius was a fixture in the palace's council meetings, delivering variations of the same speech every time he spoke. "Much has changed in the past five years," he was saying. "The people are still getting used to your reforms, and the cost of foreign wars has been difficult for many to bear."

"My new taxes have only targeted those with wealth to spare, senator," Justinian said patiently. "Besides, is the expansion of our Empire and infrastructure not worth the cost?"

"Indeed, *Augustus*," Hypatius said, "and I gladly pay what is required of me. However, I fear that, in your zeal, you may have misjudged. You have changed the ancient laws of marriage, neutering men within their own households. You have stripped the wealth and influence of us senators, as well as that of the Blues and the Greens."

"Those with wealth to spare," the Emperor repeated.

"Perhaps," the senator said. "But are we senators not the representatives of the people? Are the Blues and Greens not comprised of thousands of citizens? In most ways, *Augustus*, we are the people."

The Emperor folded his arms. "So, what do you suggest?"

"A more restrained response," the senator said. "Let the Blues and Greens mourn their champions as they see fit."

"Your advice is to do nothing?" the Empress cut in. "What then, when gangs of drunken faction men start fires and butcher each other in the streets? Your villa will not protect you from the mob, Hypatius."

"Nothing? Of course not, *Augusta*. Indeed, some of my fellow senators and I have a great many ideas. If you recall my last proposal before the senate, I—"

"Oh please, Hypatius." It was Antonina that interrupted him. "We all know that you parrot Diocles's words. It's a step backward. As if the Greens do not control enough of this city already."

"Control?" the senator said. "This is about survival. With these new reforms, the Greens are barely holding on. Is it a wonder that the people seek to return to more traditional laws?"

Antonina snorted. "'*Tradition*' is a pretty word for thuggery and the whoring of children. I was raised by the Blues, senator. I know what values the factions hold."

"Be silent!" the mouthy guard shouted. He stepped towards Antonina, hand on his sword, his face was molten with rage. "Your betters are speaking, whore!"

Belisarius stepped forward at once, his dark eyes murderous. But it was Hypatius who acted first. His hand flashed, slapping the younger man across the face.

"Shut your mouth, fool boy!"

My mouth fell open. The *Excubitor* fell back, crying out in pain. Confusion clouded his features. "Father, I—"

"Enough!" Hypatius shouted. "You will be silent."

"He's the senator's son?" I murmured to Helena.

"Doukas," she answered. "It doesn't make him more likable, does it?"

I fought back a smirk, turning my attention back to where Hypatius bowed deeply to Antonina. "Forgive my son, Mistress. Please. He is a young man, and I fear that the heat of the day has fried what little brain he has."

The Empress made a small sound, everyone's attention shifting over to her. "Antonina and I performed together in those days, senator. Is your son insulting me as well?"

Doukas's face went white, his eyes flashing to his father. The older man hurriedly bowed again. "Of course not, *Augusta*. He wasn't thinking. Apologize, boy. To everyone here."

The *Excubitor* did so, bowing jerkily to everyone in turn. His father led him away a few minutes later, the young man's face burning with fresh humiliation.

The Emperor let out a breath once they had left. "I think you're right about needing the soldiers, my love. As if these failing peace negotiations weren't enough." He suddenly looked very tired. Theodora folded herself around her husband's arm, gazing up at him with a worried expression. "Belisarius," he continued. "See to it."

He started to move towards his speaking platform; the sands below finally cleared of any debris. "Let's hope the rest of the day goes smoothly."

Chapter Eleven

An Empress's Justice

I woke up feeling strangely energetic.

Dawn's light, and the sounds of the waking city below, were starting to filter through my window. It had been a week since the deaths of the chariot racers, and the air of the capital was still heavy with tension.

I swung my feet out of bed and hurried through my morning preparations before pulling open the door. I startled Helena, who stood there with her arm raised, ready to knock.

"Good morning," I grinned.

She glowered, rapping my bare chest with her knuckles. "Don't scare me like that."

"A soldier must always be ready for the unexpected."

She snorted, but I saw the light dancing in her eyes.

We started walking through the palace, chatting about the day ahead. It was our morning training session, and I was eager to stretch my muscles. I was bare-chested, dressed only in my sandals and loin cloth.

Beside me, Helena's chest and hips were wrapped in cloth, her feet wound into light sandals. Her coppery curls were loose, fluttering over her bared neck and shoulders.

I tried to keep my attention forward, on figuring out what we would work on today. But my eyes kept finding her. I was drawn to her smile, to the curve of her neck and what lay below. I kept peeking at her body, watching the bounce of her rear and the play of her defined muscles beneath her bronzed flesh.

I said something—what, I don't remember. She laughed, and I tried to force my thoughts back to the training that was to come.

Yet, hypnotized by her company and the sway of her hips, my mind was filled with her.

I could picture the flush of her cheeks and chest after our run. The way her lips parted with each heavy breath, and how the green of her eyes would deepen as we worked our bodies.

I imagined the sweat darkening her hair and coating her flesh. I saw it drip, trickling down her body and making the muscles of her naked stomach gleam with every one of those heaving breaths.

I felt my heart quicken and I inhaled deeply through my nose, anticipating the air that would soon be filled with the intoxicatingly sour scent of her femininity.

"Are you going to answer my question?" I heard Helena ask.

"What?" I said, blinking my way back into the present.

"I asked you a question, Leo," she repeated, arching an eyebrow. "A while ago, actually."

"You did? I—uh ..." I trailed off, heat suddenly roaring through me. God help me. How did I admit that I hadn't heard a word she'd said because I'd been admiring her ass?

She laughed, the sound growing louder as my blush deepened. She stopped walking, facing me with her hands on her almost naked hips.

"Is this how it's going to be every time I try and talk with you? I guess I have to get my important questions out before you notice my ass, huh?"

I hadn't thought that I could get any redder. I stammered out an apology, stopping when another of Helena's laughs interrupted me.

"I'm just teasing you, Leo." Her eyes were bright, while she gestured down at herself. "Although, I would have thought that you'd be used to this by now."

I blew out a breath, speaking before I had a chance to think. "I don't think that I'll ever get used to the sight of you, Helena."

Her eyes flicked away, and I noticed a flush creeping up from the swell of her chest. I felt my own burning heat fade into a softer sort of warmth.

"Yeah, well, as long as it doesn't make you stop ..." She trailed off, her expression unsure.

"Are you asking me to go easy on you?" I asked, my tone teasing. "Because it will take more than a bit of exposed skin to stop me from beating you blue, shield-mate."

Her face relaxed, and the smile she gave me nearly made me shiver.

"Good," she said. "What are we going to work on today?"

We still stood in place, facing each other in the empty hallway. I scratched at my stubble, thinking out loud.

"Well, we'll run first to get our muscles ready. And then, when we spar, I think we'll try to focus on your shield. You're still a bit sloppy with it, and I—"

Helena had begun to stretch as I spoke, reaching her arms towards the ceiling. I managed to keep myself from focusing too closely on her. But I choked on my words when, with a flash of mischief, she neatly spun around so that her back was to me and folded herself at the waist.

My eyes went wide and my thoughts dribbled from my head. My vision was swallowed by the shape of her ass, the way it shifted as she bent over. I watched her near-naked cheeks drift apart, drinking in the sight of that narrow strip of cloth tucked away between them. Helena's hands were at her thigh, tugging at the ribbon of cloth she'd tied there. Though, instead of simply working the knot loose, she bent lower, spreading herself wider and drawing it down to her sandaled foot.

My breath caught, my blood roaring as I drank in the glory of her. My gaze was trapped by the tight, little flare at the joining of her thighs. Her muscles shifted as she stepped out of the cloth loop, causing my mouth to water. The veiled, swollen curl of her sex was a bundled-up birthday gift whose wrapping I yearned to rip away. What sort of taste, I wondered, would I find within?

"Sorry," she said, arching her naked back to bring herself upright. "What were you saying?"

"Shield," I answered. I cleared my throat to try again. "Shield?"

She laughed, her face a mask of reddened delight. She tied her hair back with the fabric that she'd removed from around her leg, giving me the chance to come back to myself and curse my bottomless stupidity.

"Alright," she said, brightly. "Let's get down to the sands, shield-mate."

She started to move, and after a few more seconds, my body stuttered into motion.

"That was payback," I accused.

She grinned through the flush of her cheeks, not denying it.

We spoke a bit more on our way through the palace. Helena walked closer to me, I noticed, and I was delighted every time I felt the warmth of her bare arm brush against mine.

Despite what it may seem to some, I wasn't a fool.

I could feel the growing attraction between us. We were shield-mates, bound by duty to stand beside each other. But it was more than that. Though we spent nearly every waking moment together, I felt the ache of her absence when I lay down to sleep, alone. I was falling for her. And somehow, by God's own miracle, this strong, mischievous, soul-achingly beautiful woman was growing to care for me in turn. Our arms brushed once again, and I felt my stomach flutter. I tried to hide the idiotic grin that stretched across my features.

We were not far from the Hippodrome now. We had fallen silent a few turns back, and it was into that quiet that my mother spoke.

"*This isn't right, my little lion. You know it isn't. This place ... this woman couldn't build you the home you deserve. And your father; your father died a good, honorable man. What would he say to see the choices you've made?*"

My father, I told her, would be pleased with the happiness I was finding here.

"*Would he?*" she asked. "*And what about me? Should I tell you how I wept when I learned how far you've strayed from the path we set for you?*"

I pushed her from my mind. I glanced over towards Helena and met her eyes. She smiled, though it was small. She'd been biting her lip, her face twisted into the same anxious hesitancy of before.

And in that moment, despite how closely we walked, it felt like there was a chasm between us.

As usual, we were the first to set foot on the Hippodrome's sands that morning. There was little sign of last week's tragedy; the debris had been cleared by teams of working slaves and the track had been raked smooth.

Helena and I limbered up, stretching our muscles while the cloudless sky brightened. We jogged, then ran the Hippodrome's circle. And by some unspoken signal, both of us kept to the outer wall when we came to the place where Maleinos and Velanis had died.

By the time we finished our third lap, a group of *Excubitors* had filed out and begun their own training. They didn't bother us, though it looked like Doukas, Senator Hypatius's son, had returned to train. I felt his hatred like a physical weight against my shoulders.

We'd begun to spar when yet another group entered the Hippodrome. Helena and I watched them a bit between bouts. They were builders, coming in with wagon-loads of cut wood and tools. They started to erect some sort of structure at the track's center.

"It's gallows," Helena said.

We were at the water barrel now, sweat pouring off of our bruised, dusty flesh. I looked over to where the builders worked, a few men handing planks and beams of wood up to those waiting on the medium-sized platform they'd already assembled.

"I didn't hear too much fighting in the past few nights," I said. "Nobody set any fires either."

Helena stretched, winced, and rubbed at one bicep. "The soldiers must have kept things pretty quiet. But there's always a few drunken brawls that go too far."

I grunted, taking another long sip of water.

I'd been eight when I saw my first hanging. It was part of life in the Empire, and even in Rhodos, we'd had our share of killers and thieves. There would be hangings soon, I bet, of men whose blood had run too hot after the races.

I shifted, squinting up towards the sun. "Come on," I said. "The Empress will be waking soon. I don't think we'll have time to wash before gearing up."

"Great," Helena teased, helping me stow our training equipment. "Stand for away from me then. I don't want to spend the day smelling you."

I chuckled, and we made for the palace entrance. I glanced over my shoulder one last time and saw that the gallows were mostly complete already. I felt my good mood fade. The Emperor was flexing his authority, and I hoped that it would be enough to quell whatever dissent remained.

As I walked away, however, I once again heard the crowd's chant. I felt a twinge of something in my chest, an echo of the tide that had moved the mob.

I tried not to dwell on it as I followed Helena back towards our Empress.

Chapter Twelve
The Empress Guides

The halls of the Imperial Palace were buzzing with activity. During the day, this vast complex swarmed with administrators, scribes, scholars, and the hundreds of other people needed to keep a vast Empire running smoothly. They kept to the bottom floors, moving within a hive of *tablinum*, libraries, workspaces, and audience chambers.

The upper floors meanwhile, were the haunt of nobles, senators, generals, and bishops.

Helena and I had passed many of the Empire's elite on our route through the more sumptuously decorated upper halls. These were those men whose wealth and influence allowed them to petition the Emperor directly.

While Justinian would spend his day meeting with Byzantium's great and good, the Empress met with their wives.

I was just settling into my post within the Empress's salon when I heard a pleasant knock. I opened the door, feeling my body tighten beneath my armor as I found myself suddenly facing Antonina.

"Leontius," she said. "Good morning."

She was as stunning as ever.

Her blonde hair was piled atop her head, several locks of it cascading downward to brush the flesh of her bare shoulders. The rest of her pale, luscious curves were veiled by the blue of her *stola*. The cloth was gossamer thin, clinging tightly to where her body swelled and curled.

"Should I announce myself, then?"

I started, meeting Antonina's knowing smile. I met her gaze, not missing the flicker of hunger burning within her.

"*Augusta*," I said, a bit stiffly. "Mistress Antonina to see you."

"Nina!" Theodora's voice came from behind me. "Come in, come in."

Antonina trailed her fingers along my arm as she passed, leaving me with a low laugh and a cloud of her spice-rich scent. As the two women embraced and greeted one another, my eyes shifted to Helena.

My shield-mate was also in her armor, seated at a small desk not far from the Empress's divan. A column between us stopped me from seeing the stacks of reports, letters, and notes that she was sifting through, but I didn't mind.

It was her I wanted to see.

She felt my gaze, looked up, and smiled at me. I returned her smile with one of my own, feeling my stomach vibrate with a happy flutter.

"I have a busy day today, but you're welcome to stay with me," the Empress told her friend. She pulled Antonina down onto the divan beside her, glancing towards Helena.

"Who's my first appointment?"

"Lady Irene," she said. "Wife of Governor Arethas."

"The Governor of Samos is here?" Antonina said, helping herself to a tray of sweet cakes and watered-wine. "I didn't know that the old pervert had remarried."

"She's a sweet girl," Theodora said. "Young, but intelligent."

Antonina made a small sound, biting into a sweet cake and brushing the crumbs from her breasts.

There was a tentative knock at the door. I pulled it open, revealing a noblewoman standing demurely in the hallway. She was young, having probably just entered her second decade of life. She had dark hair, with a pretty, heart-shaped face. Her skin was pale as Antonina's, already tinged pink by the heat of the morning.

"Lady Irene?" I asked, politely.

She nodded, and I let her in once I'd properly announced her.

"Irene," the Empress said, standing to greet the young woman. "So good of you to come, dear."

"*Augusta*," the girl said with a graceful curtsy. "Thank you so much for seeing me."

The Empress's feet were bare and bangled in gold, as was her habit within her chambers. Her hair was down, gold shining through her tumbling, walnut tresses. She wore a long *stola* of light, airy silk that contrasted the warm brown of her skin. The dress clung to her dancer's body, leaving her arms and shoulders bare to soak in the mid-morning light.

"Of course, of course," the Empress answered, kissing the young woman on both of her cheeks. She introduced Antonina next, the general's wife standing to embrace the woman as well.

"Sit, sit, my dear," Theodora said, gesturing to one of the chairs facing her divan. "You must be on the verge of death in that dress. Helena, would you get the Lady Irene some water?"

The young woman obeyed, seating herself and smoothing her skirts. She wore one of the more traditional dresses of the new, Christian nobility. One of those many-layered, tightly-pinned garments of somber gray that was as smothering as it was impractical. I didn't know how the poor woman could bear the weight of all of that cloth. My back started to sweat just looking at her.

"Now," the Empress said, after a few minutes of pleasantries. "What brings you to the palace today, dear?"

The Lady Irene let out a breath, carefully setting aside her cup of water. She straightened, folding her hands onto her lap before she spoke. "I came to pay my respects, *Augusta*. And to ask for your advice."

"Well then, consider the formalities over and done with. Speak freely, my dear."

Irene nodded but hesitated a moment before speaking. "It is about my husband, the Lord Arethas."

The Empress nodded. "You've been married for close to two years, have you not?"

"Yes, *Augusta*. And in that time, I have familiarized myself with the extent of his domain. I have made a study of our laws, including the new legislation put into place by yourself and our Emperor."

Theodora smiled encouragingly, waiting.

"And, it's just that ... my husband isn't running things well," Irene blurted.

Antonina laughed, and the Empress raised an eyebrow. The young woman flushed, quickly correcting herself. "It isn't that, *Augusta*. Forgive me. It's just that there is so much more that could be done to improve. We are a small province, and our people are generally happy and healthy. Yet, with a few simple changes, Samos could become one of the most prosperous provinces in the Empire."

"Well, he is the Governor," Theodora said. "As his wife, your duty is to help and advise him. The decisions, however, are ultimately his to make."

"But he won't listen to me!" Irene said, her hands twisting the fabric of her dress. "I lay out my ideas for him as succinctly as I can, and yet he dismisses them without consideration. I'm no child, and yet, he treats me as one."

"Maybe your ideas aren't that good," Antonina said.

Irene flushed, but she didn't back down. "With respect, Mistress, that is untrue. For example—"

"Yes, yes," Antonina cut back in. "I believe you. I wanted to see if there was a bit of steel in your spine."

"Pardon, Mistress?"

"That strength is important," Antonina continued. "Hold onto it, but keep it hidden."

"Hidden? Mistress, I don't understand. From whom must I hide myself?"

"Why, dear," the Empress said. "From men, of course."

Theodora smiled at Irene's bewildered expression. She shifted on her divan, leaning towards the young woman. "Men have made this world their own. It is a hard truth for us women, but it is one nonetheless. They're jealous of their place in it. An intelligent, driven woman like you is ..."

"Terrifying," Antonina finished. "Men hate the thought that we'd be just as capable at running things as they are."

Irene slumped back. "Then, there is nothing I can do? I'll just have to sit silently and watch the world go by without having ever touched it."

"That's how many women live their lives," the Empress said, gently.

"But I don't want to!" She exclaimed. "Help me, *Augusta*. Please. You and Mistress Antonina do not live so passively. How do I mirror what both of you have done?"

The Empress and her friend shared a look. It was Antonina who next spoke. "How's your marriage?"

Irene blinked. "Mistress?"

"Your marriage," Antonina insisted. "How would you describe it?"

"Good," Irene said after a few moments. She was a bit put out by the sudden change but elaborated nonetheless. "I'd say that it is good. We are civil to each other, and he never mistreats or forces himself on me."

Antonina arched an eyebrow. "Truly? With tits like yours, girl, I figured that he'd be pawing at them every night."

Irene gaped, too surprised to even flush. I managed to hold onto a cough, unable to help glancing down towards her chest. And indeed, even tightly bound and completely covered, the shape of her breasts was impressive. They were of a size with Antonina's, I thought, though it was hard to tell.

Helena, I noticed, was also craning her neck for a peek.

"How's the sex?" Antonina continued. "Do you enjoy it? Does he just pump it into you while you lie there, or do the two of you make an effort?"

Lady Irene's eyes were starting to go a bit wild. Her gaze flicked to the Empress, her expression pleading. But Theodora remained silent, watching the exchange with a small smile.

"Well?" Antonina demanded.

The young woman managed to stutter out a meaningless series of words, her expression one of sheer horror.

"I thought so," Antonina said. "You're making a mistake, you know. You need to know how to fuck if you want to get anywhere, girl. You're young, you're beautiful and you've got breasts enough to stiffen a eunuch. Don't hide them away like that; use them."

The noblewoman gaped, cheeks blazing. Antonina sighed, and without a flicker of warning, reached up to the neckline of her own dress and pulled it down.

Now I did choke, coughing as her breasts spilled out into the open air. They were as lush, creamy, and full as I remembered. Twin, rounded curves of pale softness that quivered with every one of Antonina's breaths. Her nipples, pink as a sun-kissed morning, were already starting to stiffen.

My mother shrieked in my mind, startling me. What the hell was I doing? Helena was right there!

I ripped my gaze away, feeling a fist clench around my heart. My eyes sought my shield-mate, my spike of fear fading as I met her steady gaze.

She smiled, though there must have been something panicked in my features because her smile quickly widened into a grin. She covered her mouth, her eyes crinkling in silent laughter. I let out a sheepish breath, forcing myself back to attention.

Around the Empress's divan, Lady Irene looked like she'd been kicked by a horse.

"You see?" Antonina said. She looked down at herself, her expression becoming faintly bitter. "They're already starting to sag. Tits like ours have an expiration date, girl."

"Mis— Mistress Antonina!"

Irene seemed to be coming out of her daze. Her eyes flicked to Antonina's face, then the Empress, and then towards me. Impossibly, she seemed to burn a shade redder.

"Your breasts! The guard— Mistress!"

"Oh, relax," the general's wife said. "Everyone here has seen them before. Besides, I have to show them off while they're still nice to look at." The woman cupped both of her breasts with her hands for emphasis, squashing them together to swallow the cross between them.

Irene choked.

"Quit torturing the girl, Nina," the Empress finally cut in. "Put those away."

Antonina grumbled but obeyed. Theodora, meanwhile, took a few more moments to consider the young noblewoman.

"Antonina is right, dear," she said. "You need to make sex a greater priority."

Irene opened her mouth to speak but the Empress held up a hand.

"Hush now, love. Listen for a moment. The world out there might belong to men, but the bedchamber is ours. Take charge of it. You lead him to your bed, instead of following him in. Make a fortress of your sheets, Irene; a place where you are queen."

The young woman's face still burned, but she listened with a focused intensity.

"Find what makes your body shiver," Theodora continued. "What drenches your lips and what makes you scream in pleasure. Making love is a sport of two. Insist on your pleasure as much as his own and make your bodies sing. Then, when he is drained and warm and contentedly nestled in the pillow of your chest—that is when you start making suggestions."

"It's almost too easy," Antonina said. "Once you know the trick of it. Get him used to following you between the sheets, and pretty soon he'll follow you in everything else."

Theodora's eyes sparkled, leaning towards the young woman. "Be gentle at first, as if whatever you say is just a passing thought. Don't press, but bring it up the next time you lay together, and then do it again. If he's content, he'll start to listen despite himself. Your conversations will become longer, deeper; and that's when you'll know you have him."

"I don't ..." Irene let out a ragged breath. "I'm not like you. I don't know how."

The Empress's smile was gentle. She nodded toward the woman's tightly concealed frame. "With that, my dear. Your mind is sharp, but it is your body that you must use. That will change in time if you use it well. But for now, while you are young, it is your greatest weapon."

Irene nodded uncertainly, gazing down at herself.

"It is God's gift to you," the Empress continued. "Use it, take pride, and revel in it. For it is yours, sweet Irene, and it is as beautiful as the soul it shelters."

"And remember what I said about your tits," Antonina added.

Theodora laughed softly, leaning back into her divan. "They really are spectacular, aren't they?"

Irene was silent for a moment, then I saw her loosen.

"I always have been rather proud of them," she said, hesitantly. "They're heavy but ... are they really that nice?"

"That's right," Antonina said. "Be proud of what you've got. Loosen up that dress and push them out a bit. I want to have a better look at them."

And then, slowly, as if she couldn't really believe what she was doing, Irene reached for the collar of her dress.

I shook my head, turning to face the door. This place ... there was always something new. I smiled, hearing footsteps. It was Helena coming to stand beside me. She leaned against the wall.

"She's got them out now," Helena said, too low for the others to hear. "Are you sure that you don't want to look?"

"Are they as nice as we thought?"

Helena laughed. "They're even better."

I let out a long, regretful sigh, but did not turn around.

"Ever the proper soldier," she teased. "Although, I can't help but remember how you didn't hesitate to stare at me this morning."

I winced. "Yeah, well, that was different."

"Oh, was it now?" Her cypress eyes were alight. "I'm excited for this explanation."

I reddened. "You're going to run so many laps tomorrow morning."

I expected her to laugh again, but she didn't. I glanced over and found a strange expression on her face.

"Tell me something," she said. "If you were that girl's husband, would you listen to her?"

I considered her question, answering after a few moments. "I would."

"Why?"

I shrugged. "Because she looks smart and serious. I'm sure that her suggestions are at least worth considering."

"But look at her," Helena said. "She's got her tits out in a room full of strangers."

I bristled, weirdly defensive. "Yes, but that doesn't change anything."

"Of course it does. It's not proper."

"What?" I said, leaning back. "Helena, what the hell is going on?"

"It's not what good, proper women do," she insisted.

"You sound like my mother."

"I'm sure you've had the same thought."

I was angry now. "What the fuck is this? The girl isn't stupid just because she's got her breasts out. It doesn't make her worse or somehow unworthy. Why the hell are you saying this horseshit?"

"Because it's what you believe."

"Not anymore," I growled, struggling to keep my voice low.

She smiled, and I was suddenly taken aback. I was still angry, but Helena had neatly slipped out of the feeling's focus.

"Really?" she questioned.

"Yes!" And as I said the word, I realized that it was completely and utterly true.

"Good," she said, her smile satisfied. "I'm happy to hear that."

"Why?" I demanded. "What the hell was this all about, Helena?"

"Nothing," she said, grinning into my narrow-eyed stare. "But how about I buy you a flagon of wine to make up for it?"

I stared at her for a few more moments, trying to hold on to some piece of my rightfully felt indignation. I was, however, powerless against that smile.

"Fine," I said. My lips quirked upward. "But make it two flagons."

"Deal," she said. "Then, it's a date."

Helena's smile didn't fade. She shifted towards me, a little pink staining her cheeks. My stomach burst into a thousand little embers. Here she was, beside me, closer than we'd been all day.

"And Leo," she breathed. "If I ever pull out my tits, you'd better not look away."

I stared at her, my eyes wide and mouth agape. I was unable to hear anything, save the thundering of my heart. She laughed, that full, toe-tingling sound. She slid away, but not far, her eyes bright and merry.

I let out my own breath, smiling and shaking my head at the wonder of this place.

Because in that moment, with Helena beside me and the sound of these four laughing, gasping, *joyful* women all around me, I couldn't hear my mother's voice at all.

Chapter Thirteen
An Empress's Command

"This was a disaster," the Emperor said. "This entire fortnight, ever since those fools killed themselves on the track."

Justinian sunk into a thickly padded divan, rubbing at his eyes. The Empress lowered herself beside him, running her fingers through the hair on the back of his head.

"It's not been that bad, love," she said. "We're making headway with the Sassanids."

"Christ," he groaned. "Don't remind me about the Persians. They're pricklier than a sackful of porcupines, and King Kavadh's demands are getting more outlandish by the day!"

We were in the Empress's sumptuously decorated salon, the imperial couple having retreated here after a midday session with the Senate. I was at my post by the door, fighting to keep my back straight.

We were deep into August now, and it had been a long day.

"And Hypatius," the Emperor said. "You heard him today, like a wolf smelling blood. He spoke well, the bastard. I saw too many of those other old fools nodding their heads along with him."

"All he has is fear," Theodora said, still stroking her husband's hair. "That will pass in time."

"Perhaps, but we may not have that time. If war breaks out again with the Persians ..." The Emperor let out a long breath. "Maybe we are pushing things too hard, Theodora. Or going too fast. We've changed much in our five years on the throne."

"Change that has been for the better," the Empress said. "You remember how it was."

"Aye, well, traditions die hard."

Theodora snorted. "Fear of change isn't a tradition. Our predecessors were weak. The Blues, the Greens, and those senators have long held onto much of the wealth and power. Of course they don't want things to be different."

"Don't forget the men of the Empire," Justinian said, bitterly, "whom we are apparently oppressing more than our slaves."

"I refuse to believe a law against a father selling his daughter into bondage is oppression," the Empress snapped. "Neither is the condemnation of rapists."

"How is it that Hypatius said it? 'Men are being run over roughshod by their wives in full defiance of our traditions and those of Christ himself'?"

"And those of 'God' Himself," Theodora corrected, pressing her lips together. "As if women aren't themselves creatures of God. How is keeping womankind in this soft sort of slavery not the greater sin?"

Justinian let out another long breath. "I know that we're right in this, Theodora. I'm just tired. And with yesterday's botched executions ..."

"I know," the Empress said. She pulled her husband down into her lap, trailing her fingers over his jaw. "We don't meet the Ambassador for another hour. Rest, my love."

Justinian protested but he soon relaxed beneath his wife's gentle hands.

I turned to stare out at the balcony. The sky was bright, the sun just beginning to descend from its zenith. I couldn't hear any noise from the city, which was strange, as things had not exactly been quiet.

They had finished setting up the gallows three days ago. The stage had sat empty until yesterday, when the Emperor had ordered a swift round of executions. More than a dozen men, Blues and Greens alike, had been hanged without much ceremony or fanfare.

This morning, however, Helena and I had returned from our training to find the Empress already waiting to leave. Two men had escaped justice, she'd told us on the way to the senate chambers. A Blue and Green. They were holed up in a church, surrounded by some of Belisarius's men.

And therein lay the problem. As long as they stayed within the church's walls, they were safe from any sort of secular interference. And the longer they stayed there, making a mockery of the Emperor's will, the more a people already on edge would seethe.

The Empress's voice pulled me from my thoughts. She motioned me over to where Helena had already joined her by her divan. Both women smiled when I approached, the Empress, bare-footed in a thin dress, and my shield-mate in her *stratiotai's* kit.

"Leontius," the Empress spoke softly. "You look tired."

I forced a little stiffness into my spine, matching her tone of voice. "I am fit for duty, *Augusta*."

She smiled. "As you always are, my soldier. Though, neither of you have had much rest, have you?"

I exchanged a glance with Helena.

The Empress continued. "You train every morning, and attend me all day until I go to sleep. Even then, there are nights when one of you guards my door. You need rest."

Neither of us spoke, sensing that the Empress had more to say. She was looking down at her husband now, her smile a little sad.

"Like my husband. There is always something that needs his attention. I'm happy he has these moments, but it is not enough. And so, I am imposing a night of relaxation. On all of us."

"Highness?" Helena said.

"Once the day's duties are done, I will retire to my husband's chambers. There, I will spend hours making love to him and ensure that, for this night at least, he thinks no more of our Empire." Her smile ticked higher. "Perhaps I'll even invite Nina and Bel, or one or two others."

I squirmed, my face red. Luckily, Helena was there to speak. "They are trustworthy, but even so, Highness. We should—"

"Not concern yourself with it," Theodora interrupted firmly. "The *Excubitors* are fully capable of guarding us on their own. Go down into the city, spend some of your wages. With the way things are going ... it may be a while before you have another chance."

"*Augusta*," I started.

"No, Leontius, enough. I will hear nothing more of this."

I shut my mouth and bowed.

A night off; the thought electrified me. I thought about all that I could do. Where might I go? Who might I see? I had a few friends in the city and a few places where I used to relax, before my time at the palace.

The Emperor awoke. We accompanied Theodora as the royal couple went to Justinian's chambers so he could change his simple toga for more regal attire, befitting his meeting with the Sassanids. Theodora went with him; Helena and I stayed outside the door.

As I pulled the door closed, I became sure of one thing: no matter how I spent these next few, precious hours of freedom, I wanted to spend them with Helena. She was beside me in the suddenly quiet hallway, already looking up towards my face. I met her gaze, and my heart started to pound.

"Tonight, would you—" I coughed. Why in God's name was my throat so dry? "Would you like to go down into the city? With me, I mean," I added hurriedly. "Together."

Heat crawled up my neck. Why the hell had I said it like that? I'd just ruined it. No way she would ever—

"Sure," she said.

A faint blush rose to color her cheeks. She smiled, reaching one hand up to brush at a lock of her hair. I saw the warmth in her eyes, and I suddenly felt like I would float away.

"Let's go into the city," Helena said. "Together."

☧

Evening came, and I let out a ragged breath. A tremor shivered through me, the force of my will doing little to ease my shaking hands. My body was shutting down, my mind lost in a fog of paralyzing terror. But I was *stratiotai*, a veteran of war and death; I could knock on a beautiful woman's door.

And I'm proud to say that, after only a few more minutes, I did.

"One second!" Helena called from within her room. "I'm almost ready!"

I was still a mess of panic and snarled nerves. But when she emerged and I saw her smile, my entire being eased.

"Hey," she said.

"Wow," I answered.

She laughed, "Is that it?"

Helena was in a *tunica* that was cut a little lower at the neck than my own. It was loose, belted at the waist, and ended just above her knees. The cloth hugged the muscles of her shoulders and the swell of her chest. It was dyed a deep green, the color making her eyes appear more vivid, and adding a burnished depth to her tumbling waves of copper hair.

And though the garment was mostly utilitarian, on her, it was finer than the richest sort of gown.

"Wow," I said again.

Helena was so beautiful, so bright with life and color, like a field of grass after rain.

She sighed theatrically, the light shifting within her cypress eyes. "I can already tell that this night will be a bit short on intelligent conversation."

I laughed, stepping back to let her into the corridor. "We're soldiers, Helena. The Empire doesn't need us to do more than grunt and hit things."

"I see," she said. "So, what about those of us who can speak using two or more syllables?"

"Well, sir," I grinned, holding out my arm. "You become officers."

She laughed. Two bright, delighted spots of pink appeared on her cheeks. She slipped her arm in mine, and together, we started through the palace halls.

"I do like ordering you around," she said. "Although, you don't always listen very well."

"That's what your sword is for, sir."

She flashed me a grin. "I did land a pretty good hit on you this morning, didn't I?"

"I let that one through," I told her.

"You're such a liar!"

I laughed as, side by side, we left the Empress's wing and headed towards the palace's main gate. Our surroundings faded away, faces and hallways blurring past me as we spoke. I was fully absorbed in her, in the feel of her beside me. I delighted in the sound of her voice and laughter, thrilled at the warmth of her touch.

We had almost reached the main gate when a familiar aristocratic voice pulled us from each other.

"Well, look at this," Doukas said, his eyes flicking between us. "The coward and his little woman. Are you finally tired of playing soldier then, girl?"

The senator's son was alone, though his voice was loud enough to hook the attention of many of the passing servants. He swaggered towards us with a sneer, wearing a *tunica* made to emphasize his muscled limbs.

Beside me, Helena's face flooded with crimson. She ripped her arm from mine, glaring at Doukas.

"Ah, don't be like that," he said. "Isn't it so much easier to hold onto a man than to try to be one?"

"What the hell do you want?" I said, my anger rising.

"Watch your fucking mouth, dog," he growled. "I'm an *Excubitor*. Don't think that either I, or my father, have forgotten how you attacked me. You'll pay for that."

I was a heartbeat away from smashing Doukas's face in for the second time when some instinct drew my gaze to Helena. Her fists were clenched tightly, her entire frame wound tight. At first glance, she looked to be radiating fury, but something in the burning twist of her face caught me.

There was anger there, yet it was colored strangely. There was a depth to it, a flavor to her rage that went beyond mere insult. Helplessness, perhaps? Shame? Or was it some blend of the two with a healthy dose of self-loathing and humiliation thrown in?

I wasn't sure, but at that moment, I knew that this wasn't my battle to fight.

"Shield-mate," I said, drawing her gaze. "Do you mind dealing with him?"

She frowned.

"I'm sore from training," I clarified. "You really did pummel me this morning. So, just get rid of him, and then we can go get those flagons of wine you owe me."

"What?" she said. Confusion swirled over her features, masking her ugly feelings of doubt.

Doukas laughed. "You fucking coward. Do you think that I won't break this bitch just because you're hiding behind her?"

I smiled, taking a few steps back. "You don't stand a fucking chance, golden boy. Don't take too long, shield-mate. I'm thirsty."

Rage mottled his features. He snarled wordlessly, reaching to shove Helena out of his way. She reacted without thought, ducking beneath the blow as smoothly as any veteran. Then, as if tucked behind a shield, she straightened and rammed her shoulder into him.

Doukas was knocked back, and I grinned to see Helena's face flicker from surprise to disbelief before settling on triumph.

The senator's son's face registered many of the same emotions, and he seemed to really notice Helena for the first time. His eyes narrowed.

"You look familiar, bitch," he said, stepping back to her. "Have I fucked you before?"

Helena met his eyes without flinching, her body loose and ready. "How's the face, Doukas? Do you want me to break a few teeth this time?"

"I'll kill you, slut," he growled, looming over her.

The air grew heavy, but Helena didn't bow beneath its weight. Doukas's eyes darted over her, unused to her lack of reaction. And the longer he hesitated within that pregnant silence, the more uncertain he seemed to become. I leaned against the nearest wall, not trying to hide my smirk.

"Doukas!" a voice called, cutting through the tension. An *Excubitor* had appeared at the end of the hallway. He was in his golden armor, gesturing towards the senator's son. "Come on," he said. "We're due on patrol soon and the captain wants a word with us. Hurry up and get in your armor."

The presence of the other *Excubitor* seemed to fortify Doukas's spine. He spat at Helena's feet and sneered at me. "This isn't over."

When we were once again alone in the hall, Helena spun towards me, a wide grin tugging at her flushed cheeks.

"Did you see his face!" She crowed, laughing in delight. "I've been wanting to do that for years!"

I laughed with her, pushing myself off the wall. "Too bad you weren't really holding your shield. That shove was perfect!"

"That bastard! I fucking got him!" She did another happy spin, moving towards me with light dancing in her cypress eyes. "And you! Were you really going to let me fight him alone?"

I shrugged. "You didn't need my help."

"But I could have," she said. "He's a lot bigger than me, and he's got more fighting experience."

I snorted. "Helena, you're four times the soldier any of those rich pricks are. Trust me, I'd have bet everything I owned that—"

She didn't let me finish, stepping into me and pressing her lips to mine. She kissed me, a shock of such gentle softness that I felt the rest of the world fall away.

We broke apart, and I saw a thousand flickers of feeling within her wide, cypress eyes. There was happiness, pride, tenderness, a bright mischief, and a hundred other things that spread through her like a vast canopy.

Then, I watched that canopy shift as she smiled. And in the glory of her being, I caught a glimpse of that beautiful, nameless wonder growing tall within her.

"What were you saying?" she asked, snaking her arms around my neck. She smelled of cedar and salt, of sea and sun. "It sounded nice."

I laughed, my heart drumming with joyful disbelief. My hands found her waist, and I pulled her close. She was so warm, her body melding into mine. "I don't remember."

I kissed her, that second touch made clumsy by the smiles we both wore.

"You're going to have to lose that idiotic grin," she told me.

"I can't help it," I said.

She shifted against me. I lost myself in her eyes as I slipped a hand through her tumbling locks of copper hair to cup her cheek.

"I've been waiting too long," I finished, leaning down towards her lips once more.

And it was this kiss, long and slow and without reservation, that made my spirit sing. I was breathless when we parted, my head filled with the taste of her. Her eyes shone, and she let out an airy little laugh.

I pressed my forehead against hers, holding her to me. I closed my eyes, my every breath filled with her scent. Then, I felt her shift, her mouth reaching up toward mine. I met her eagerly, my lips already craving the velvety sweetness of hers.

"You know," she murmured afterward. "I can tell that you haven't bathed today."

I winced. "Sorry. I didn't have time after we got off duty."

"It's okay, I didn't either, to tell you the truth. I didn't think ..."

"Me neither," I admitted. "And I wanted to see you quickly."

"Hmm," her breath swirled past a bitten lip. "Well then, we should probably go take a bath."

I nodded, unable to speak past my suddenly dry throat.

Chapter Fourteen

Oaths Beyond the Empress

We were stepping through into the Empress's bath chamber before I could really wrap my head around what was happening.

The room was empty, though the tiled pool had already been filled with steaming water. Great clouds of humidity billowed through the space, moisture quickly beading onto our skin.

We stripped down to the training wraps that we both still wore as loincloths, leaving our *tunicas* on a long wooden bench. Helena was a bit faster, drifting barefoot towards the water while I was removing my sandals.

"Leo," Helena said when I'd straightened. She was standing within the clouds of steam, facing me from only a handful of paces away. She smiled, and though her next words were spoken softly, they resonated through me.

"Don't look away."

Then, she reached a hand up to the cloth that bound her chest, pulling on a single loop. My heart hammered against my chest like a smith at his anvil, sending sparks of heat flashing through me.

The cloth slowly unraveled from around her chest.

Helena's eyes, deeper than ever before, never left my face. She shifted her body beneath the unwinding loops of cloth, drawing me further in. I glimpsed her nakedness through the tumbling lengths of fabric.

And with every heartbeat, with every one of her breaths, more of her was revealed to me.

I saw the soft valley of her chest, deep enough to lose myself in. The flesh of her breasts was smooth, stained pink by heat and moisture. They curved gently outward, and I caught a glimpse of a nipple through the still-falling curtain of cloth. It was bright, shockingly pink next to the warm bronze of her flesh.

"Well?" Helena asked.

She flexed the naked muscles of her stomach, shifting to let the last of the cloth tumble away. The motion swung her naked breasts from side to side. Air was lodged in my throat, stopping whatever answer I might eventually find. I was mesmerized by the ripple of her chest, trapped within its sway.

Her breasts were full, straining against her warm, soft skin. They were heavy and pert, the steam clinging deliciously to their rounded shape. Her nipples, round and stiff, were two rose petals lain upon a silken blanket.

"Do I still have to repeat myself?" she teased, light dancing in the depths of her cypress eyes. "I'm going to get tired of that."

The breath I released was ragged and frayed along the edges. "Get used to it. I don't think I'll ever be able to look away from you again."

Her smile softened, and I saw the heat rise to color her cheeks. Embers flew within me, making my stomach buzz. God, she was beautiful. Stomach-flutteringly, heart-poundingly, soul-shatteringly beautiful.

Helena moved towards me, her bare feet gliding over the tiled floor. I met her halfway, jerky where she was graceful. We stopped before each other, not quite touching. I gazed into her. And now that the moment was here, my head was a roiling storm of wants and doubts and needs.

I heard my mother's voice, shrieking about the error I was about to commit. My life had forked the day I'd won that footrace. I was no longer on the path I'd been set to walk, shown something new by an Empress and those that surrounded her. I didn't know if it was right to continue down this trail. I didn't know which path was right, and perhaps I never would.

But what I did know was that Helena was here, and right now, the thought of there being any space between us sickened me to my very core.

"Leo, I'm standing here with my tits out. If you don't kiss me in the next three seconds, I—"

So I did, pulling her to me and kissing her more deeply than I had before. She returned my fervor, making a small sound in her throat. Her naked chest pressed against mine, the rest of her melding into me.

Her fingers explored me while we tasted each other, trailing down my naked sides. She traced the lines of my ridges and scars, leaving a tingle of gentle heat in her wake. Her hand eventually slipped down to my navel, her fingers digging into the wrap at my waist.

I started, suddenly aware of the fire between my legs. I was hard. God help me, I was so fucking hard. My manhood bulged painfully against my loincloth, pushing into the tightness of Helena's lower stomach.

Her kiss became hungrier, her fingers brushing my hardness, tugging more and more insistently at the cloth that caged me.

I *ached* for her. Her scent, her touch and her taste and the glory of her body—she made my blood sing. I burned for her, longed to cool myself within her cracks and crevices. But not yet.

I wasn't ready, not when I could see the bruises and sweat that still stained her body. She stiffened when I accidentally brushed a bloom of discolored flesh, and I felt the tremble of her tired muscles against me. The training that let her stand up to fools like Doukas caused her so much pain. Her body suffered for it, and it wasn't right for me to take from her now.

Not before I gave.

I pulled away, breaking our kiss and twisting so her hand fell away from my manhood. Surprise flashed across her features, then hurt.

"Leo, what—"

Her question turned into a squeak as I scooped her up into my arms. She threw her own arms around my neck, and I felt the bare flesh of her legs and back press against my limbs. I looked down in time to catch her glare.

"What are you doing?"

I smiled, starting to move. Her arms tightened.

"Leo!"

"You stink," I said.

She choked, and I grinned at the sight of the outrage in her reddening face. I squeezed her a little tighter, cradling her against me.

"But don't worry," I added. "That's what we're here for, right?"

She glared at me for another heartbeat. She wanted to say more, but I suspected she already knew some of what I intended.

I stepped into the pool a moment later. The water was hot, but not uncomfortably so. I was waist-deep after a few more steps, lifting Helena a bit higher.

"I'm going to put you down," I said, reaching the long, carved seat where the Empress typically lounged.

She nodded, letting out a small groan of pleasure as the hot water enveloped her. I made sure that she was comfortable, lowering her gently onto the sculpted seat.

"Come join me," she said, leaning her head back. "It's nice."

"In a minute," I said. And then, on a whim, I bent down and kissed her forehead. "Relax."

She made that small sound again, settling herself lower. She closed her eyes, lips curling lazily up into a pleased smile.

Within a few heartbeats, I was out of the water, heading towards a nearby corner. There were two stone massage tables there, not far from the desk at which Helena normally sat.

The Empress came down here nearly every day. When she did, a pair of muscled body-slaves usually waited for her by these tables. They weren't here tonight, thankfully, but the soaps, oils, perfumes, and soft towels they used were.

I came back into the pool, bearing a few strips of rough cloth and the softest, most buttery bar of soap I'd found. I lowered myself down by Helena's feet, soaking and then lathering up the first piece of cloth. Helena's eyes were still shut, her breathing steady. She was relaxed, luxuriating in the simple pleasure of the bath.

"Helena," I said when I was ready, reaching beneath the water to touch her leg.

"Hmm?"

"Just lie still."

I ran my palm along the shape of her leg, moving from the tips of her toes to the swell of her thigh. I learned the shape of her, finding every cut, every bruise, and every scrape. Helena let out a pleased sigh, shifting her leg towards me. Her skin was so smooth, so tight over her muscles.

With the soap-lathered cloth, I started scrubbing at her skin. I worked up from her foot, washing the sweat and dirt from her. I was slow and thorough in my ministrations, careful around her scrapes and bruises.

I bathed her lower body up to the loops of cloth that were still bound around her waist, skipping up to her stomach once I'd finished both of her legs. Her stomach muscles were taut, rippling beneath my hands as she arched her back towards me.

"Don't forget my breasts," she murmured, not opening her eyes.

I chuckled, not missing the slight curl of her lips. I began with the underside of them, running along their rounded edges. God, but they were soft and pillow-like, the flesh silken. And as I ran my hands over them, my fingers couldn't resist a few gentle squeezes.

I was as thorough here as I'd been with the rest of her, making sure that even her rosy nipples were clean.

Helena's smile didn't fade.

When all that remained was her hair, I slowed even further, beginning by wetting it with water from my cupped palms. I was careful not to let any trickle down her face. And when her hair was dark and saturated, I lathered my hands with soap and cleaned that too.

She shivered as my fingers massaged her scalp, shifting languidly where she lay.

"Alright," I said once I'd finished. "Are you ready for the next part?"

She cracked open an eye, peering at me through slitted lids. "What is it?"

"You'll see," I said, slipping my arms back beneath her back and legs. Then, ignoring her little mewl of protest, I lifted her out of the water. She snuggled into me, keeping her eyes closed until I walked us over to one of the massage tables.

"Oh, Leo," she purred, finally peeking at where I'd brought her. "I love this idea."

"I thought you might," I said, placing her down on a few towels I'd spread out earlier. "Lie on your stomach."

She obeyed, stretching cat-like over the toweled surface. Her eyes fluttered shut, resting her head in a pillow of her arms.

I hesitated a moment, standing there above her. Her body glowed with the soapy water that still clung to her, giving the bronze of her skin a deep, burnished look.

Embers spun faster within me, burning hotter, and I felt my body respond. She was a vision, stretched out before me. I admired the arch of her back and the swell of her hips, my eyes settling on her near-naked ass. It curved gracefully into the air, veiled only by the thin strip of cloth still buried within.

"Is looking all you're gonna do?" Helena's voice was muffled by the pillow of her arms. She shifted, making her flesh quiver.

I coughed, forcing myself to focus. I dried her with one of the soft towels, dribbling scented oil onto her back. I started to rub it into her, and she melted into the table with a sigh.

Again, I worked slowly, spreading the oil along her warm flesh. I was no body-slave to know just where to press and sculpt. But I was *stratiotai*; I knew the feel of knotted muscle and how to smooth it back into place.

"Roll over," I said, having finished with her neck and shoulders. "I'll do your front as well."

Helena turned her head, glancing up at me through a curtain of darkened copper hair. Her eyelids were heavy.

"That does sound nice," she said. And with another long blink of her pleasure-hooded eyes, she pushed herself up. Her breasts came off the covered stone, swaying pendulum-like through the heated air. Instead of lying on her back, however, Helena sat upright. She stretched, her feet dangling above the tiled floor.

"You don't want to?" I asked. I took a step back, leaning against the edge of the second stone table.

"Oh, I do, more than anything. But ..." She reached down, fingers plucking at the cloth that was still wrapped around her waist. "Wouldn't it be easier without this?"

My throat was suddenly drier than the Persian desert. Unbidden, my gaze slid down the naked curves of her body, coming to rest of the snuggly wrapped swell of her sex. She shifted her oil-slick thighs, opening herself up to me.

I tried to swallow, but couldn't.

My hardness was a bar of burning metal between my legs. I felt the weight of her eyes on me; I could picture the way her breath escaped through parted lips, but I couldn't tear my gaze from her center. I could see the veiled outline of her lush, silken folds pressed tight against the wet layers of cloth.

She laughed, the sound low, and from deep within her. "I guess that's a yes."

Her fingers slipped into the wrapped loops of cloth, tugging on the edge. She was on her feet a moment later, the wet cloth noticeably looser, though it still clung to her hips and navel. She swayed into the space between us, gliding towards me. Her loincloth hung in long loops now, only held in place by the loose grip of her fingers.

I sat back on the table, making space for her between my knees. I didn't speak, reaching out to grip her waist. I pulled her close enough that her steam-moistened nipples brushed my naked chest. We stared into each other, and my heart ached at what I found there.

I saw that thing: that vast, unknowable, beautiful, *wondrous* thing that grew within her. It filled her now, there for all to see. I blinked wetness from my eyes. My throat closed up, blocked by a hundred embers of all-consuming tenderness that had been swirling up from the deepest parts of me.

She was so beautiful; so gentle, so warm and so strong. God, but she was everything, the answer to every question I'd been too afraid to ask. I …

"… love the way you look at me, shield-mate," she said.

Helena brought her free hand up, trailing her nails through the rough hair along my jawline. I smiled, relishing even this small connection between our bodies.

"Shield-mate?" I said, teasing. "Is that what we are, even here?"

Her expression changed, the softness leaving her face. It was as if she'd suddenly been doused with ice water.

"Shield-mates stand side by side. Together, Leo, that's what you told me." Helena shook her head, taking a half step back. "If you can't do that here, then I …"

At that moment, as she looked away and I saw that vastness retreating from her gaze, I understood.

Men and women were not created equal. The Bible spoke of it. It was a truth so central to most of our lives, that most of us looked right past it.

But not Helena.

She'd never married and had eschewed the life that so many of her sex were forced into. She'd fought for her place, for the chance to do something different. She'd no doubt sacrificed for it, lost friends and family for it. And despite everything, she was terrified of losing it. Because in the Roman Empire, a man stood before his woman. Not beside her.

She took another step back, pulling away from me. My grip tightened around her waist. I didn't let her go. We were here, together within this place we shared. Shield-mates. And it was only now that I realized how much that word also meant to me.

Helena as my equal? It felt so right. Truly, unmistakably right.

"Helena," I said.

She looked back up to me, so unsure. I let those embers within me swirl up until they danced behind my eyes, hoping she would see the fullness of my words.

"Do you swear yourself as my shield-mate, vowing to stand beside me?"

Her eyes widened, staring at me mutely with an expression of such fragile vulnerability that I almost swallowed what I next spoke.

"Do you promise to stand together against the future; to face your enemies and mine with our shields locked?"

She blinked rapidly, her eyes shining with unshed tears. I could no longer speak past the lump that had returned to close my throat. I watched her, hoping that it would be enough.

Then, she leaned her chest into mine. Her arms rose to wrap themselves around my neck. I heard the wet strip of cloth she'd been holding tumble from her waist to the floor. But the sound was distant, easily ignored within this endless moment between our beating hearts.

"Do you, Leontius, swear yourself as my shield-mate? Do you vow to stand beside me?" Her voice was so soft; that wondrous vastness there behind her eyes. "And do you promise to believe in me; to trust that I'll hold that place beside you, and face what comes with your shield locked onto mine?"

I nodded, my voice rough. "I swear myself to you, shield-mate."

"And I swear myself to you, shield-mate," she said, tears spilling down each of her cheeks.

Then, our lips found one another's. We kissed, falling deeply into each other. I opened myself to her, and she to me. And together, we guided the other through every part of ourselves.

When we finally parted, my head spun with the taste and the knowing of her.

"A kiss to seal an oath," she breathed, her arms still around my neck.

I smiled. "We're bound together now, shield-mate."

She nodded, eyes bright. "I have another for you."

"Oh?"

She leaned fully into me, her cheek sliding against my own so that she could whisper into my ear.

"Do you promise to make love to me?" Her breath, her body on my skin made me shiver. "And tonight, do you vow to hold me in your arms while I sleep?"

"I swear it," I said, leaning in towards her, my heart hammering in my chest.

"Ah," she said, dodging away. She put a finger to my lips, her eyes bright. "This one needs a special kiss."

I blinked, puzzled. I tried to speak, but she pressed her finger down harder.

"Shh." Her other hand came to rest against my chest, pushing onto me with insistent strength. "Lie down."

I obeyed, liking the way her bottom lip had curled up between her teeth. I shifted to lay down lengthwise on the table, the stone wet and shockingly cool against my naked back.

Helena drifted around towards my head, her fingers trailing up my chest.

"Helena, what—"

Her hand slid back over my mouth, cutting me off. She was behind my skull now, and I had to crane my neck backward to see her.

"No talking," she said.

Her eyes were on mine. Her breath swirled through parted lips, a deep scarlet blooming beneath her flesh. She leaned forward, her copper hair tumbling down towards me, her hands on the stone beside my shoulders.

"Don't move," she breathed. "Not yet."

My chest ceased its rise and fall, my breath locked within me. Her naked breasts hung there, just above my face. They brushed against each other, the crack between them deep enough to smother me. Her nipples, those pink, perfect petals, brushed past the tip of my nose.

"I don't want to hear your promise to me, Leo."

She stretched over top of me. Her breasts swung away, her nipples slipping over the flesh of my chest. Her hands shifted and I watched the tight ripples of her stomach slide past.

"I want to feel it."

Then, in a show of fluid grace, Helena was completely on the table, her knees on the stone. They started right beside my head, but as she kept moving lower, they shifted into place on either side of my shoulders. The naked arch of her navel slid past my gaze. I saw a patch of dark hair; my first glimpse of the full, uncovered beauty of her.

"I want you to show me your sincerity," she said. "As I prove my own."

And then, with one more agonizingly slow shift of her body, she was over me. She held herself a scant handbreadth from me, letting me feast on the sight of her. Her center was a lush seam of curling velvet, soft when the rest of her was so tight. Her pubic hair, dark and gleaming with moisture, was verdant. A forest of curls that was as wild as the cypress green of her eyes.

Those embers swirled faster within me, gathering together. My heart slammed against my ribs like a battering ram.

Helena's knees shifted a fraction, and in some distant corner of my mind, I felt her fingers pulling at the cloth wrapping my waist. But I was frozen, breathing in the heady scent of the sweat that still clung to her sex. That movement, that minute adjustment, had opened her. She was spread wide before me; her silken lips parted to reveal the gleaming, dew-drenched warmth within her.

My mouth flooded with saliva, my eyes watering as I refused to blink away the sight of her. I felt a small sound escape me. A moan? A whimper? I wasn't sure. But at that moment I thought of it as a prayer—an exhortation to God and this, the most perfect of His creations.

"You promised to make love to me," she said.

Her breasts pressed against my navel. I groaned, as suddenly, the tightness between my legs disappeared. Helena had pulled away my loincloth, I realized, freeing my cock. She made a small sound of pleasure in her throat, wrapping the warmth of her palm around my shaft.

Then she started to stroke me, working my still-damp member up and down. I felt her inhale my scent; the dripping folds of her slit quivered with her airy sigh of anticipation.

"So, kiss me, my shield-mate," she murmured, her breath tickling my tip. "Speak your oath into my body."

Another groan rumbled out from me as, a moment later, Helena's tongue flicked out to taste my cock. Her hand continued to work, pulling my skin down from around the head of my penis. She spread her saliva over that too, wrapping her tongue around me in languid swirls.

The sensation freed me from my paralysis. The embers within me came together into a veritable flame.

My hands came up and I dug my fingers into the flesh of her ass, spreading her even wider before plunging in. Her pussy was a steaming jungle; a rolling ocean. Her soft, moisture-beaded pubic hair tickled my face as I dove through her dewy folds. I closed my eyes, melting into her, into the taste that flowed from between her legs. Helena pulled me into the satiny dampness of her mouth, and I luxuriated in her liquid serenity.

Where the Empress and Antonina had scalded me with their heat, Helena soaked into me with a soothing coolness. She was the rain-drenched forest, the salty spray of the sea. She was more sour than sweet, tasting of the scent that drifted from her body when we trained. She tasted wild, of movement and sweat, and the sun on tired muscles.

I ran my tongue through to her depths, feeling her every little gasp and quiver. She settled herself more fully onto my face as her head bobbed slowly up and down on my cock. I explored her fully, carefully. And, remembering my promise, I used my lips and tongue to speak to her of my devotion.

After some time, I felt her mouth come up from me. She let out a breathy moan, arching her body upward. Her weight pressed down on me, her ass slipping from my grasp and closing over my face. I was suddenly smothered in the dark of her, drowning in her taste and her scent.

God, she was so wet. Her moisture-slick folds slid over me, coating my beard and face as her hips started to roll. I couldn't breathe, couldn't see, but I didn't care, losing myself within the deepest parts of her. And when it felt like my lungs would burst, she lifted herself off of me.

I let her go, my chest heaving. I pushed myself onto my elbows as Helena spun to face me, her knees on either side of my hips. She smiled, a curling, pleasure-softened expression.

I reached up, running my palm along her cheek. I pulled her smile down to my own, kissing her deeply. Her body slid into place against me, the falling curtain of her hair shielding us from the world beyond.

"There," I said once she had pulled away. "Now, it's doubly official."

She laughed low in her throat, that vastness within her eyes. "Make love to me then, my shield-mate."

With that she lowered herself down onto me, sheathing my spit-gleaming cock within her.

She moaned, her body swallowing me whole. I slid my hands down to grip her hips, leaning my head back as she began to move. Helena rode me, her body a silken wave. Her hips rolled in a gentle rhythm. I fell into it, moving my body with hers.

I ran my hands up and down her figure. I kissed her mouth, her breasts, her nipples, her cheek, her neck, and then back to her lips. She was so soft. Her lips were as cool as falling snow. She tickled my ear with her breath, the air escaping her in little gasps that rolled in time with the slow undulation of her hips.

Helena and I made love.

There was only her, the feel of her against me, and the fire that was growing in my chest. She felt it too, because together, our bodies soon quickened. The placid sea stirred, the silken wave of our rhythm churning faster and faster. We built upon each other; the fire roared through me, while her body swayed and roiled like a storm.

Then, she stiffened. Something relaxed within her, and I felt myself slip free. She lifted herself, and through the swinging curtain of her breasts, I saw the storm of her body burst.

She squirted, the sea's spray pouring out from between her legs. Her wetness splashed onto my stomach, warmer than the air around us. I was transfixed, watching as her body clenched and trembled, her every motion sending more of her spattering onto me like rain.

Helena's face was suddenly scarlet, her expression twisting into something between horror and shame.

"God, Leo, I'm so sorry! This happens to me sometimes, I can't always control it." She was speaking quickly, shifting as if to push herself off of me. "God, why now! I'm so sorry, I know that this is so disgusting. Please, Leo, I'll clean it. Just don't—"

The flames became an inferno, searing away my every thought. My hands clamped tightly around her hips. Blood roared in my ears, a scalding heat searing the inside of my throat.

I *burned* to drown myself in her.

I jerked into motion, pulling and sliding my body down the table until my face was once again beneath her lush, dripping pussy.

"Leo, what!? Don't—" Her voice became a breathy squeak as I dove back into her. I drank from her, lapping at her delicious sourness with long strokes of my tongue. I could hardly breathe, my nose crushed into the soft curls of her pubic hair. But that didn't matter. My arms flexed, grinding her steaming, soaking folds harder against me.

"Leo! Stop it!" She panted. "What are you ..."

Her voice trailed off into an airy moan. My tongue plumbed the depths of her with nothing of the careful exploration or calculated flicks of before. I drank from her like a man dying of thirst, feeling the fire burn hotter and hotter within me.

"Leo ..." Her thighs clenched around my skull. "This is ...this is so ... so ... ah ..."

That last word became a deep, back-arching, toe-curling moan. I felt it thrum through her body. Her fingers wove themselves through my hair, gripping me tightly. I loosened my hold, letting her slide herself back and forth over my mouth and nose.

I took everything I could from her, desperate to ease the burning.

Helena whimpered. I felt a tremble wrack her body, her fingers tightening in my hair. She ground herself into my face, her breath ragged.

"Fuck, Leo. I can't. I—"

She cried out, throwing her head backward. Within her, I felt something loosen. Helena was the storm once again, her scream like thunder. And from between her legs, the clouds broke.

Her wetness flooded into me, filling me with the taste of her sour-sweetness. I pulled my mouth from her lest I drown, closing my eyes as her rain soaked my face and hair. When the storm eased, I opened my eyes to find the soft jungle of her pubic hair a mere tongue flick away, moisture still dripping from her steaming folds.

"My lion," Helena panted. Her naked breasts heaved and her eyes were glazed with pleasure. "My hungry, hungry lion."

But I wasn't yet finished. A growl rumbled out of me, the dull roar of the inferno. My cock twitched, afire with the same blazing heat, burning like a freshly forged sword. And it was in Helena's soaking pussy that it needed to be quenched.

I groaned with need, shoving myself back along the stone surface until my hips were once again below hers. She laughed from above me, letting herself be maneuvered until the tip of my cock pressed against her moisture. "Drench me," I panted before I thrust into her.

I slid into her effortlessly. God, she was wet. She was so fucking wet.

She gasped, throatier this time. She arched her back, grinding her hips into mine, her hands planted on either side of my shoulders. Her tits hung low and heavy, swinging pendulum-like above me. I pulled her down, burying my face between them. I kissed and sucked, forcing myself fully into her pillow-like softness.

I thrust into her again and again, faster and faster. She mewled, shuddered, and moaned. I slipped out from between her breasts, grabbing her hips. Her body melded itself to mine, her heavy tits squashed against my chest.

Her ass rebounded against my hips, a rhythmic thunderclap that grew deafening as I plunged my cock deeper and deeper into her. She shifted. My member slipped from her soaking center, a gush of her wetness spraying out after it.

She soaked me, once again coating my cock and hips and stomach with her fragrant rain. My entire body shook with the growl that rumbled from me, my thoughts melting away. I grabbed a fistful of her hair, yanking her lips down to mine. She mashed her mouth against mine our tongues fighting to wrap the other in its embrace.

Gone was the gentle sway, the tenderness. Her body writhed in my grip. Her hand slipped between our sweat and squirt-slickened bodies, gripping my cock and forcing it back into her. I growled into her throat, feeling the tip of me skip off her silken ridges to impale her fully.

She shuddered, her pussy flexing around me. She slammed her hips down to meet my next thrust and the next. We kept our lips locked, hammering our bodies together again and again and again as we raged against and into each other with elemental fury.

We were fire and storm; lion and shark.

And then, when there was only the heat and the sweat and the pounding of our bodies, I exploded.

I roared silently, my body clenching tight. I pumped all of myself into her, her body riding wave after wave of billowing heat.

Then, it was gone, and we collapsed.

My chest rose and fell in great bellows. I was empty, completely spent. She had taken all of me, quenching me in her cool wetness.

Helena lay atop me; the flesh between us was hot, sticky from our passion. She shifted, letting out a languid sort of sigh as my cock slipped out of her. She slid into the crook of my arm, resting her cheek against my chest.

I let out a pleased rumble, pulling her close. I traced swirling patterns along the small of her back with my fingers, smiling when I felt her shiver.

"That tickles," she said.

"Do you want me to stop?" My voice was hoarse.

Her breath tickled the hair on my chest. "No."

I laughed softly, folding my arm so that I could run my fingers along her ribs and shoulders. We lay in silence for a while, letting our bodies cool.

"Did you mean it?" she said, at last. "Everything you said."

"Hmm?" My eyes had been growing heavy. I rubbed at them, feeling the stiffness of my body as I shifted against the stone. "What?"

Helena didn't answer, so, I blinked myself awake. I slipped a hand beneath my head, speaking a few heartbeats later. "Look at me."

She stiffened, not moving until I called her name. She raised her head slowly, her face carefully blank. I could see a flinch already forming at the corners of her eyes.

"Is this because you want my tongue in your pussy again?" I asked, flatly.

She blinked, her expression going slack.

"Well?" I demanded. "I'm getting pretty tired of always repeating myself you know."

Helena choked on her next breath. A flush crawled up her skin, and she was laughing within the next heartbeat.

My expression of mock severity faded into a wide smile. I pulled her back down to me, kissing her laughing lips. She relaxed, her body curling back into mine.

"Side by side, shield-mate," I told her. "Your shield locked to mine."

She nodded, her face just above mine. "You're right, I'm sorry. It's just ... no. Never mind."

"I don't swear oaths lightly," I said. I raised my hand, brushing a lock of hair back from her face. "And I don't think you do either."

"No," she said, that vastness filling the green of her eyes. "I don't."

"Good," I said, and this time, she leaned down to kiss me.

It was a while before we separated, though her face twisted when we did. "God. Your lips still taste like ..."

I grinned up at her, feeling the first flicker of those embers swirling back to life within me. "I'm not surprised. I nearly drowned."

Her face burned scarlet. She let her forehead drop to rest against my chin. "God, Leo, I know. I'm so sorry. I totally lost control there."

I laughed, tugging her head down into the crook of my neck. I massaged her scalp with my fingers, pleased when she let out another little sigh.

"I guess I should apologize too," I said. "I don't know if that ending really counts as 'lovemaking.'"

She raised herself back up, propping herself on my chest to gaze into my face. "I don't care. Those last few minutes were ..."

"Amazing," I finished.

She smiled, biting at the corner of her bottom lip. She ran her fingers through the hair on my jaw, scratching at the remaining dampness.

"It really didn't bother you, then? When I ... you know."

"Soaked me?" I grinned.

She flicked my nose, "I'm serious."

I looked into her, hoping that she could see the heat gathering within me. "Helena, seeing that, and feeling how you ..." I shivered, my flaccid cock twitching. "It drove me completely wild."

"You're sure? Because it always happens when I get close. I can hold it back sometimes, but tonight— "

"Don't," I told her. "Not ever, shield-mate."

Her smile was like the sun on glittering waves. She kissed me, and when she pulled back, light danced within her eyes. "What makes you think this will happen again?"

"Oh?" I said, shifting my body beneath hers. "Don't I still have a few promises to keep?"

"Hmm," the sound came from deep within her. "You do."

"Well then," I said. "I was planning on going to wash myself in that bath. And then, taking you up to my bed chamber."

Helena shifted, her naked flesh sliding against mine. The first stir within the ocean's stillness. "I'm not tired."

Those embers at my center came together, a tongue of flame flickering to life. I let it burn behind my eyes, running my entire palm down the arch of her back. "Me neither."

"My lion," she purred. "Always hungry."

She brought her lips down to mine, whispering two more words in the moment before they met.

"Devour me."

Chapter Fifteen

Out in the Empress's City

My breathing slowed. I felt the darkness deepen as my thoughts drifted away and swirled into whatever stuff dreams were made of.

The soft warmth at my side shifted. The hairs along my side rose, cool air sliding in to replace the kiss of Helena's naked flesh.

"Are you asleep?" she murmured.

I felt her breasts press against my chest, strands of falling hair tickling my shoulders. She ran her fingers through the hair on my jaw, gently scratching me with her nails. I leaned into her hand and shivered when her fingers trailed down the curve of my neck.

I made a small sound of pleasure. "Not anymore."

"Good."

I could hear the smile in her voice. Her naked leg slid along mine, and a heartbeat later, she pressed her smile onto my lips. She kissed me, pulling me into her soothing, crystalline depths.

My arms wrapped around her, eliciting a breathy little laugh.

"My lion. Are you still hungry?"

"Mmm, maybe a little?"

"Ah," she purred, full of hidden promise. "Well, in that case ..."

She slipped from my arms, the bed creaking as she rolled off. She was gone, and the absence of her warm body was a bucket of cold water.

I sat up, blinking in the candlelight. "Helena, what the hell?"

She grinned, her fingers working a lock of her hair into a small braid. "Come on, it's still early. Let's go eat."

I stared at her flatly, her grin widening. Her cypress eyes were bright. "You said that you were hungry, didn't you?"

"I did," I answered. "But you know what I ... That was cruel."

Her grin melted into a laugh, and her skin flushed. She swayed towards me, her still naked curves rolling like the waves beneath a ship. She sat in my lap, letting me loop my arms around her waist.

"You make it too easy, my shield-mate."

I raised an eyebrow. "Oh—so, it's my fault, then?"

"Obviously," she answered, eyes dancing. "You trained me to go after weakness when I see it."

It was my turn to laugh. I rose to my feet, lifting her in my arms. She threw her arms around my neck, her laugh joining mine to fill my small sleeping quarters. I kissed her before setting her down.

"I am hungry, shield-mate," I said. "And it just so happens that there's more training we can do tonight."

"Should I get my armor?" she asked, her eyebrow climbing.

"No," I answered, my smile wolfish. "But get your fists ready. I'm choosing where we eat."

"A soldier's tavern?" Helena said, an hour or so later. "I've been in one of these before, you know."

"As a *stratiotai*?"

"No," she said, something flashing across her face. "Not as a *stratiotai*."

I was an idiot. The *Excubitors* had never accepted her. Of course, they never would have invited her out for a drink.

"Helena, I—"

"—don't like the look of this place," she cut me off. She gave me a smile that was meant to be teasing but was a hair too strained. "Are you sure it's any good? It smells like puke and sour wine."

I hesitated a moment before letting the matter drop.

"That's the smell of success," I told her. "Kostas runs the best wine house in the city. Well, the best that a few *nummi* a day can afford."

"The Empress pays us enough to go somewhere less ... successful."

"You'll like it, trust me. The wine tastes like horse piss, but ..." I let the tension build for a few heartbeats. "He's the only one in the city that makes decent *pitaroudia*."

Pitaroudia was a mash of chickpeas and other vegetables fried together into little balls. It was a staple from back home, and it had taken me ages to find this place.

Her eyes widened. "He's Rhodian?"

"From around Alyki Bay," I said, happy to see the reaction I'd been hoping for. "On the western side of the island."

Her smile, as she followed me in, became one of honest excitement.

The streets had been quiet as we'd passed, oddly subdued. But Kostas's place, I was happy to see, was lively.

Drunken soldiers weren't spilling out of the door, but there was enough of a crowd that we had to push our way past a few people. I led Helena to the back, where old Kostas scowled from behind his bar.

"Kostas," I said, leaning against the bar. "I promised this Rhodian lady some *pitaroudia*. Are you going to disappoint her?"

"Rhodian?" he said, suddenly a lot less grouchy looking.

"From Lindos," Helena said.

We chatted for a bit, swapping the latest bit of island news that we had while Kostas poured us a couple of flagons of dark wine. The food would be ready in a few minutes, he told us.

"She's paying," I said when I spotted Kostas's young son.

The kid was coming back with an empty drink tray. I hooked him by the arm, leading him away. I put a silver coin in his hand, promising him another if he'd fetch something for me. Helena looked at me curiously when I returned, but I kept my mouth shut against her silent question.

"*Centenarius*!" I heard a voice call. "Leontius!"

I turned, already feeling a grin stretching my features. At a nearby table, five men were waving towards me. They wore happy smiles, their cheeks rosy with wine.

"Sergius! You old bastard! What the hell are you doing here?"

Sergius, a crusty old *stratiotai* with more scars on him than most had years, made a show of cupping one ear. "Can't hear you so good, sir! Come here and whisper it to me!"

The men at his table laughed. I did too, shaking my head.

"Friends of yours?" Helena asked.

"Men from my old cohort," I said. "Come on, I'll introduce you."

Helena's body tightened. I saw the same expression as before flash across her features. Resignation? Consternation? I wasn't sure, and it was gone just as fast.

"Sure," she said, stepping forward and forcing me to move after her.

The men rose to meet me, and I greeted each with a rough embrace and rougher words. Sergius, Gratian, Suda, Maurice, and Niketas, as good a squad of *stratiotai* that had ever served in Justinian's legions.

"Boys, this is Helena," I said as we sat in the chairs pulled over for us. "My shield-mate. She guards the Empress with me."

Sergius blinked. Maurice set down his wine while Suda and Niketas glanced at each other in disbelief. Helena, however, seemed to loosen, the faint crinkle of something disappearing from the corners of her eyes. Gratian, horse's ass that he was, guffawed.

"Come on, *Centenarius*," he said. He was seated on Helena's other side and took the opportunity to drape one arm around her shoulders. "You can't expect us to believe that sweet little thing fights beside you?"

Whatever else I could say about Gratian, and there was a lot, I couldn't fault his eye. Helena was a vision in that green *tunica*.

"You think I'm sweet?" she said, lips curling into a small smile.

"Sweet enough to eat," he said. His eyes roved up and down her body. "How much?"

Helena stayed silent, relaxed, that small smile never leaving her lips.

"I'm good, too." Gratian insisted. "You'll see. My cock's so good that you should be the one paying me!"

He snickered through his leering grin. I shook my head when Sergius opened his mouth to interfere. Although I needn't have. Because, an instant later, Helena's fist crunched into Gratian's throat. He gagged, falling backward, his chair crashing to the ground. The tavern fell silent, all eyes on Helena as she slowly stood. Her eyes swept the room. There was a heartbeat of silence, and then two. Her lip suddenly quirked.

"Nobody touches before they pay."

The room exploded with laughter, covering the sound of Gratian's moaning. Helena sat back down while I moved to help the man pick himself off the floor.

"I'll kill her," he choked. "I'll fucking kill that bitch."

"Shut up," I said, loud enough for the others to hear. "She'd gut you like a fish. And I'd cut off whatever bits my shield-mate left of you."

I pulled him up and hissed into his ear. "You stupid bastard. Helena is the Empress's personal guard. Do you want your head to decorate the palace walls?"

Gratian's face blanched. He started to stammer something but I pushed him away. "I told you to shut the fuck up. Go get us some more wine."

"Whatever Kostas hasn't pissed in for me," Helena called.

Sergius's grin was wide. "Good punch, that. It's the only way to get him to shut his hole."

"Aye," Niketas said, draining his cup. He burped. "Finally, some fucking peace."

"*Centenarius*," Maurice said, leaning forward. "No offense to your lady, but a shield-mate? Are you sure about this?"

"This lady," Helena said, "can speak for herself. Look me in the eyes and tell me what you mean."

Maurice complied. "You're a woman. You're real pretty, I'll give you that, but you don't know what this means."

"I don't need a cock to piss standing up. Why would I need one to hold up a shield?"

Maurice smirked. "Cute. But it's more than that, it's—"

"Wait, you can piss standing up?" Gratian interrupted, returning with the wine faster than I'd expected. His voice was hoarse. "Seriously?"

The others groaned.

"That wasn't the point, Grat," Suda said. "Although, now I am a bit curious ..."

"It's easy," Helena said, winking towards him. "And I guarantee that I can piss better than Grat fucks."

Laughter rolled around the table. Even Gratian snickered, though heat crawled up his face. He lifted the jug of wine, filling Helena's cup and then mine.

"So, what the hell are you talking about, then?" he asked.

"If she can really be Leo's shield-mate," Maurice said. "If she can fight."

"She knows what it means, Maur," I said. "She's good, too. Fast. And she's got some sense, unlike you thick-headed bastards."

"If the *centenarius* says so, then that's good enough for me," Sergius said. "What do you say, boys, we gonna keep her around?

"Let's drink!" Niketas said, grabbing his cup.

Sergius banged the table, hoisting his own cup into the air. "To Helena!"

"Helena!" We roared, slamming our empty cups down a few moments later.

These were rough men who lived rough lives. They were killers who earned their coin in the grinding crush of the shield wall. They respected a foul mouth, a hard fist, and loyalty to one's brothers. They were *stratiotai*.

And when Helena, her cheeks flushed a happy red, clacked her cup with a still sheepish-looking Gratian, I saw them start to think of her as one too.

Our *pitaroudia* arrived, and we fell to bickering over the platter of fried balls of ground-up chickpea, onion, and mint.

"Leo never told me that he was a *centenarius*," Helena said, speaking through a mouthful of food.

I snorted. "That's because I'm not. These idiots just call me that."

"The crest don't make the *centenarius*," Suda drawled. "Ain't that right, Serg?"

"That's the damned truth, lad," the older man replied.

I rolled my eyes, the rest of the boys snickering into their cups. Sergius liked to share whatever kernels of wisdom popped into his head. We'd all heard this particular one a hundred times already.

"We call him that because of Callinicum," Sergius continued, clarifying.

"Ah," she said. "You were all there?"

He nodded. "And my bones would be decorating some Persian's trophy shelf if it wasn't for the *centenarius* here. All of ours would."

The mood sobered, each of us remembering. I looked down to my hands, seeing the flecks of old, old blood beneath my fingernails. The ones I could never seem to clean.

"Was it bad?" Helena asked.

"Aye," Sergius answered. "The old *centenarius* was a right stupid prick. He got himself killed in the first charge of the Sassinid horsemen. Leontius here took over after that. Things were real shaky for a bit, but he kept us from scattering. And when the general decided he'd had enough of watching us die, Leo got us retreating."

Nobody spoke for a while, memories holding us. Some of us put wine to our lips, others stared with unfocused eyes. The mood remained dark until Gratian, bless his fool soul, blurted out, "Fuck, but *Centenarius* Demetrius was a *prick.*" That brought out a few chuckles. Niketas let out another burp, and Maurice swatted the back of his head. Most of us felt lighter after that.

It didn't do any good to dwell on the past. The things we'd done, the friends we'd lost ... It wasn't good to remember. *Stratiotai* had to live for the moment.

Maybe that was why I'd always been such a terrible soldier.

☧

It was approaching midnight when Sergius hauled himself to his feet. He blinked bleary eyes, motioning to the others. "Right boys, we've got patrol in the morning. Let's get moving."

The men swallowed their last mouthfuls of wine, said their goodbyes, and stumbled away with varying levels of coordination.

Sergius watched them go with a shake of his head. He rifled through a pouch at his side for a moment before turning back to me. "I've got something for you here, *Centenarius.* It got to the barracks a few days ago."

He held a folded envelope out towards me. My stomach clenched. It had only been two months since I'd sent out my own letter, and while possible, it was surprising to receive a response so fast. For an instant, I dared to hope that this might be something else.

But my name on the folded envelope was written out in my mother's blocky hand. I snatched it from him, quickly stuffing it away and out of sight.

"It was good to see you, Leo," Sergius said. He pulled me to my feet and pounded my back in a rough embrace. "Don't forget about us rankers while you're dining with nobles."

"Take care of yourself, Serg," I said, returning his embrace. "And, thank you."

"We're on garrison duty," the old soldier grinned. "What's going to happen in the capital?"

Sergius surprised Helena by pulling her into a hug next. "Keep your shield tight to his. Our *centenarius* always seems to be around when shit is the deepest."

"I'll keep the sword from his back," Helena said. "Though, it might loosen him up a bit."

The older man laughed. "It was good to meet you, lass. And remember, you've got a brother in old Sergius." With a last little wave, he ambled out and into the deepening night.

"You were right," Helena said, settling back. She popped the last of the *pitaroudia* in her mouth. "This is a great place."

"Even with Grat here?" I asked with a smile.

"Even still," she said, her lips curling upward. She put her elbow on the table, leaning her head against her palm. "I'm happy that you introduced me to your friends. It was ... nice."

"It was," I said. I shifted in my seat, wanting to move my chair closer to her. But the movement jostled the letter in my pocket. Suddenly, my mother's words weighed more than a boulder. I shifted again, an awkward jerk of my body that accomplished nothing.

Helena's smile softened. She took pity on me, scooting over until her leg pressed against mine. I let out a breath, leaning back in my chair. We sat in silence for a while. I closed my eyes, enjoying the warmth and the quiet murmur of the few remaining patrons.

"This was always my favorite part," I said after a while. I opened my eyes to find Helena waiting for me to continue. "A place like this. With the others, once the campaign was done. It's ..." I trailed off, trying to order my thoughts. How could I explain this to someone who'd never been to war? How did I tell her of the constant tension, of the anxious expectation that came with knowing that somewhere, beyond the light of your campfire, someone wanted you dead?

Kill or be killed; there was none of that in this tavern. I could drink with my friends, without wondering which of them I would lose. Or what I would have to do.

It was just "... different," I finished.

Helena didn't laugh. She didn't smile or tease. She just watched with eyes that took in so much of me. She leaned into me, resting her head against my shoulder.

"Different," she said, letting out a long breath. "I like that."

My eyes suddenly prickled. I blinked furiously, trying to clear the wetness seeping into them. I turned, leaning my chin against her hair, breathing in the scent of her. I shifted my arm to pull her closer.

"Leo," she said. "What would you do if you weren't a soldier?"

"I ... I don't know," I said. "I've always been a soldier."

"But could you do it for ten more years?"

"What else would I do? My father was *stratiotai*, and his father and his father. I don't know anything else."

Helena shifted against my shoulder, her hair tickling my neck.

"What's your plan once you've retired?"

I bobbed my shoulders in a small shrug, careful not to disturb her. "Go back to Rhodos. My mother is a seamstress. I'll help her run the shop."

"And marry a 'good' woman?" She said, her tone edged with mockery.

I didn't answer, though I tightened my grip on Helena. For a heartbeat, her body was stiff. Then, she let out another long breath, relaxing against me.

"What about something like this?" she asked, gesturing around us. "A tavern."

"Running a wine house?"

She pushed off of me, suddenly more animated. "Why not? You could open a soldier's tavern on Rhodos; make a place for old *stratiotai*."

"A peaceful place," I murmured.

"Exactly!" She grinned. "It's a good idea, right?"

"I'd have to learn how to make *pitaroudia*," I said, feeling a smile tug at my lips.

"I'm sure Kostas will give you his recipe."

I laughed. "I'm a soldier, Helena, not a cook. I think I even burned water once."

"You are a soldier," she said. Her eyes held mine. "But you can be something else."

I looked away, swallowing.

"You'll think about it?"

"Sure," I forced some lightness into my tone. "But only if you promise that you'd go out and catch fish for me every day."

Helena stiffened, her face suddenly bright red. Not the reaction I'd been expecting. Her eyes flicked over my face, searching. "You don't think I'd be better as the cook? Or serving drinks?"

"No," I said, not having to force my smile. "You belong on the sea, right?"

Her eyes were so wide. I felt my heart start to beat faster. That vastness, it was there, rising to the edge of her, on the verge of breaking through.

"Leo," she murmured. "I—"

She was interrupted by the thump of a pouch on our table. I looked over to find Kostas's son standing by our table. The kid looked exhausted but triumphant.

"You found what I asked for, then?" I said.

He nodded, holding out a grubby hand.

"Good man," I grinned, flipping him a silver coin.

He disappeared without another word, and I quickly disengaged myself from Helena to put the lumpy, medium-sized pouch away.

"It's a surprise," I told her. "For later."

She arched an eyebrow but didn't press me. She downed her last mouthful of wine, letting out a happy sigh. "We have to come back here."

I nodded, bringing my own wine to my lips.

"It's nice to see that you can relax without my pussy in your mouth."

I choked, spraying out a mouthful of wine. Helena laughed, that deep, joy-filled sound. She pounded my back as I coughed myself hoarse. My face blazed, and I felt the eyes of the remaining patrons turn towards me.

"Leo," she said. "You're defenseless."

I coughed, glaring at her through watery eyes.

"Come on," she said. "Let's get back to the palace."

We walked out into the night, breathing in the city's quiet. Although, it did not last long. We were but a handful of blocks from the wine house, when, out of the dark, we saw the fire. And heard the baying of the mob.

Chapter Sixteen

An Empress's Past Shared

The baying of the mob. The glow of fire.

After a few moments of debate, Helena and I decided to move towards it. There were no screams of pain, no real sounds of violence coming from the streets ahead. We would see what was happening, we decided, before returning to the Empress.

We came into a square with a small, torch-lit church planted solidly at the northern end. A few squads of armored *stratiotai*, perhaps forty men, stood with swords drawn before the single door. They were imperial legionaries, though I did not recognize any of the grim-faced men.

Surrounding them was the mob.

The seething body of humanity filled the square. There were men, women, and children. The old and the young and the in-between. Their roar was the pounding of the surf, the blue and green flags they held, the rolling of the waves.

The mob was hurling rocks, taunts, and empty flagons of wine towards the imperial soldiers. They ebbed and flowed like a tide, backwards and forwards, as the guards stuttered out and edged back.

Helena and I pushed our way to the rear of the crowd, ending up close to where a wild-eyed man screamed from the top of a heavy crate. I gripped Helena's arm, leaning close to shout.

"Is that where the escaped prisoners are?"

She nodded. "Saint Akakios church. Should we help the guards?"

I shook my head vehemently. There was no way that I was getting involved in this. If the *centenarius* here had any sense, he'd be pulling his men back.

And, sure enough, the soldiers started to march away. The crowd roared, a fresh wave of stones and broken pottery raining down on the retreating men.

"See!" the man beside us shrieked. "They're weak! The Emperor is weak! No more taxes and no more oppression! Power to the Greens! *Nika*! *Nika*!" The man pumped a sword into the air, a weapon that he shouldn't be allowed to have, let alone be able to afford.

His rallying cries were lost in the crowd's jubilance. Their voices were that sea surging through rock: a disjointed, chaotic maelstrom of sound that crashed into and swirled around itself. I heard calls to free the prisoners, to end the costly wars, and to remember the charioteers that died. Men screamed at the perversion of change, while cries of *Nika* rose like plumes of spray from the boiling tides.

The church doors opened. Two men emerged, welcomed by the crowd's roar of joyful defiance. These were the two escaped prisoners: a Blue and a Green. I saw more unexplainable swords thrust into the air. The two colors blended, united by a single call of conquest.

"*Nika*! *Nika*!"

Helena and I exchanged glances, my fear and unease mirrored in her expression. We retreated from the square a few moments later, hurrying away from the crowd and looping around towards the palace. We avoided any knots of people we encountered, breathing out a sigh of relief when the walls of the palace finally came into view. Our pace slowed. The walls were well-lit, with wary-eyed *Excubitors* patrolling the parapets.

"Things are really getting bad," I said.

Helena nodded, her expression serious. "We need to speak to the Empress. The weapons they had ..."

She trailed off, unsure, as I was, of the significance of what we'd seen.

"Aye," I said. "Let's get behind these walls."

The gates, two massive doors of heavy, iron-banded wood, were sealed shut. I hammered my fist against them, stepping back into the pools of light provided by two, over-hanging lanterns.

"Who's there?" an *Excubitor* called from above, poking his head over the parapets.

"It's us," Helena called back. "Open up."

The man took in our faces, eyes shifting to peer into the surrounding darkness.

"It's you," he said. "You two alone? Why are you out so late?"

"None of your business," Helena said. "Let us in. We have to see the Empress."

"Yeah, alright. I'll just come down and do that, then." He gave us a smile that set the hairs of my neck prickling. "Don't go anywhere. I'll be down in just a minute."

He vanished without another word, though we could hear the rattle of his armor as he stomped down a flight of stairs. I settled in to wait, wondering at my sudden sense of unease.

"How long does this usually take?" I asked.

"Not long," Helena said.

I waited for her to say more, but she didn't continue. Her attention was on the parapets. She was chewing her lip, eyes distant.

"I think," she eventually said, "that I've seen him before. I'm pretty sure that he's one of Doukas's friends."

I groaned. "Fantastic."

"Do you think he'll try something, again?" Helena asked.

"Probably," I said, blowing out air. "Especially if he comes with friends." Then, I shook myself, holding my arm out as if a shield was strapped to it. "Alright. By my side then, shield-mate."

"Yes, sir," she said, flashing me a quick grin. "*Centenarius*."

"Don't you start."

She laughed, sliding into place beside me. She hesitated a moment, before planting a quick kiss on my cheek. I smiled, an expression of pleased idiocy that I still wore when the gates swung open a few moments later.

Our instincts, unfortunately, proved to be accurate.

"Well," that familiar, prissy little voice said. "There seem to be beggars at our door."

Doukas was there with four other *Excubitors*, including the man who'd spoken to us from the parapets. The bastards were all armored, with swords at their belts and hastily-grabbed clubs in their hands.

"What are you doing here, Doukas?" Helena drawled. "I didn't think you'd want to see us again."

"I just want to talk," he said, leading his rich friends a few steps forward. They waved their clubs menacingly, spreading out a bit but too stupid to try and surround us. Helena and I stayed put, though I gripped her arm.

"If anything happens," I hissed. "Follow my lead."

She jerked her head up and down before speaking. "We don't have anything to say to you. We're the Empress's Guard. Let us through."

Doukas smiled like a child ripping the wings off an insect. "Ah, Copper, don't be like that."

Helena stiffened, sucking in a breath. Doukas's grin widened.

"I knew that I'd fucked you before, bitch," he said. "Seeing you earlier really jogged my memory, and then when the boys and I got to talking ... Here." He unhooked a pouch from his belt and tossed it towards us. It hit the cobbles with the metallic jingle of coins.

Helena had started to tremble.

"Three and a half *follis*," Doukas purred. He nodded to the coin purse. "That's what you cost, right? It's all there. Why don't you scoop that up and come into the alley with me?"

"And I'll take a roll after that," the man from the wall grinned.

"What the fuck is this?" I growled. "Pick up your fucking money."

"Paid is paid, runner," Doukas said. "It's not fair that you're the only one who gets a turn." He took another step forward, slapping his club into his hand. "That's how she's getting you to train her, isn't it? I can't say that I blame you. Copper's little cunt is magic."

A third man snorted. "You're exaggerating, Doukas. This slut was just another hole."

"Shut the fuck up," I said. "All of you."

Doukas laughed. "She didn't tell you, eh coward? Our Copper here has been on her back since she was old enough to take it. We've all had a dip in her."

Helena bowed her head.

"God, that bitch loved to work a cock. Do you remember, Copper, how I made you scream?"

I looked over to Helena, blood roaring in my ears. She was still shaking. She peered at me through the falling curtain of her hair, and one look into her shattered eyes told me all I needed to know.

It was true.

"*Look*!" My mother screamed into my mind, her words made heavier by the letter in my pocket. "*She's a whore! Didn't I say it? She's just another wicked, painted actress! This filthy creature doesn't deserve you, my little lion. Come home. Come back to where you belong.*"

"You're nothing but a dumb little slut, Copper," Doukas said. "You were never a match for me."

Emotions surged through me. My mother continued to blather in my head, gloating and spewing a litany of righteous condemnation and vitriol. I shoved all of that aside. I was *stratiotai*, and now wasn't the time to get lost in my head. I tightened my grip on Helena's arm. "Ready, shield-mate?"

"Come on," Doukas said. "Get rid of the runner then we'll remind Copper of her place."

"Helena!" I roared, startling everyone. "Shield up!"

She snapped her gaze back up, in time to see the others charging toward us. I grinned, feeling the eager thunder of my heart.

"Are you ready?" I asked.

"Yes," she answered.

"Then, run!"

I yanked her backward, forcing her into a spin and pulling her after me as I bolted from the gate. I dragged her away, accelerating quickly.

I don't care who you are, two soldiers in *tunicas* cannot beat a squad of armed and armored men. Even if it was these five shit-eaters. The *Excubitors* roared, giving chase. Helena, I was pleased to see, found her footing after a few stumbling steps. We stretched our legs, pulling far from the palace walls and into the night. We lost ourselves in the city's darkness, streets and buildings blurring past us as we ran. My heartbeat slowed after a few minutes, the sound of pursuit fading behind us.

Away from danger now, my thoughts began to swirl. Pieces clicked together in my mind, this final truth doing so much to explain the mystery surrounding my shield-mate's past. She was a woman dressed as a soldier; the Empress's guard with no real combat training. Her old friendship with Theodora and Antonina, her complete lack of bashfulness, and even her bawdy sense of humor could be explained. Helena had been an actress.

She must have known the Empress and Antonina from those days. Both of those women, I knew, had grown up desperately poor on Constantinople's streets. The Blues had taken them in when they were old enough, putting both women to work in their brothels and stage productions.

Helena's father had been a fisherman, and her mother had died in the weeks following her birth. They would have been poor, likely only ever a few bad days at sea from starvation. And for a young woman in the capital, there were very few ways to help ward off hunger.

So, she'd started to sell her sex.

Copper, I thought, a stage name. A brothel name. I imagined the shine of her hair by candlelight. The name fit her.

The pounding of our feet on the cobbles was a familiar beat. I realized that we'd fallen back into our rhythm, running side by side at the pace made natural by our daily training. My mother's voice started to leak back into my thoughts, all spite, judgment, and hatred. But the comfort of the run and the feel of Helena in her place beside me helped smother my initial surge of revulsion.

I let the air flow in and out of my lungs, Helena's breath cycling with my own. Nothing had changed. She was still there, right where I wanted her to be. The shape of her still fit as smoothly as it had before.

I felt those ugly emotions drain from me.

She was my shield-mate. And when I looked back into myself, I saw nothing of the furious disgust that my mother demanded I feel.

So, Helena had been a whore? That was nothing compared to what I had done.

I hadn't been paying attention to where we ran, following wherever Helena led. She guided me through the city, past empty squares and street corners full of shouting people. We eventually came to a quiet place, the buildings here older and shabbier than most.

We ran until we came to the sea.

We were far from the palace now, at a small dock along the edge of the Marmara Sea. It was one of those warm, cloudless summer nights. The moon was bright against the inky darkness of the water.

Helena slowed to a walk, and so did I. I kept beside her, stepping onto a short wooden pier. Neither of us spoke, though even in the deepest night, a dock was never silent. The sea lapped against the wooden pilings. Boats creaked, thumping rhythmically against their moorings. I breathed deeply, comforted by the scent of salt and old fish. It smelled like Rhodos, like home.

"This is the last place I saw my father," Helena said, coming to the edge of the pier. "He left one morning in his little fishing boat and never came back. I was thirteen years old."

She was silent for a few moments, gazing out and away from the city. I stood with her, feeling the sweat on my body start to cool.

"I know what you're thinking, Leo. Just say it."

She'd taken a step back from me, her arms crossed over her chest. She couldn't meet my eyes, and she curled away from me as if avoiding the blow she was sure I'd give her. She was ready to take my scorn, disgust, and condemnation. That expression on her face, so different from the brightness of her smile, broke something in me.

She'd sold her body for money. She'd been a whore, but I was a butcher. A killer. How was it that, of the two of us, it was she who felt vile? Why should she be the one to cringe from *my* revulsion?

"Say it, Leo," she said. "Come on!"

Her voice had risen, tinged with the desperate need to end this wait. To let whatever was going to happen, happen.

"Will you sit with me?" I said, lowering myself to the dock.

I didn't look at her, staring out at the sea with my legs dangling until I eventually felt her sit beside me. I pulled out the pouch that I'd gotten from Kostas' son, teasing it open and handing it to her.

"Here," I said. "Have one."

Helena peered inside, staring back up at me in disbelief. "Honeyed figs? Are these honeyed figs?"

I nodded. "They're your favorite, right?"

And then, all at once, her expression of raw vulnerability and confusion vanished and was replaced by one of rage.

"Honeyed figs?" she screamed. "You got me honeyed fucking figs?"

She slammed the pouch into my chest.

"I'm a whore, Leo! I fucked any man that paid me. You find out, and now you're giving me honeyed fucking figs?"

Her face was bright, even in the darkness. Her eyes flashed with a wild mix of a hundred different emotions. I wished that I knew what to say. "Helena, I—"

"And I was good at it too," she spat. "Like those fucking pigs said, I was one of the best. I had generals, senators, and Goddamned lords lining up outside my door. And you know why?"

Her fists, her body, all of it was clenched so tight. She was on the verge of shattering, like all the joy I'd seen break behind her eyes.

"Because I fucked them senseless. I did it all, Leo, anything they wanted. I'd take everything they could give me and then beg for more. And, when they were done, I'd hold their sweaty bodies and whisper that I'd never had it so good." Her face twisted. "And you know why? Because men always tip better when you stroke their egos as well as their cocks."

I ignored the churning in my gut and the pointless jealousy that reared up in me. I didn't know what to do, what to say. So, I said the first thing that came to me. "Were you ever going to tell me?"

The question, I saw, was a knife through her armor. She slumped, turning away, back out to sea. "I don't ..." she started, then swallowed. "I don't know. It's that ... remember the day we met?"

"When you came out to escort me to the Empress?"

She nodded. "Doukas and the other guard did their usual shit, but you ..." Her voice cracked, but she kept speaking, trying to blink away the tears gathering in her eyes. "You didn't laugh at me, Leo. You didn't smirk or roll your eyes ... You called me sir, and I mean ... You treated me with respect as if I really was ..."

She trailed off for a few moments, her fingers clenched tight in her lap.

"It was nice, Leo. It was really, really nice. And then with the training and everything else, and after tonight ... I just ... I just wanted to see."

My heart was steady in my chest. I remembered the way she'd looked at me in the tavern, the way she'd taken in so much of me with those cypress eyes.

I took in all of her now, and despite the letter in my pocket, my mother's voice had never felt so distant. "Well," I said. I pulled one of the sticky fruits from the pouch, holding it out to her. "Let's see."

"Leo," she said, her eyes full of tears. "Why?"

Because you're amazing, I thought. Because you're so beautiful. You're so strong, bright, and filled with so much life. You understand me, and when I'm with you I feel such peace. You're more than your past, and you're so much more than the world says you can be. And oath or no, whatever the future holds, I will do everything I can to keep you by my side. Your joy may be broken, Helena, but mine lies with you.

I wanted to say that, and so much more. But I was *stratiotai*, and so I spoke with the words I knew. "Because you're my shield-mate."

I could see something fracturing beneath her features, like a wall of sand about to be burst open by a wave. She didn't move, and so I reached out and unwound her fingers from the cloth in her lap. I put the honeyed treat into her palm.

"Leo," her voice cracked. She cradled the little piece of fruit in her lap. "I'm a whore."

"You were a whore," I said. "You became something different."

"I'm dirty. I'm not good, I'm not proper. I'll never be fit for y—" Her voice broke again. Her fingers closed tightly on the honeyed fig, her eyes screwing shut. "Who'd ever stand beside a whore?"

Then, she wept.

She curled around herself, shoulders shaking. Tears streamed down her cheeks. I shifted close, gathering her in my arms. She resisted at first, but I didn't let go. I held her head to my chest until she reached up to clutch at me with her empty hand.

I didn't speak, didn't murmur sweet words into her ears. I just held her, letting the pain that drained from her soak my chest. It was amazing. I felt so light, as if Helena's tears were washing away what remained of my doubts. I felt hope, real hope for the first time in so many years. This wondrous woman had done so much. She'd been a whore, and I'd been a soldier. She'd become something different, something new.

Could I do the same?

In my head, I saw a room filled with tables. It was there, by a market square that looked out onto the sea. A place built by four hands instead of just two. Who'd want to stand beside her, she'd asked. What a ridiculous thing to say. I didn't want to be anywhere else.

"Do you, Helena, swear yourself as my shield-mate?" I felt her body stiffen. "Do you vow to stand beside me? And do you promise to stand together against the future; your shield locked onto mine?"

She pushed herself off of me. Our gazes met, and I saw a new world behind her eyes.

"Well?" I asked.

She nodded, jerking her head up and down.

I matched her nod. "Then, I swear myself as your shield-mate, vowing to stand beside you. I promise to believe in you; to trust that you'll hold that place at my side."

I cupped her hands around the honeyed fig in her lap.

"And tonight," I said, "and however many nights we have. I vow to hold you in my arms while you sleep."

A heartbeat later, her lips were on mine. She kissed me, and I could taste the salt from her tears.

"You don't care?" she said when we finally parted. "You really don't care?"

I smiled. "I'm a soldier, Helena. I've paid for it, like every other man in the legion camps."

She shook her head. "This is different. Leo, I ... I won't just be some tart on your arm. I refuse to be."

"I know," I said. "I want more."

"I'll never be the proper woman. For your future, Leo. I don't just want to stay home with children while you're out in the world. I won't do that."

I laughed. "I know!"

"I'm serious! I'm not right for you, and people will always know what I am. I'm dir—"

"God, Helena!" I interrupted. "Enough! Christ on his cross, but I'm sick of hearing that."

"It's what everyone says," she said. "And what they'll say about you too."

"Nobody talks like that about the Empress. Or Antonina."

She snorted, and my heart warmed to see some of her old fire. "They're married to the most powerful men in the Empire. We're nobody. People will talk, Leo."

I inhaled deeply of the salty air, letting out a long breath.

"Have you ever killed anyone?"

"What?" she asked.

"Have you?"

"No. But what does that have to do with anything?"

"Because I'm a killer, Helena. I don't think I was even seventeen when I became one." I turned my gaze downward, holding out my war-calloused palms. I could see it there, the old blood. "I was a recruit, marching with my new unit towards the border with Persia. I was on watch one night when some bandits, or just desperate villagers, attacked. I remember them being so thin, armed with clubs and sickles and knives. It had been a hard winter, I think. It looked like they could barely hold their weapons."

I don't think I'd ever told anyone this story before. The words flowed out of me like water draining from a long-festering swamp.

"The first man I killed had a wild beard. And this ragged tunic. I remember that so clearly: the fucking tunic of all things. It was almost an accident, you know. He swung his hoe at me, and when he missed, it was like he stumbled into my sword. Another man screamed when he saw it. He was a lot younger, his son I think. Or nephew; they looked alike. He charged me, and I killed him too."

"Leo," Helena said. "You were attacked."

"I was, and I kept telling myself that. But then a few years later we went to war with the Sassanids. We marched towards their cities, and I couldn't really use being attacked as an excuse anymore." I clenched my fingers, trying to hide the blood I saw dripping from them. "I've killed so many, Helena. Fathers, sons, husbands—any who came in front of me. So much blood ... and no matter how many times I wash my fucking hands, it's always there."

I looked back towards her.

"You're dirty? With what I've done, I'll never be clean again."

"You were at war," she said. "You had no choice."

"That's true," I said. "I did it to survive. And so did you."

She blinked, a few more tears spilling from her eyes. I continued to speak, forcing words past the lump in my throat.

"So, no, I don't care about your past. I don't care what you've done, or what my mother or those pampered fools in the palace say. Because when I look at you, Helena, all I think about is the miracle that brought a woman like you to the side of a butcher like me."

"You idiot," she said, a watery smile curling her lips. She let herself fall forward, her forehead coming to rest in the crook of my neck. "You don't know what you've done."

I took a moment to wipe the wetness from my eyes. "I know that I spent a fortune on honeyed figs that aren't being eaten."

She shifted against me, finally bringing the fruit up to her lips. "This one's a bit smooshed ..."

I laughed again, deeper than I had in a long time. She raised her head, her tear-reddened eyes twinkling in the darkness. I planted a kiss on her lips, this time tasting nothing but honey.

"Come on," I said, pulling her up. "Those idiots should be off-duty now, and it's been a long night."

Neither of us spoke as we made our way back to the palace. We were exhausted, wrung out from a flood of emotions. Newly-discovered feelings swirled through me, but I lacked the energy to even acknowledge them. For now, I was content to walk beside her. Our arms brushed against each other, and I felt her fingers slip between my own.

The city was finally quiet, the not-yet rioters having laid down their heads. Though, it was a heavy sort of silence. It was the stillness after the crash, the inhalation before the roar. And as we came into the streets nearest to the palace, we saw the word *'Nika'* painted on more than one door.

Chapter Seventeen

The Empress Dreams

The morning bell sounded, calling all of us palace workers to our posts.

I groaned, cracking open eyes that were gummy from lack of sleep. Helena shifted in my arms, pushing herself up. She stretched, and I watched the muscles play beneath the naked flesh of her back.

"Time to get up," she said.

I made another tired sound, feeling her absence as an uncomfortable spot of coolness. I pushed myself onto one elbow, trying to claw the sleep from my eyes. We'd returned late, with everything that had happened the night before. I'd be surprised if we'd managed to get more than three hours of sleep.

"It's too early," I said.

"Are you suggesting we should neglect our duty?" she teased.

Helena was seated on the edge of my bed, peering back at me through a curtain of her hair. The light of the morning sun touched her tanned skin, making it glow, and transforming her auburn locks into strands of liquid fire. There was a small smile on her lips, though I could see that she was wary.

She knew better than I that, at times, words spoken in the dark could not abide the light.

We were due another long conversation, but not right now. I was much too tired for that. So, instead, I flopped my arms around her and pulled her back down.

"Leo!" she squawked, squirming against my chest. "Let me go!"

"No."

I pillowed her head in one of my arms, pulling her closer to me and tucking her in just right. I let out a long sigh of contentment, closing my eyes and breathing in the scent of her hair.

"Leo …" I could hear the smile bubbling beneath her serious tone. "We're not going to have a lot of time to gear up."

"Don't care."

She laughed softly, letting herself settle against me, her warm body molding itself to mine. "I'd never have gotten into your bed if I'd known how lazy you are."

"It's your fault," I mumbled, her hair tickling my face. "Too warm. I'll be better next time."

"Oh? Are you sure that you'll even be able to afford a next time?"

Her tone was teasing. I felt the tension in her body, however, a guardedness that would not leave so quickly.

"Mmm," I said, opening my eyes and kissing the side of her head. "I don't know. Maybe we can just go for a run, then."

With herculean effort of will, I forced myself to sit up, slipping my arms from around her. I stretched, my face cracking open in a massive yawn. Through watery eyes, I saw Helena lying on her back. Her hair was a cloud of burnished fire around her head, her bared breasts caressed by the light spilling through my window.

"A run?" She asked.

"And then we can go fishing."

She arched an eyebrow, and I grinned. "I'm hoping that after all that, you'll be tired enough to just curl up beside me without thinking."

She pushed herself onto her elbows, letting the thin blanket slide down her naked stomach. "You don't think that I can keep up?"

"Oh, you definitely can." My grin got wider. "But I'm a terrible fisherman. And I'm impossible to teach."

She laughed and I leaned down to kiss her lips. I meant to pull away quickly, but Helena had another idea. She threw her arms around my neck, dragging me down to the pillow.

Our kiss deepened and I felt my exhaustion flee as her smooth leg slid against mine.

"I guess we'll have to go out often," she said when we finally did part. "If you're that slow to learn."

I smiled. "Maybe, every day."

"My lion," she breathed, bringing her palm to my bearded cheek. "How did I ever find you?"

"By getting out of bed," I said, looking at her pointedly. "You know that we don't have time to stay here all day."

Helena stuck her tongue out at me. She pushed me aside, slipping out of bed and stepping fully into the sunlight.

"Careful, shield-mate." She stretched, her body wrapped in nothing but the morning. "Because my price just doubled."

I laughed, feeling myself respond to the sight of her light-soaked curves. I let my eyes roam the shape of her, from the knowing curl of her lips to the swell of her large breasts. My gaze skimmed down the ripples of her stomach to the verdant tuft of hair peeking out from where her legs flowed into each other.

My heart quickened as my mouth dried. I remembered the taste of her and the steaming softness of her wetness against my face.

"You didn't hear what I said again, did you?"

I blinked. "What?"

She laughed, shaking her head.

I tore my gaze from her body with no small amount of difficulty, settling back on her expression of amused exasperation. "Did you say something?"

"Completely hopeless," she said, scooping up her discarded *tunica*. "I need to start charging you for looking. Then, at least, you wouldn't be completely useless to me."

"Better put that on, then," I said, "before I give you everything I have."

She looped the green cloth around the back of her neck, instead, thrusting her naked hips out in a pose of casual seduction.

"Keep looking," she said, her cypress eyes alive with a shifting brightness. "I want to buy a fishing skiff."

I laughed, delighted by the sheer wonder of this woman. My chest buzzed with an airy sort of warmth. She enchanted me, this person who dared to be more than the world said she could.

"Toss me my *tunica*," I said, shifting to the edge of the bed. "I don't want to be late because of you."

"We don't have time for breakfast," she said, ignoring me. She'd slipped into her garment, bending down to retrieve mine. "I still need to bind my chest. You're going to have to help me with—"

Her words were cut off by the letter that tumbled to the floor. I cursed, the pleasant tingling in my chest and limbs gone like the laughter in a widower's heart. I'd forgotten that the damned thing had been in my pocket.

My mother's letter.

Helena picked it up, turning the plain envelope over in her hands. "This is what Sergius gave you?"

"Yeah," I said, coming to my feet. I pulled my *tunica* over my head. "Just put it on the desk."

Helena didn't move. "Is it important?"

With barely a glance, I plucked the letter from her hands and tossed it onto the desk. "No. It's just a letter from my mother."

I made to move towards my armor stand in the corner, but she stepped in front of me. She placed a hand on my chest, meeting my gaze with those eyes that took in so much of me.

"It's nothing, really. Now, come on." I made to move past her again but she didn't let me. "Helena, we have to—"

"I would give anything," she interrupted, "*anything*, to get a letter from my father. I don't even know if he's alive or dead."

My eyes flicked up to hers, and then away again just as quickly. "Helena—"

"It's none of my business," she spoke over me, yet again. "But sometimes we don't get the chances we think we will."

"Yeah, I know." I let out a breath. Of course I knew. How could I not? I was a soldier. "It's just ..." It's just that I wanted to stay happy.

Those eyes softened with understanding. She looped her arms around my neck, pressing the warmth of her body against mine, holding me tight. My hands rose to grip her waist. I swallowed, trying and failing to speak past the lump in my throat.

"To stand together against the future," she murmured. "Your shield locked onto mine." She pressed her lips against my skin and pulled back, her arms still around me. "I swore that oath. And don't think that

I'm going to let anything keep me from it." She smiled. "Side by side, shield-mate. I'm with you in this."

I snorted, blinking the wetness from my eyes. "We've been reminding each other of those words a lot."

"We're Rhodian, Leo. We're more stubborn than most."

"Stubborn?" I said, finding my smile and pulling her back to me. "Or are we just a little slow?"

Her eyes danced. "Maybe it's a bit of both."

☧

We slipped into the Empress's chambers a few moments before our shift was set to begin. We'd skipped breakfast, helping each other into our armor with much frantic tugging of straps and calls of hurried encouragement. We'd only just taken position on either side of the entrance to the hall when the Empress emerged from her sleeping quarters.

"*Augusta*!" I said, stiffening into a salute.

Beside me, Helena rolled her eyes. "Good morning, Empress."

Theodora's lips curled into a smile.

She swayed towards us, her body shrouded in purple silk. The fabric of the light *stola* clung to her, revealing the shadowy contours of her curving shape. Her sun-darkened flesh and walnut hair gleamed, burnished with lavender-scented oil.

Her normally bare feet were wrapped in delicate sandals, her steps still no louder than the swish of her near-translucent dress. Gold glinted as she glided through pools of sunlight, sparkling off of the thin wires that she'd woven into her hair, the chain at her throat, and the bangles she wore wrapped around her arms and ankles.

Theodora came to us in purple and gold: an eagle of Rome, swathed in the colors of Empire.

"A good morning, indeed," she said, her eyes sparkling as she took in the air between Helena and me. "How was your night?"

"It was good, Empress," Helena answered. "Thank you."

"Oh, come now," Theodora said. "You know I need more than that."

I coughed. Pink bloomed on Helena's cheeks, lighting her smile. "It was very good, Empress." Her eyes flicked to me for an instant. "The morning too."

"Then, I am pleased," Theodora said. She took another step nearer to us, close enough that the floral scent of her oiled flesh washed over me. "Now, tell me, how did he taste?"

Helena met my gaze, and I saw again that vastness beneath the shifting cypress of her eyes. "Like honeyed figs."

The Empress laughed, leaning over to press a kiss onto Helena's cheek. "And will you be so sweet for me, my Leontius?"

"*Augusta*?" I asked, heat rising to my cheeks.

She lay a hand on my forearm, her smile curling at the edges.

"Must I always remind you?" Her voice was low, her hand sliding up my arm. "I too will have my taste, my soldier."

I was frozen stiff, paralyzed by a roiling mix of exhaustion, the Empress's heady scent, confusion, and not a little bit of panicked concern. My gaze went right to Helena, desperate to see what thoughts might be written on her face.

My shield-mate met my eyes with an open smile. She saw through me, of course. And because I didn't look away from her, I saw the moment that her face flickered with impish delight.

"Dora?" she said, moving to my other side.

She'd left her spear behind, matching Theodora's movement by running a hand along my forearm. Her palm was warm, and I was filled with sudden apprehension. The Empress arched an eyebrow, waiting.

"Perhaps we might grant him the Patriarch's Indulgence?"

A flicker of very real surprise crossed Theodora's features. She opened her mouth, shut it, and then looked at me and back to Helena.

"Already?" the Empress said.

Helena shrugged, her smile remaining in place. Her eyes flicked back to me. "It was an ... eventful night."

"Interesting," the Empress murmured, her fingers squeezing my forearm. I coughed once again, awkwardly shifting. I didn't want to interrupt, despite being achingly full of questions "The indulgence, my Leontius, is something from our past." The Empress watched me closely, searching the feelings flashing across my face. She smiled after a moment. "You continue to surprise me." She turned back to Helena, a curl of heat blooming beneath her flesh. "But yes, that's a good idea. I'll see to it." Her hand lingered on my arm a moment longer, her bottom lip caught between her teeth. Then, the Empress shook herself and stepped away. "But that will be later. Right now, our city is on the edge of disaster. We have work to do."

She moved towards her divan while Helena moved past me and back towards her spear.

"What's the indulgence?" I hissed, my blood running quickly through my veins.

Helena grinned, her entire face stained with that same red heat. "You'll see," she mouthed.

I glared, but she just winked at me before heading over to her small desk.

"Don't bother," the Empress said. "There are no appointments today. Let in anyone who comes, my Leontius."

I saluted.

The Empress lowered her silk-wrapped body onto her divan. Though she lounged within the cushions, she was as regal upon it as on any ornate throne.

"We'll be here until just past midday," she said. "Then, we'll go meet with my husband. We've sponsored another chariot race; it will be held this afternoon. Justinian hopes that it will calm things down again, though we still have to work on the speech he will give."

"Empress," Helena said, moving to stand behind her. "About that. Last night we saw—"

Theodora held up a hand, cutting her off. "Later, Helena. I've already received reports of what happened. We will discuss this with my husband. For now, however, I expect us to be busy."

And indeed, those words proved to be prophetic. No sooner had Helena settled into her post than I heard the first knock on her door.

It was a man I didn't know, introducing himself as a lord of a place I didn't recognize. The Empress had just finished welcoming him when I heard another knock. It was a pair of matronly women this time, coming to sit in what would grow into a sizeable gathering.

Throughout that long morning, visitors came and went. I saw bishops, merchants, lords, and ambassadors, coming singly or in groups. They were staying somewhere within the palace's interminable guest wings and the unrest prevented them from leaving.

The Lady Irene came by, accompanied by a man that I took to be her husband, Lord Arethas. She greeted me with a smile and a faint flush to her cheeks. I was happy to see new confidence behind her eyes and surprised to see that the dress she wore was cut low, exposing a generous slice of her chest.

The lord Arethas, for his part, looked at his young wife with a mix of outrage and bewilderment. It was evident that Lady Irene had taken some of the Empress's advice, and her husband did not know how to feel about it.

Throughout the whole morning, the Empress met with dozens of people, showing nothing of the fatigue that she surely felt. And in his own reception chamber, I knew that the Emperor would be doing the same.

For it was people, and what they gave of their wealth, time, and bodies, that moved the Empire.

An Emperor only ruled so long as his people tolerated him, and the annals of Rome's history were soaked with the blood of those men who'd forgotten this truth. Theodora was no such despot. She spoke with each visitor, listening to their fears and grievances. She offered her own words in return, promising to look out for them and their families. She assured them that while things may have changed, the future was undeniably bright. She thanked each for their loyalty, drawing out pledges of continued support, swearing that her husband would never ask of them more than they could pay.

The Empress reminded all who came to her that the dream of Rome died only when there were none left who believed.

Chapter Eighteen

Enemy of the Empress

"My guards were out in the city last night," the Empress said. "They can confirm some of the captain's reports. There is real wealth, real organization behind some of these dissenters."

"Traitors," Belisarius growled. The dark-haired general's cheeks were red with anger. "*Augustus*, let me bring my legions into the city. I can have the worst of the factions hanged by nightfall."

The sun had risen past morning. We'd escorted the Empress to her husband's *tablinum*, a space where he could conduct his business surrounded by books and scrolls. Helena and I were posted along the wall behind where Theodora sat with the others at a large table. A few *Excubitors* were in the room too, meeting our eyes with varying degrees of hostility.

The Emperor Justinian massaged the bridge of his nose. "I'm not going to let *stratiotai* loose in my own capital, Bel. The people aren't our enemy."

"They're burning the city down around us!"

"Captain," Theodora said before her husband could speak. She addressed the nervous-looking commander of the city guard. "We've had riots before. Why haven't you been able to keep the peace these past few days?"

The guardsman bowed low. "Your pardon, *Augusta*. I have few men under my command, and the Blues and Greens are well-entrenched in most parts of the city. In the past, they've done a lot of the work in keeping their own neighborhoods orderly. Now, however ..." He trailed off into a grimace.

"Now, they're the bastards doing all the damage," Antonina said from where she sat beside her husband. Belisarius's wife swept her blonde hair back from her face, sifting through a stack of reports on the table in front of her. Antonina accompanied the general nearly every time he went on campaign. She was well used to helping him untangle the mess of paperwork that taking any sort of decision inevitably produced.

"You cannot control the city, then?" the Empress asked.

"Forgive me, *Augusta*, but I cannot. Not on my own. I've lost dozens already in the attempt."

"Then let me bring in the legions," Belisarius repeated, his fist slamming against the table. "We're letting the mob run us over!"

"Enough!" the Emperor snapped. "I am not slaughtering hundreds because a few nobles are stirring up discontent! We are an empire of laws, and I will not taint our efforts with the senseless spilling of blood."

The two men glared at each other. They were men of power, both used to getting their own way. But of course, only one was Emperor.

Belisarius looked away. "Of course, *Augustus*."

The Empress let out a breath. She dismissed the captain with a few words of thanks before standing from her chair and going over to her husband. She leaned into him from behind his chair, wrapping her arms around his chest.

Justinian slumped back. "The Blues and the Greens; why did my damned predecessors have to cede so much to them?"

Theodora kissed him on the cheek. "We always knew that curtailing them would be difficult, love. Don't lose sight of what we are trying to accomplish."

The Emperor took a moment to lean into her touch. Then, he let out a long sigh and straightened. "Okay. They want me to pardon the escaped prisoners, right? Will that satisfy them?"

"Seems like the minimum," Antonina said, fanning her summer-reddened face. "They've already escaped, so what's the harm?"

"The harm," Belisarius said, "is that they were condemned to die."

"Bel is right, my love," the Empress said. "You spoke of upholding our laws; what message does it send to those watching us for weakness if we capitulate on this now?"

I shifted in my place against one of the walls.

They had been at this for more than an hour, a series of officials, titled aristocrats, and soldiers streaming in and out of the Emperor's *tablinum*. They'd been summoned to give their official opinions, testimonies, and reports: the mass of information intended to aid the Emperor in handling the developing crisis.

Or not handling it, as seemed to be the case.

I turned away, looking out the open window. I could see the sloping roofs of the Hagia Sofia and the Patriarch's residence. The city stretched beyond, baking in the afternoon heat.

The planned chariot races were due to begin soon. Suddenly, there was a loud knock at the door. One of the *Excubitors* on duty outside poked his head in. "Senator Hypatius is here, *Augustus*," the man said.

"What?" The Emperor responded. "This is a closed meeting. Send him away."

The guard hesitated. "Of course, *Augustus*. He says that he's come from the city, however. And that he holds a list of the people's demands."

Justinian and his wife exchanged a glance. "Very well. Send him in."

"Your Imperial Majesties," the senator said, entering the room and sweeping his robes out in a deep bow. "Thank you for seeing me."

"Out with it, Hypatius," Belisarius growled. "We don't have time for your pretty words."

"Of course, general," the senator said. He approached after a nod from the Emperor, pulling a roll of parchment out from a fold of his robes. "I'll speak plainly. Representatives from the Blues and Greens approached me earlier today. We sat down together to speak of their grievances. This is the result of that meeting."

He set the parchment on the table. The Emperor, Belisarius, and Antonina set upon it like wolves, ripping it open and devouring its content. The Empress, however, watched the senator.

"You're uninterested in the people's demands, *Augusta*?" Hypatius asked.

"I already have a good idea as to what they are, senator," she said. "I'm more interested in what role you play in all this."

The man smoothed his robes. "That of simple messenger, *Augusta*."

"But why you? And who were these 'representatives' you met with."

Hypatius shrugged. "I'm not sure. But I've worked hard to cultivate a reputation as a fair man who is agreeable to reason. So, perhaps that is the reason the representatives sought me out."

"Indeed," the Empress said. "It must be your ... reputation."

The senator bristled, but the Emperor chose that moment to speak. "This is absurd! The dismissal of my prefect, John, and my *quaestor*? The full pardon of the prisoners and the repeal of my new laws?!"

"Not every single one of your new laws, *Augustus*," Hypatius cut in, smoothly. "I believe those changes most desired are spelled out."

"No," the Emperor said. "Not all. Mainly those concerning women and the change in the aristocracy's share of tax."

"The people are aggrieved, your Majesty," Hypatius said. "You've stripped the Blues and Greens of power and have changed many of the basic tenants of our laws. Add to this the ruinous cost of our campaigns in the east, and surely you must understand some of the people's plight?"

"I'm not agreeing to any of this," the Emperor growled.

"*Augustus*, please," the senator said. "There is wisdom in giving a little to gain a lot."

Antonina snorted. "Explain to me the wisdom of completely folding over?"

They continued in this vein for some time, arguing back and forth until we left for the Hippodrome.

Hypatius accompanied us through the halls of the Imperial Palace, one of several prominent citizens who had been invited to watch that afternoon's races in the presence of the Emperor.

The stadium was full when we arrived, the crowd a roiling mass of anger. When Justinian stepped into view, they began to roar, drunk on wine and the victories they'd already had against the city.

The Emperor called for quiet, assuring the crowd that he would answer their resentments. It was several long minutes before the mob was still enough for his voice to be heard. He began his speech as the first of the charioteers emerged on the sands.

Theodora had not yet taken her seat, remaining back by Helena and me while her husband spoke. There were a dozen or so *Excubitors* in the box as well, there to ensure no harm came to the Imperial family and their guests.

Hypatius approached the Empress while Justinian was halfway through his prepared words. "The Emperor is wise to give into these demands."

The Empress didn't let any of her anger show. She'd argued hard against any sort of concession. "There are some things that he will not bend on. No matter how much of your *wisdom* you share."

The senator's eyes moved about, checking that none but we were within earshot. Disdain flooded his tone. "You mean the repeal of your laws?" He smirked. "I fear that it is only a matter of time, Empress."

"Victory is an ugly color on you, Hypatius. But it is a bit premature, is it not?"

"Premature?" The senator swept his arm out. "Look at this. The people cry for change! Will you keep forcing your unwanted beliefs onto so many who want nothing of them?"

"Unwanted?" the Empress said. "The elevation of women is good for the Empire as a whole, senator. Are we, too, not God's creatures?"

"Of course, though none other possess such delusions of grandeur."

"Only those born to privilege see equality as a loss."

"A privilege," Hypatius said, "that was granted to us by God. And how wise a decision it was. Did a woman's choice not already cost us the paradise of Eden?"

"Ah, of course," Theodora said. "That old tale. What a stupid girl she was, to listen to the serpent and hide her naked perfection. As if clothing herself against a man's crawling eyes could ever bring some sort of comfort."

"A wholly false interpretation," the senator sneered. "But I suppose that we should trust a whore's mind to see lust as the root of all things."

I tensed, my anger flaring. I made to step forward, but the Empress flicked her open palm towards me.

"I was a whore, senator," she said, "and so you may trust me when I say that it wasn't women who came to me with minds full of lust."

"As you well know," Hypatius said, face reddening. "Eve's sin was disobedience: her refusal to submit herself to man and God. A sin which you seek to drive us back into."

"Was it not God who made me Empress?" Theodora said. "It is by His divine authority that I rule."

"Your authority," he spat, "comes from trapping a powerful man between your legs. You would determine the course of our Empire through the ungodly use of your sex!"

"My husband is no slave to his desires, Hypatius. Great men do not possess the flaws of the majority."

Hypatius' eyes flashed, but the Empress wasn't finished.

"And surely, senator, a man like you can come up with something other than that tired lamentation? God has granted gifts to all his creations. Is it not the most pathetic sort of weakness that the man who lords over his family with the strength of his arm suddenly cries sin when his own base lust is used against him?"

"Our laws are clear," Hypatius said through gritted teeth. "Do not expect us to sit quietly by as you trample over nature and tradition."

"Ah, so it is 'us' now?" Theodora said. "How easy you speak of disobedience when it is the sin of another. Your Emperor, the one who you have sworn to obey as your master, has commanded that you cease this insurrection."

The Empress's expression was hard, her back straight and clad in purple. She looked down towards the senator from an eagle's height. "Do you, too, as Eve once did, refuse to submit yourself?"

Hypatius didn't respond, glaring at the Empress with barely-held fury. But she wasn't finished speaking. She leaned forward. "You cannot see past your own failings. You're weak, and your insecurities disgust me. Men like you make us out to be frail, simple creatures that are good for nothing more than venting your lust upon and bearing your children. Your fragile egos cannot bear the thought that a woman might, in truth, be a stronger, more intelligent, more capable being than you will ever be."

The Empress moved towards Hypatius with the deadly grace of the raptor's dive. Her words, filled with the eagle's unshakable pride, pinned him like talons. "But I will liberate us. I will show all of you what a woman can really be."

She reached out to run a finger along Hypatius's jaw. He flinched back at the sudden contact, looking away from the Empress's languid smile. "And be sure," she purred, her silken chest so near to his, "that I will use every weapon in my arsenal to do so."

"Vile woman," he hissed. His face blazed. "You don't know what's coming, you stupid whore. I'll—"

The mob's rising roar swallowed his next words. I turned in time to see the crowd flooding onto the sands of the Hippodrome.

"*Nika! Nika!*"

They crashed against the palace walls, swords and axes and sickles flashing in the summer sun. The Emperor shouted, but the mob didn't hear. They pounded against the walls, flames rising from where men held torches to the stadium's wooden stands.

The Hippodrome was burning, smoke rising with the thunder of the crowd's battle cry.

"*Nika! Nika! Nika! Nika!*"

We were under siege. And when I looked back towards the Empress, Hypatius was gone.

Chapter Nineteen
An Empress Besieged

"Have you ever been under siege, my Leontius?"

I turned at the sound of the Empress's voice, stiffening into a salute. "*Augusta*!"

She rolled her eyes. "And a good morning to you too. Has three days of confinement truly done nothing to ease your sense of propriety?"

"That's like asking whether the sight of the sun makes fish want to fly," Helena called from where she stood by the door.

"Oh?" Theodora said. "And what do fish have in common with our Leontius?"

Helena grinned. "Neither of them can actually comprehend the question."

The Empress laughed, and I leveled my best glare toward my shield-mate. This, of course, had the unfortunate result of drawing laughter from her as well.

"We're under siege," I reminded both women.

The Empress came to stand beside me at the window. She lay a warm palm against my forearm and gazed out.

Beneath us, Constantinople burned. The sky was choked with a haze of smoke and ash. The mid-morning sun appeared dark, hanging in the sky like a disk of smudged bronze. The fog was noxious, cloying; it blocked the sun's light, though it did nothing to shield us from the summer heat. Rather, it seemed to trap and magnify the heat like some great oven, so that the already thick air turned positively suffocating.

"So much destruction," the Empress said. "The labor of decades and centuries gone, just like that."

"Augusta." Then, after a moment's hesitation, I added. "I caught a few glimpses through the smoke. It looks like there's a lot less damage further out."

She squeezed my arm, smiling without feeling. "I suppose that makes sense. It's not their own homes they wish to burn, after all."

I followed the Empress's gaze as she took in the shattered villas, pavilions, and monuments that now surrounded the Imperial Palace. Many of the ruins still smoldered, adding their own unique, charring stench to the air.

The *Praetorium*, the military headquarters of the Empire, had been gutted. A centuries-old courthouse had been torn down, its statues shattered. And in the distance, where great Hagia Sofia had once stood, there was nothing more than an empty patch of sky. Theodora stared at that empty place for several long moments, eventually pulling the heavy golden cross from between her breasts to press it against her lips.

We could see the edge of the Hippodrome from the Empress's window. And though its venerable stones were scarred by fire and rage, it still rose high above the city. It was at once a reassuring reminder of the Empire's might and the cradle from which its destruction might have been birthed.

"You never answered my question," the Empress said.

"Augusta?"

Theodora smiled. "Have you ever been besieged?"

"Your pardon, *Augusta*," I said, flushing. "No. I've only ever been on the attacking side."

"Hmm," she said. "And what do you think our chances are here?"

"They're good, *Augusta*. In a lot of ways, it's harder to sit around outside the walls than within. It takes a lot of will, discipline, and organization to properly besiege a fortress."

"Things that you don't believe our citizens have?"

I shrugged. "They're focused now, *Augusta*. But that becomes more difficult as days turn into weeks."

"Hmm," she said. "Perhaps."

We could see them from up here, the mob. They swirled through the streets below, stained with soot and fueled by wine and victory. They were not so much an organized force as a writhing mass of blue and green with iron in their hands and cries of war on their lips.

Nika! Nika! Nika! I could hear them now, the crowd pulsing with their chant of conquest. They were swirling about the Hippodrome's entrance, keeping clear, as of yet, of the palace's walls. They seemed to be going into the arena, funneling into the still-smoking interior.

"It's hard to believe," the Empress said, "that so few of my husband's guards can keep out so many."

"Three hundred *Excubitors* is not so small a number, *Augusta*, when put behind strong walls."

"Neither are those extra few hundred that Belisarius called in, I suppose." She squeezed my arm one more time before letting go. "I shall defer to your judgment then, my Leontius. Now, trapped nobles and dignitaries will soon begin to pester my husband. Before I go to help him, however, I wish to see what the crowd is doing."

I saluted. "Your will, *Augusta*."

Then, Theodora straightened. She became the Empress once again, striding back through her quarters and disappearing through a doorway. I could hear her calling for her maidservants, summoning them to her wardrobe.

"Where are we going?" Helena asked.

I finally moved to join my shield-mate by the single door.

"The Hippodrome," I answered, stiffening into place. "The crowd is going into it."

Helena chewed her lip for a few moments, fingers drumming along the haft of her spear. She stared out towards the smoke-stained sky for a few moments before taking a step towards me and kissing me on the cheek.

I raised an eyebrow. "What was that for?"

"In case I can't do it later."

I didn't like the direction her thoughts were heading, so I plastered a look of indignation onto my face. "I refuse to let that be the last time you kiss me. That was terrible."

She'd been in the process of stepping away, but my comment brought her up short. The cypress of her eyes shifted a shade brighter when she caught sight of my expression.

"Terrible? I didn't have to kiss you, you know."

I sniffed. "You may as well not have."

Both of her eyebrows popped up. I laughed and then I reached over to loop my empty hand over her waist, pulling her to me. Her lips curled into a smile, a faint bloom of red rising to her cheeks.

"While on duty?" she teased. "You really have changed."

"It's your fault," I said.

Then, I leaned down and kissed her. Our breastplates ground loudly against each other, but I ignored it. My entire focus was on Helena, on the softness of her lips, the warmth of her skin, and the feel of her opening herself to me. She made a sound low in her throat, her tongue darting forward. I responded in kind, tasting her, plunging ever deeper into the feel of her lips.

My body was alight when we finally parted. I didn't look away from the shifting vastness behind her eyes.

"There, wasn't that better?"

She shifted against me, sliding one leg along mine in a motion that was as smooth as the tide. There was a new depth to her now, a rising ocean to match the heat I felt curling within me.

"My lion," she murmured. "Always hungry."

"Well," the Empress suddenly said. "I guess that we were wrong, Helena."

I wrenched my neck around. Theodora was watching us from the doorway, hands resting on the swell of her hips.

I leaped back, now burning with an altogether different sort of heat. I babbled a stream of nonsensical apologies, which I was sure that neither woman heard over the sound of their laughter.

"We were wrong, Highness?" Helena eventually said. "How so?"

The Empress grinned. "It seems like some fish really can fly."

The sound of the mob grew as we moved through the palace.

The three of us marched single file. Helena was in the lead, her boots ringing loudly against the stone floor. The corridors were quiet, kept clear for passing soldiers by the Emperor's orders.

My shield-mate and I were armored for war. I'd checked every strap of our breastplates and greaves before leaving with the Empress. We'd strapped on our heavy shields and cinched our helmets atop our heads. Swords hung from both of our waists, complementing the spears in our hands.

Theodora, for her part, moved silently in the space between us. She'd garbed herself in a light, sheer purple dress. The hem of her garment trailed behind her, long enough that I had to be careful where I set my feet. She once again had strands of gold woven into her walnut tresses, the gleam matching that of the warm chain that disappeared between her breasts. As we emerged into the light of the Hippodrome, she shone with the colors of Rome.

A squad of *Excubitors* stiffened to attention as we stepped into the Imperial Box. Their leader stepped forward, hammering a fist into his breastplate.

The Empress nodded her head.

"Have any yet tried to climb through here?" she asked, speaking loudly over the sound of the crowd below.

There were thousands of them, a roiling mass of blue and green that heaved with the current of unseen tides. They were packed together, writhing and churning, near as numerous—to my eyes at least—as the grains of sand over which they stood. Their roar was the pounding of the surf, their fury like the ocean's storm. The iron of their spears, swords, sickles, and hammers glinted in the sun, like so many droplets in the sea.

"No, *Augusta*!" The man shouted back. He nodded to the bows and long spears that his men carried. "But we'll be ready if they do!"

Theodora smiled her gratitude, the expression making the guard blush brightly. I suddenly felt a strong sort of kinship to this man.

Helena fell in beside me while the two exchanged a few more words. Her face was flushed red, and I knew from the sweat coating my back that I looked the same. The heat was brutal, the feeling not helped by the smothering weight of all our armor.

I took a few moments to look around. The fire had marked everything. What only a few days ago had been large seating galleries of wood was now a charred ruin. Vast piles of still-smoldering timber had spilled over many of the remaining rows of seats, cracking the stone and creating an impossible maze of char and smoke.

"I brought you something," Helena said from beside me.

I looked over to find her holding out a square of folded paper. It was an envelope, one I recognized.

My mother's letter, still unopened.

"What?" I said. "Why do you have this?"

She just smiled, and in that smile, I saw the sadness that I'd sought to avoid back in the Empress's chambers. She'd been asking me about this letter for the past three days. This morning, when our schedules had finally allowed us to wake up together, I guess she just took it from my desk.

I didn't reach for it. I didn't want it. I didn't want things to change; I wanted to be happy and stay like this forever. But Helena's eyes never left mine. And that sad, broken smile ...

Just in case, it said.

It was only right, I thought, finally taking it and stowing it beneath my armor, that I'd receive my mother's letter here. That I'd feel this weight in a place where the air was so heavy with the stench of ash and violent apprehension.

Helena stepped away and I didn't look at her again. The Empress had finished speaking with the guards and started towards the edge of the Box. I quickly moved after her, Helena barely a step behind. We placed ourselves before her, shielding her in case anyone below had a bow or was particularly adept at throwing stones.

Nothing flashed towards us from the seething crowd, though I almost wished that something would. My thoughts were numb, my mother's letter pulling all of me under. I swept my gaze over the roiling mob, desperate for any sort of disturbance to focus on.

Luckily, or perhaps not, I soon found one.

A ripple of calm was spreading from the Hippodrome's far corner. Out from where I'd once seen Maleinos and Velanis emerge came another chariot. This one was wide and looked heavier than those typically used to race. It was large enough for two passengers. I saw a driver, slowly guiding a team of four white horses through the crowd.

The other figure stood straight. He was dressed in a robe that was dyed both blue and green. He held his arms out, and people fell silent before him.

"Hypatius," the Empress hissed. "The fool has turned traitor then."

"Not just him, Highness," Helena said from beside me. "There's a group on foot following directly behind him. I recognize Senators Lucas and Narses in there."

"Indeed," the Empress answered. "Those goddamned fools."

The men were making no effort to hide their identities. I recognized a few more lords, powerful merchants, and even a bishop or two. These men must be the core of Hypatius's support and were, if I had to guess, those responsible for all the swords and spears I saw flashing amongst the crowd.

When the chariot finally halted, the mob was as silent as an ocean of several thousand could be. Hypatius noticed the three of us watching from the Imperial Box, and I saw his lips curl into a sneer before he turned to address the crowd.

"Good people!" he shouted, holding up his arms. "My fellow citizens. I am honored to be speaking to you today, on this, the dawn of our new golden age!"

The crowd boiled, shoving fists, flags, and weapons up into the air. Hypatius basked in the adulation, continuing once the cheering had abated. "You have done the work of God these past nights. You have shown the world, and our leaders, that we are a people with a will!"

Hypatius was an orator well-used to shouting down his opponents on the Senate floor. His voice was loud, powerful, and thrummed with the yawning depths of his passion. "We have the will to shape our world, to make it better! We are a people wise in our knowing, secure in the word of our God. We are a people that knows what is right! And for too long, we as a people have been kept silent!"

The mob roared.

From behind me, I heard the Empress tsk. "Hypatius has always been a tiresomely effective speaker."

"I tell you, brave citizens of the Empire, that our star is waning. For decades, our world has been crumbling at the edges. We've been sliding backward, our realm in danger of falling to the same blackness that consumed our first capital in the West. But we are not to blame! Look, my people! Raise your eyes and see the greatest author of our degeneration!"

I stiffened as suddenly the weight of a thousand and more eyes fell upon us. No, not upon us—upon the Empress.

"Theodora," Hypatius sneered. "Wife of our Emperor."

All around him, the crowd hissed and booed. The Senator lifted his head, his voice rising to speak over the mob's anger.

"She is our Empress, but she was not born to the purple! Tell me, who amongst you remembers her career as an actress?"

The people laughed and jeered.

"Who amongst you remembers her on stage, baring her tits and flaunting her naked sex? Or perhaps you remember her from the brothel, where she'd spread her legs for anyone with a few silver coins. And this, my wise, my *good* people, is who leads us!?"

The crowd spat, roiled, and shouted. Their flags and weapons ripped through the air, a thousand and more seething waves.

I snuck a peek back at the Empress. Her expression was cold, her shoulders straight and her back unbent. She looked down upon them as would an eagle, a creature secure in its majesty and unconcerned with the scorn of those beneath the shadows of its wings.

"Wolves gather at our borders!" Hypatius roared. "The Persians and savage tribes of Arabia take from our eastern provinces with impunity; while in the west, Vandal and Orstrogothic hordes mass with knives sharpened for murder!"

The Senator gesticulated with every word, his face red with feeling.

"And here, in our capital, the price of grain has doubled! Gangs of foreign criminals haunt our streets and pestilence reaps us with its pox-blackened scythe. These are times of strife! God is testing us! And who do we have to lead us?" Hypatius paused for a heartbeat, his words ringing through the smoke-scarred Hippodrome. "Rome's greatest whore!"

The mob screamed.

A hail of debris rose towards us. There were stones, rotten fruit, and empty flagons of wine flung with rage-strengthened arms. Helena and I raised our shields, protecting the Empress. A few of the better-aimed stones thumped against them.

"We need to go, *Augusta*!" I shouted. "It's not safe!"

"Not yet."

"Our enemies mock us! God turns his back on us! And in her gilded chambers, this vile whore laughs even as she strips everything from us!" Hypatius, swathed in green and blue reached his arms into the sky. He raised his head, gazing up towards the heavens. "But I say to you, righteous people, that it's not too late. We can reclaim our glory! We can be strong once again! We can do away with these perverted laws and go back to the traditions that once made us great. We can conquer!"

"Nika!" The crowd roared, stabbing fists and weapons and flags into the air. *"Nika! Nika!"*

"Let's go," the Empress said. "I've seen enough."

We finally turned away, moving past the now nervous-looking squad of *Excubitors*. But even as we stepped out of the Imperial Box, Hypatius's words followed us.

"We can take back our Empire! We can seize it from those who would pervert it! So, take it, my people! Fight! Conquer! Together, we can show them that blue and green are mightier than purple and gold!"

The rest was lost in a wordless roar. It faded slowly as we made our way through the palace halls. I took the lead this time, moving quickly towards the Emperor's *tablinum*. Not one of us spoke, and what servants we passed hurried aside in the face of our grim expressions.

We were almost halfway to our destination when a new sound reached my ears. I froze, though I was pushed a half-step forward when the Empress walked into my back.

"What—"

"Quiet!" I barked.

My heart thundered, and I was only distantly aware that I'd snapped at the Empress. What was that sound? It had been like—

Then, we heard a much louder sound: a crash of splintering wood. Right on its heels was the clash of metal, followed immediately by a piercing, blood-soaked scream.

"They're in the palace!" I cried. "Run!"

Chapter Twenty

The Empress's Vow

I CHARGED DOWN THE hallway, Helena and the Empress sprinting behind me.

Doors and junctions blurred past, my boots skidding around every corner. I hardly felt the weight of my mother's letter now. I was lost in the immediacy of the moment, my mind empty of all but our survival.

I was *stratiotai*, and this is what I knew.

I finally slowed when we came to a T-junction in the corridor. I stopped when I saw that both passageways were empty, though sounds were coming from every direction. I heard rough laughter, the splintering of wood, and screams of anger and pain.

I clenched my teeth, fingers flexing on the haft of my spear. I'd hoped to find allies by now, someone who had either information to guide our steps or a sword with which to fight beside us. Or both. Both would have been nice.

But we hadn't encountered anyone, and careening blindly around the palace was a sure way to get ourselves killed. I had to get the Empress to safety, though I knew she wouldn't like my decision.

I turned at the sound of tearing cloth. Theodora had a knife in one hand and was ripping it through the hem of her purple *stola*. Within moments, she'd cut her legs free; the dress now ended in a ragged line just above her knee.

"Damned thing's impossible to run in," she said, handing the knife back to Helena. She stepped high with one leg. "That's better."

Sweat sheathed her dancer's limbs. The Empress bundled the excess cloth in one arm, using the other to sweep her tresses back from her reddened face.

"Let's go," I said, gesturing to the right with my spear. "We don't stop until we're back to our quarters."

"My husband is not in my quarters, Leontius," the Empress said. "I will not abandon him."

"With all due respect, *Augusta*, my duty is to you. The Emperor has his *Excubitors*, while you have only the two of us. We are vulnerable here. We have to go."

"I'm not leaving him," she insisted. "Besides, if we make it to his *tablinum*, we'll be in a larger group."

"*If*," I said. "Your husband's meeting chamber is nearer to the main entrance. We can't risk it."

Damn, we didn't have time for this. I could still hear the chaotic swirl of screams and crashing metal. Were the rioters getting closer? It was impossible to tell with the way sound traveled through these fucking hallways.

Theodora opened her mouth to speak, but I cut off her. "No! I'm sorry, *Augusta*, but we don't have time. We're going to your quarters."

Her eyes flashed. I saw in her gaze the strength and iron-bound determination that had brought her from the horrors of poverty to the highest station in the Empire.

"And if I refuse?"

My duty was clear and I met her eyes without flinching. "Then I'll sling you over my shoulder and carry you there."

The tension ratcheted upward, but Helena stepped between us a mere heartbeat later. "He's right, Dora, we have to go. Justinian has a full squad of soldiers with him. He'll be fine, but not if he hears that something happened to you."

A shriek shattered the air. This one was close. That decided it.

"Let's go!" I barked.

I turned towards the Empress's quarters. I didn't look back, hearing the slap of her sandals and the jingle of Helena's armor directly behind me.

I careened around another corner, pumping my arms to maintain my speed. Then, two men spilled from the junction that we were racing towards.

In a flash, I took in a dozen details. Both men were bearded, their eyes wide, wild, and a bit glazed from the same wine that stained the rough *tunicas* they wore. They stumbled around to face us, shouting. I saw strips of green cloth wrapped around their biceps. And in their hands, each bore a blood-soaked sword.

"Through them," I roared. "Don't stop!"

The men braced themselves. The hallway was narrow and left no room to leap out of our way. To their credit, they stood with blades ready, facing me with surprising bravery. But that didn't matter. I was *stratiotai*, armed and armored for war, and these men were not.

My spear took one man in the gut, folding him around the weapon's haft. My arm twisted from the shock of the impact, and I let go of the spear, tucking my shoulder behind my shield to crunch into the second man barely a half-step later. His sword flew from his hands, the force of my charge sending him tumbling away.

"Keep going!" I shouted, not dropping my speed.

The man I'd impaled had started to moan, but I was quickly past him and trampling over the writhing form of his companion. The moan warped into a high shriek of pain, the sound like claws tearing into my mind.

I'd killed him.

He may as well have been defenseless for all the chance he'd had. I could feel his blood splattered against my hands; another layer of filth that I'd never wash away. I was a monster and a butcher. The letter in my pocket—

I wrenched my thoughts back to the present, packing all my horror, doubt, and self-loathing away for later. There'd be time enough for that if we survived the next hour.

I kept running.

Several tense minutes later, we neared the Empress's wing.

One last corner and we were before the door, stepping into the small reception chamber that led to the Empress's private rooms. I swept my eyes over the familiar space, lingering for a heartbeat on the deeply cushioned chair where I'd once shifted so uncomfortably. My first audience with the Empress.

It seemed like a lifetime ago.

I shook my head clear, turning towards Helena and the Empress. My shield-mate was breathing evenly, her spear unbloodied. Her skin was flushed, but she watched me from below her helmet with eyes that were clear and ready. Theodora's gaze was no less direct. She'd dropped her purple bundle of cloth, I noticed, replacing it with a bloody spear.

"*Augusta*," I said. "Is that ... my spear?"

"Indeed," she said, thumping the butt onto the stone floor. "I pulled it out of that man as we ran past."

"You ..." I trailed off.

Her sandals were soaked in blood. I remembered the way his moan of pain had suddenly morphed into an agonized shriek. A picture of the Empress grasping the spear with both hands flashed through my mind. I saw her plant her foot into his ruined guts, her shoulders flexing as she yanked the weapon free.

The Empress arched an eyebrow. "Don't look so surprised. This is my home; I have no qualms about defending it."

"Yes, but—"

"Do we really have time for this, Leontius?"

I clicked my mouth shut. She was right; it was only a matter of time before more rioters found us.

"We don't," I said. "Helena, get the door open and then help me drag this furniture over. We're going to barricade it."

She nodded, moving to obey.

"And me?" the Empress asked.

"*Augusta* ..."

Her eyes flashed. "We don't have time for your tiresome sensibilities, Leontius! I'm here, so put me to work!"

I grit my teeth and squashed my reservations into the same corner where I'd packed the thoughts of my mother. "Look out the window," I said, moving to the room's single divan. "Tell me what you see. And then go around the corner and keep watch."

I dragged the wide chair past the door Helena had just opened and into the hallway beyond. This was the single passage that led to the Empress's salon. It was narrow, free of any sort of encumbrance, and about a couple of dozen paces long.

This was where we would hold them.

I didn't know how many people had invaded the palace, but in this space, it wouldn't matter. Well, it would matter less. This corridor was narrow enough that, with our shields locked, Helena and I would block its entire width. The mob would have to come at us from the front, funneling themselves into a space where my shield-mate and I would have every advantage.

They could still dislodge us if they were persistent enough, of course, but I aimed to make that as costly an endeavor as I could.

"I can see into the courtyard," the Empress called. "The gates are open."

"Not broken?" I asked.

"No," she answered, grimly. "Wide open. People are streaming in, but there's fighting down there too. Belisarius's soldiers, I think, pushing their way to the gatehouse."

The gates were open. Someone had let the bastards in.

"Go keep watch, *Augusta*. Warn us when any come near."

Helena and I worked quickly, hauling everything we could into the hallway. We piled the furniture up, keeping the way mostly clear, ready to shove things into place as soon as the three of us were behind it.

"Is this going to work, Leo?" Helena asked.

"Not forever," I grunted, lifting a cushioned chair up high to toss it onto the pile. "But we just need to hold until those gates are closed."

Helena hesitated, poised over a small table. Her eyes found mine. "You're sure those soldiers will make it?"

"No." I moved towards her, lifting that small table halfway off the ground. I smiled. "But that hope is all we have."

She chewed on her lip a moment, then nodded. She reached down, and together, we carried the table through the doors.

We were able to work for another minute before Theodora came racing back into the chamber. "They're coming! Dozens of them."

I cursed. "Did they see you?"

She grimaced in response.

"Into the hallway, then. Go!"

We hustled through the door, Helena locking it behind us. Without a bar to drop down across it, it wouldn't hold long, but I'd take every minute we could get.

The rioters shouted as they spilled into the room. We shoved what we could of the furniture into place directly behind the door, finishing right as it shook with the first blow.

"We have a few minutes," I said, moving back until I stood with the two women. "Is your armor still tight, Helena?"

She nodded her face a mixture of fear and bloody-minded determination. "Should we grab more furniture from the salon?"

I shook my head. "The door won't hold long. I don't want to risk being out of position. When they break through, we're going to hit them fast and hard."

Her eyes widened. "You want to charge them?"

I bared my teeth, feeling every thundering beat of my heart. "All that debris in front of the door will trip them up when they come through. We're going to hit them while they're unbalanced."

I looked back toward the door. It was rattling on its hinges as fists, shoulders, and the hilts of weapons crashed into it. "We're better armored," I continued, speaking quickly. "We're better armed. They can't get around us here, but that just means that all of their weight will be on our shields. If they're stubborn enough, it's that weight that will eventually kill us."

I could picture it, Helena and I shoved back step after step, our strength fading as the fighting dragged on. Eventually, we'd be pushed back into the Empress's salon, surrounded, and killed.

We needed to break them before that happened.

"Make them pay for every step they take. Kill or wound, it doesn't matter. Any rioter we put down will tangle up the others, making it harder for them to really push into us." I met Helena's gaze. "Remember, we're playing for time."

She let out a breath, but her nod, when it came, was sharp.

"Very well," the Empress spoke up. "Helena, may I borrow your knife once again?"

"*Augusta*," I said. "Is there somewhere in your chambers that you might hide?"

Behind me, I heard the deep thunk of an axe striking wood.

"I'm not going to hide, Leontius. Your knife, Helena."

"*Augusta*," I said, watching her take Helena's knife. "You can't stay here. Please, go into your chambers."

She ignored me, bending down to cut another few strips from the ragged hem of her dress. She swept her walnut and gold tresses back, tying them off with one of the lengths of purple. "Not only will I stay," she said, once more taking up my bloody spear. "But I'm going to fight."

Wood splintered, axe-blades bursting through the door. Rough laughter and eager shouts spilled into the hallway.

The last of my patience broke as well.

"This isn't fucking pretend!" I shouted. "People are going to fucking die here! Go to your chambers!"

I expected defiance, an eagle of Rome rising to scream at whoever dared to question its majesty. Instead, the Empress smiled.

"And tell me, my Leontius," she said, gently. "If you and Helena fall, will I be any safer cowering beneath my bed?"

"Our duty is to protect you," I growled. "Whatever happens, it'll be worse here."

"I disagree," she answered, still in that disarming tone. "A long time ago, I swore that I would be mistress of my own destiny. I won't sit back while others decide my fate."

Theodora stepped close to me. She smelled of smoke, sweat, and lavender. She touched my arm, looping another strip of purple cloth around my bicep as she continued to speak.

"I've made a real life for myself, one that I believe will allow me to finally put some good into the world. I won't let them take it from me."

"*Augusta* ..." I tried. "You could climb from a window. You could go to the docks and catch a ship."

"No," the Empress said. "I won't run, and I won't hide. I will fight, and if the worst should happen, well ..."

She cinched the strip of purple around my arm, her movements sure, her eyes flashing with the iron of her will.

"I may not have been born to the purple, but I will die in it."

More wood splintered, axes and swords and hands tearing at what was left of the door.

Theodora leaned into me. She pressed her palms against my chest and kissed my bearded cheek. "For what you're about to do, you have the gratitude of an Empress."

Then she moved over to Helena, tying purple around her arm and repeating those words. We had seconds before the rioters broke through.

I flicked my eyes to the purple silk around my arm. So be it.

"Helena, give me your spear," I said. "*Augusta*, move with us but stay a few steps back. Stab through whatever gap you see."

She nodded, and I turned with Helena to face the door. I took her spear.

"You remember what to do, shield-mate?"

"No big moves," Helena answered, drawing her sword. "Shield up. Thrust, don't cut."

"Stay tight against me."

"Side by side," she said. "Together."

God, but I was in awe of these women. I was in awe of their strength, their determination, and their composure under this most terrible sort of pressure. How many more such women lived within our Empire? How much greater would our world be if they were allowed to thrive?

It was an idea worth dying for, I thought. And though these might be my final few minutes, I thanked God for the miracle that had brought me here.

I met Helena's eyes for what might be the last time, allowing myself a heartbeat to stare into that beautiful vastness within her cypress gaze. I had the urge to kiss her, to press my devotion into her lips.

But my mother's voice, folded away in an envelope that was suddenly heavier than all the world, pulled me away.

Then, the door shattered.

Men burst into the hallway, tripping over debris and their own momentum. They scrabbled at the piled furniture, roars of triumph and cries of *nika* turning into confusion and shouted curses.

My blood screamed through my body, my breath coming faster. Helena was tense to the point of shaking, her jaw clenched tightly enough that I thought her teeth might crack.

"*Stratiotai*!" I roared, slamming the butt of my spear onto the floor. "*Stratiotai*!"

I slammed it down again and again; a pounding drum beat. Helena's gaze darted towards me, her eyes wild.

"Where is your heart?" I bellowed. The mob was quickly pushing through our barricade, but I stayed in place. My spear hammered its steady rhythm. "Show them, *stratiotai*! Show them!"

At my side, Helena brought the flat of her sword crashing against the flat of her shield. She did it again and again, matching the beat of my spear. Her body loosened, ready; her breathing steadied, falling into that same rhythm.

"Rome's heart beats!" I shifted my grip on my spear. "*Stratiotai*! Let them hear!"

Behind us, the Empress brought her own spear down, and our space was filled with the legion's war-thunder.

The first of the attackers stumbled through the furniture and into the open hallway.

I stepped forward, moving with the pounding beat. I cocked my spear back and launched it forward.

It harpooned into a wild-eyed man waving an axe and blue flag. He crashed back into his companions, the weapon jutting from high on his unarmored chest. His scream and thrashing body added to the entranceway's chaotic heave.

"Show them!" I drew my sword, slamming it against the face of my shield: once, twice. "Show them!"

I charged, and at my side, Helena moved with me. The stones of the hallway blurred past, and my vision tunneled, locked on the milling horde of blue and green.

We screamed and thundered into them.

My shield crunched into a man, blasting him back into the press of invaders. I didn't slow, the violence of my charge driving me forward. Helena was with me, and together, we hammered into the roiling mass.

But there were so many of them. They were packed too tightly, and after a mere handful of paces, we rebounded off what felt like a solid wall of bodies.

"Hold!" I bellowed. "Hold!"

Men screamed and cursed. I heard the roar of my pulse, the sound of smashing wood, and the howls of the injured being trampled underfoot.

I bellowed wordlessly, grinding forward, my body taut. Helena was with me, her metal hip against mine. Our shields overlapped, separated, and then clacked back together, fighting the weight of the mob.

Hands clutched at my shield's rim, and weapons scarred its surface. A few weak blows slipped around it to ring against my helmet, shoulders, and armored shins.

Nika! Nika!

My heart crashed against my chest. It was so loud—louder than the thunder of a thousand marching feet. I couldn't think, couldn't doubt, and couldn't fear. I existed solely within those beats; within the scream of my muscles and the pressure of Helena's shield against mine.

And the feel of the sword in my hand.

With another wordless scream, I stabbed my blade up beneath my shield. The weapon punched through something soft. I ripped it free, spilling a gush of hot liquid, and feeling a weight slide off my shield.

Helena's sword was in what space there was between our bodies, stabbing into the cracks that separated us. I had an instant's reprieve, a single heartbeat in which to notice her. She was screaming, her face red, her sword red, her body rigid.

Her shield was falling, so, in the moment I had, I shoved my own higher up against hers. It was all I could do before more weight slammed against me and I was killing again. We were slightly out of sync now, leaving us vulnerable, but I pulled my attention away, trusting her.

She was my shield-mate. She wouldn't let us fall.

Nika! Nika!

I wasn't sure which of us was the first to step back, but it didn't matter. We moved as one, our swords punching out again and again and again.

Nika! Nika!

We were forced back another step, and then two. My sword arm was a blur, pumping in and out. I tore my knuckles open against the wall on my right. Blows rained down on me, but I hardly felt them.

Nika! Nika!

Then, a moment of true danger. A huge man, reeking of wine and the stink of his dead companions, hooked an axe along the top of my shield. My sword cut towards him, but a shift in the mob caused me to miss. He yanked back, jerking me forward.

Hands closed on me, pulling me into them, away from Helena. I heaved backward, but they didn't let go. I was out of position, would be torn down in a moment if I couldn't—

A bloody spear ripped over my shoulder, its tip skipping off the big man's jaws and cutting into his throat. He screamed, and bubbled, and the pressure against me eased. Then, the spear pulled back behind me, stabbing forward an instant later to sink into another's flesh.

I managed to tear myself free, my shield locking back into place with Helena's. We fell back another step, killing, moving as one.

Nika! Nika!

We killed, stepped back, and killed again.

Nika! Nika!

We saved each other's lives a thousand times, shifting our bodies and shields to cover each other.

Nika! Nika!

The blood, the stink, the stones, and the screams. All of it swirled within me, layering over the pounding of my heart and burning of my muscles.

Nika! Nika!

We thrust and we stabbed. We killed again and again.

Nika! Nika!

Death, so much death. But the weight never fell away.

Nika! Nika!

Those words became my own, thrumming through me. I made them my entire being.

Nika! Nika!

Victory; I would take it from them!

Nika! Nika!

I would rip it away. I would fight for it. I would never fucking stop, never fucking surrender.

Nika! Nika!

Conquer! I would conquer!

Chapter Twenty-One

An Empress Stained

As suddenly as the crash after lightning, the weight was gone.

I didn't immediately react. My mind was a storm of pounding fury, my breath ragged in my ears and my body frozen and tense.

After a few heartbeats of nothing, my soldier's instincts forced me into motion. I lowered my shield, becoming aware of my shrieking muscles. I groaned, swayed, and would have fallen over had another body not leaned into me.

Helena. My shield-mate. Her eyes were glazed and her breath was the uneven, gasping hitch of a body pushed beyond all limits. But she was alive. She was here beside me, and together, we steadied each other enough that we could each stand on our own. I blinked my vision into focus and raised my head.

We were in a charnel house. Dozens lay dead before us in a carpet of blood and pale bodies that stretched from our feet to the splintered entrance to the hallway. Their bodies were cut open and gutted, their insides spilled onto the surrounding stones.

And the stench.

It was shit and misery and death, a miasma of horror worse than any sort of butcher's yard. Beside me, Helena coughed, staggered to the side, and retched. I just swayed in place, breathing through my mouth.

"They ran away," a voice rasped. "They all ran away."

It was the Empress. She was just a handful of steps behind us, leaning heavily onto the haft of her spear. Her limbs shook with exhaustion.

"*Augusta*," I croaked. "Are you hurt?"

Blood stained the sweat-darkened purple of her dress. Thick droplets of blood were splattered along her chest and shoulders. It oozed from between her fingers, trickling down from the splintered tip of her spear.

"Ah," she said, seeming to notice herself for the first time. "No. I … I don't believe any of this is mine. And you?"

She reached a hand up to push at the strip of purple that held back her hair, leaving a streak of red behind on her forehead.

I didn't answer, refusing to look down to examine myself; I wasn't ready to see. I forced myself to stare down the hallway instead, distracting myself with thoughts of survival.

And indeed, it appeared as if the Empress was correct. Nothing moved within the corridor, and I could hear nothing in the room beyond the shattered door. The invaders had fled, and not a moment too soon; looking behind me, I realized that we had been pushed nearly all the way back to the door to Theodora's salon.

From the side of the hallway, Helena groaned. She managed to push herself upright, leaning heavily against the wall, her face wan.

"Helena," I said. "Are you—"

I coughed, feeling a wave of bile rise through me. The smell was horrific, made so much worse by the thick summer air oozing through the narrow windows. My stomach writhed, but I clamped down on it ruthlessly. Not yet.

Helena was covered in blood. Her chest, legs, and sword arm were caked in death, her face and neck splattered with it. I staggered over to her, moving despite the weight of the blood I'd spilled and the letter beneath my armor. "I'm fine," she said, trying to smile. "I'm fine. It's just, how—"

She turned and threw up once again. It was a hacking, heaving sort of retch, the kind that left you shaking. I came to stand beside her, pressing my hip to her side—all I could do without dropping my sword and shield. She leaned some of her weight into me.

"Leontius," the Empress said, moving to join us. She lay a hand on the unarmored part of Helena's hip, providing what comfort she could. "Is it safe to move?"

I blinked, stirred, and shook my head. "Not yet. We still don't know what's going on in the rest of the palace. This is still the safest place for us."

Theodora nodded, turning her head to gaze down the length of the passageway. An ocean of red dotted with pale islands of green and blue. "It seems remarkable," she said. "That we survived against so many."

"These weren't soldiers, *Augusta*," I said, exhaling. "They were potters, blacksmiths, dockworkers ... They were drunk, pushed onto our swords by those further back. They were badly led, unarmored, and most didn't even have any weapons. They were just ..."

"People," Theodora finished for me. "Dead because they believed in something strongly enough to fight for it."

I shifted my gaze back to Helena. She was still bent into the wall, her eyes screwed tightly shut and her frame vibrating with repressed feeling. She'd just gone through her first battle, and every single thought and feeling that she'd pushed aside while in the midst of it was tearing into her.

My own soul felt raw, overused, and stretched near to the point of snapping. I could feel my own crash coming, though experience let me push it away. For a time, at least.

"We believe as well, *Augusta*," I said. "In you."

The Empress smiled, though it was one that I'd yet to see her wear; it was an expression of unyielding certainty, of iron-hard conviction, the whole of it framed by a profound sense of grief. It was the smile of the lonely farmer taking his axe to the rabid skull of his favorite dog.

She stepped forward to kiss my cheek. "I'll be back with a bucket of water."

The Empress slipped into her private chambers, leaving Helena and me alone. My shield-mate had managed to straighten herself, though her body still shook. I watched as she breathed deeply, the lines of her face growing more relaxed with every exhalation. She was eventually able to open her eyes and meet my gaze. I felt something crack within me, like the first axe blow that had split the door.

She was still her.

Though tears traced the lines of her cheeks and something had changed within the cypress of her eyes, nothing had been lost. I still recognized her. She was still the woman I—

"I'm sorry," she said.

"Helena, I—what?"

"I'm sorry," she repeated. "I'm here weeping like a child. But I'll get stronger, Leo."

I blinked.

"I promise," she said, looking away. "I won't hold you back for long. I just ... I promise I'll be stronger."

Then, despite the blood coating my limbs, the letter I bore, and the charnel house stink of the hallway, I laughed. I laughed, and I laughed, and I felt myself draw back from the edge.

Helena's face went scarlet. "Fuck you," she hissed, turning to march away.

"No!" I gasped, lurching to step in front of her. "I'm sorry. It's not that! It's—" I devolved into another peel of laughter. And though Helena's face burned a shade brighter, she didn't move away.

When I finally mastered myself, I stepped a bit nearer to her. I looked into her eyes, my face relaxing into a smile. "Helena, you wonderful, amazing, beautiful, and hopelessly blind woman. You're the strongest person I've ever known."

She snorted, though I saw something shine within her eyes. "You weren't the one crying and puking."

"No," I agreed. "Not yet."

"It's coming?"

I nodded.

She made a small sound, moving nearer to me. "Then, I'll be here when it does."

The Empress returned a few moments later with a bucket of water and several strips of clean, white cloth. We dropped our weapons and washed the worst of the blood and sweat from our hands and faces. Helena and I discovered that we'd each suffered a myriad of cuts, and, to my horror, the Empress proceeded to tend to our injuries.

"Leontius, enough!" she snapped, as I tried to squirm away. She looked ferocious in her still-bloody dress, her hands clamping down on me. "You risked your lives for me, the least I can do is clean and wrap your wounds."

"*Augusta*," I tried.

"Stop," she said, taking up a clean rag. "I'll be quick. I have some experience if that reassures you."

I frowned, glancing over to Helena.

"At the brothel," she said. "When the men were too rough; Theodora would patch us up."

"You didn't have a guard?" I asked. "Or a bouncer?"

"Not until Helena grew a little older," the Empress said, pulling over a clean strip of cloth. "Your arm now, Leontius."

"*Augusta*, I can handle—" Her glare silenced me, and I meekly held my forearm out for her to inspect.

"Thank you." She took my arm, her fingers strong and sure. "Please don't keep fighting me on this. I'm having difficulty sitting still, to tell you the truth. I keep ... well, no matter."

I relaxed, submitting myself to her care. The Empress fell silent, unwilling to explain further. But she didn't have to; the stiffness in her limbs and the tension at the corners of her eyes mirrored my own.

Our day wasn't yet done.

The Empress had almost finished checking over Helena when I heard the sound of boots on stone. The two women heard it with me, and we moved as one. Helena and I had our shields strapped on in moments, the Empress having collected our swords for us in the meantime.

We jogged towards the shattered entrance, my limbs stiff and my heart beating faster.

"Mary's tits!" A voice loudly swore. "It fucking reeks here. Are you sure we're going the right way, Serg?"

"I thought you'd be used to the smell of your own sack by now, Grat."

"Oh, it stinks, does it? How about you come lick it clean for me, Niketas?"

Helena and I slowed, exchanging incredulous looks. We stopped before reaching the first body, my eyebrows high in disbelief.

"Shut your hole, Grat," I heard Sergius growl. "You too Nik. Shields up, lads, we don't know what we're going to find here."

"Why have we stopped?" the Empress said. She'd picked up her broken spear haft. "Are these our men?"

"They're Leo's friends," Helena said with a wide grin. "From his legion days. How long have they been in the palace?"

The tension rushed from me in a wave, leaving my body light and trembling. I sucked in a deep breath.

"I'll give it a few licks too, Grat!" I roared. "I'm tired of breathing it in!"

I heard a series of startled curses, while behind me, the Empress laughed. There was a stampede of pounding boots and then a squad of armored soldiers appeared in the shattered doorway.

"*Centenarius*!" Sergius laughed. "You're alive! The Empress?"

"She's here as well!" I called back.

The men whooped, cheering and thanking God as Sergius turned back to them. "We found them, boys! You, run back and tell the general. Maurice, take two watch the hall."

The two women and I moved back as Sergius led his men towards us. What followed was coarse laughter, back-slapping, wide-eyed realization, and a whole mess of clumsy bows as the Empress stepped forward to introduce herself.

Theodora smiled through the men's stammered greetings. She thanked them each in turn, shifting from a high, courtly accent to the less polished voice she'd have grown up with. It was the language these soldiers knew, and the Empress left blushing cheeks and sheepish smiles in her wake.

The gates, we were happy to learn, had been sealed. Though, as of yet, nobody knew who had let the rioters in. The mob still rampaged through parts of the palace, though they'd been beaten back from the outer wall. Belisarius was in command of the palace's fighting men, coordinating the squads like Sergius's that were sweeping through the halls.

"And my husband?" The Empress asked.

"Safe, *Augusta*," Sergius answered. "Last I heard, at any rate. The General was with him when the enemy broke in."

"Thank you, soldier," she said, laying a palm on his forearm.

"*A— Augusta*!" Sergius stammered, and I grinned to see the grizzled old veteran flush.

"Well then, gentlemen," Theodora said. "I believe that I will leave you here. I have to wash the stink of Gratian's balls from my skin."

A few of the men snorted, trying to choke down on their laughter. Grat, for his part, looked positively horrified. He mangled a few words, his entire face blazing a scarlet. He hadn't produced anything more than a gargle before the Empress slipped away with a wink and a small laugh.

"Grat," Sergius said in the moment of silence after her departure. "You're a fucking idiot."

"It wasn't me!" Gratian exclaimed, his eyes wide with panic. "Serg, I—Nik, and ... the Empress! She ..."

"Dumber than a sack full of rocks," Serg said, shaking his head. "Start piling these bodies outside. The rest of you grinning monkeys can help."

"Oh, don't be too hard on him," Helena said. "I was worried that he'd start talking about his cock again."

Gratian fled, followed by the laughter of his squad mates. Sergius shook his head again, but I saw a smile part the hairs of his worn beard. "Aye, well, we can thank the Lord for that." The old soldier's gaze shifted to the doors to Theodora's salon. "The Empress ... she really fought with you?"

My face twisted into a grimace. "I tried talking her out of it, but I didn't have time."

"What a woman," Sergius said, amazed. "And you, Helena ... not a lot of *stratiotai* could have held back so many."

"Leo did most of the work," she said.

Both Sergius and I snorted.

"I'm an old soldier, lass. I know what it would have taken to do this." Sergius suddenly stiffened, saluting her with a fist over his heart. "*Stratiotai!*"

Helena saluted back, her face flushing. I grinned, sure that she was about to squirm with suppressed pride.

"Come on," I said. "Let's go help the monkeys."

Chapter Twenty-Two

To Spurn an Empress

Despite my offer of help, Sergius categorically refused any assistance with clearing the dead bodies.

They'd barely fought, he said. And they were itching to do something after three long days stationed in the palace. This was the least that they could do.

Neither Helena nor I had had the energy to argue, and so we'd taken off our helmets, unstrapped our shields, and sat back against the far wall.

"I guess that now it's official," Helena said.

"Hmm?" I asked.

We were seated near enough for our legs to touch, my body throbbing with pain and heavy with exhaustion.

"After today, we're officially shield-mates."

I tilted my head towards her. "We became shield-mates a lot earlier."

"Sure, but now we've fought together. I held my place at your side." And despite the horror of what we'd had to do, I heard the fierce pride in Helena's voice.

"I knew you would. I've trusted you for a long time."

"Oh yeah?" she said, shifting to rest her sweat-darkened head against mine. "Since when?"

I leaned more of my weight into her, resting my shield hand on her thigh. I could feel the eyes of the others drifting towards us as they worked, and could picture their knowing grins.

But I didn't care. I was with her.

"Remember the first day we trained together? How difficult you were being?"

"Difficult? Is that what it's called when your gender makes everyone treat you differently?"

"Hmm," I said. "That, or simple laziness."

She swatted me with the back of her hand, swearing as her knuckles rapped on my breastplate. I laughed, squeezing her thigh.

"When you swallowed your pride and your anger," I said. "When you decided to set all that aside and let me train you. That's when I knew."

She snorted, shaking out her sore knuckles. "Well, all I remember from that day is how much you enjoyed hitting me."

"You don't remember when I said the words, 'you're my shield-mate'?"

"No," she said. "You must have done something mean to make me forget."

I laughed. She brought her hand down atop mine, and I turned it so our fingers intertwined. Her thumb drew a swirling pattern along my skin and I let myself get lost in the hypnotic motion.

With her here, it felt like I could accomplish anything. Like I might truly leave my old life behind and walk a new path. What might I do with this woman at my side? Where might I go? What might I build with her hands working alongside my own?

A little tavern by the sea, perhaps.

"Helena," I said.

I shifted my hand in hers, and in doing so, my thumb came to rest atop hers, stopping the circle she was making. I pulled my vision back into focus.

"Leo," she answered, and I heard the soft smile in her voice.

"I—" But my words were cut short, pressed back into me by a sudden weight. Blood— there was blood beneath my nails.

I was suddenly reminded of where I was, of what I had done. The charnel stink of the hallway and the emotions I'd tucked away flooded back into me. I heard my mother weep inside my head. I started to shake, my lungs squeezed tight.

I couldn't take my eyes off the blood that still crusted my hand.

"Leo?" Helena said, shifting so that she could look at me. "Are you ok?"

I didn't answer, freeing her hand from my filthy grip. I shifted from her, pulled away by a crushing weight against my side. I clawed at the pocket beneath my armor, ripping something free.

My mother's letter.

I opened it with unsteady hands, revealing a single slip of yellowed papyrus and my mother's blocky letters.

My little lion, it said. *Come home.*

I stared at the page, blinking stupidly. Five little words. Was that all? I turned the folded papyrus over, my fingers smudging its surface.

That was it.

I felt the mad urge to laugh. This was what I'd been afraid of? *Come home*? I wasn't some lost child who needed the comfort of my mother's arms.

I grit my teeth, reading those words again and again. I ached to tear into the offending letter, to rage and scream and damn my mother to hell.

I'd been expecting something like this but ... What the fuck did this mean?

I was happy. For the first time in my fucking life, I was happy. I was the Empress's guard, sitting beside a woman who was nothing but good. With her, I had a vision of a future where I wouldn't have to kill anymore.

I wasn't fucking lost.

"Leo?" Helena whispered.

She was beside me; she'd read the letter too. She once again wrapped my trembling hand in one of hers, murmuring warm words. My eyes were again drawn to the shape of that hand, to the clean flesh of her fingers.

I wasn't lost.

"I'm here," Helena said, still low enough that I could pretend I didn't hear. "Your mother ..."

She tightened her grip, her fingers warm against mine. They should be filthy, I thought. Her hands should be black with the stain of all she'd done. She'd been a whore. She'd given her body to so many, spreading her legs for anyone with a handful of coins.

Today, she'd killed. Her hands should be like mine ... but they weren't. Helena's hands were clean.

How were they so clean?

My heart beat faster, and I parted my lips to let my breath pass. Was I lost? Why were Helena's hands so clean? I felt myself unravel like a spool of yarn tumbling down a mountain.

Come home.

Was that the answer? No, it didn't make sense. I wasn't supposed to go home. Not yet. My father never had.

"Leo," Helena said. "Talk to me, I'm here."

I shifted my gaze to hers but didn't really see. "My father ..."

"Yes?" she said. "What about him? He was a soldier, right?"

"Come home ... my father never came home."

"He died?" Helena asked.

I managed a nod. "A long time ago."

He'd died not long after my fifth birthday. He'd left on campaign one spring morning and had never come back. From then on, it had just been my mother and me. But she had never stopped speaking of my father. He'd been larger than life, she'd said. He'd been loud, as much when he laughed as when he roared his anger. He'd been strong, diligent, and the person my mother had loved the most in the world.

Her lion, she'd said, golden and proud.

"*And you'll be just like him one day, my little lion. You'll be so strong and so good and you'll make him so, so proud.*"

I'd heard those words nearly every night when I was a child. She'd say it while we had dinner, and then again when she'd tuck me into bed with a hand stroking my hair.

Helena was still speaking, but her words washed over me. I looked back at my hands. Had my father's hands been so filthy? I thought that they must've been; he'd been *stratiotai*. He'd killed.

Come home.

He'd never gone back. He'd done his duty; he'd sacrificed all of the love, happiness, and comfort he had in the world for it. He'd supported my mother and me with his soldier's pay.

And when he'd given up his life for that money, my mother had done the same. She'd given up everything so that I might live. She'd nearly killed herself in those first few years after his death. I remembered how she'd begged and worked long hours for whoever would pay her.

I remembered her smiling through hollow cheeks, watching me eat the only little bit of bread we had.

Life got a little better once she'd managed to scrape enough together to open a little shop. She was a gifted seamstress, and it wasn't long before the wealthiest ladies of Rhodos became regulars in our little store. But even then, I remembered the nights she'd work with a rag close by, ready for the moment her fingers would start to bleed. The hunger was worth it, she'd always say, watching me train with sword and shield. No pain was too much to see her little lion take the shape of his father.

I saw again her happy, tear-soaked smile. The day I'd joined the legions had been the happiest day of her life.

I pushed myself to my feet. Helena rose with me, but I hardly noticed.

My parents had done so much for me. They had suffered and had given everything of themselves to put me on this path. And now I wanted to quit for a fucking tavern? Is that how I'd repay my parent's love?

No wonder my hands were so dirty.

"Leo!" Helena said, her fingers tugging at mine. "Please, tell me what's wrong. I can help."

I let out a long breath, my eyes far away. I pulled myself from her, no longer shaking.

"I'm fine," I said, inhaling the stench of death.

Helena stepped before me, but I didn't see her. "You're worrying me, Leo."

"I'm fine." The sound of my mother's weeping filled my head. She spilled tears of joy, happy beyond words to see her little lion finally turn back to the path of his father. "I just remembered where I'm supposed to be."

"Where you're supposed to be?" Helena's hand closed around my arm, squeezing. "What are you saying? Talk to me, Leo, I'm your shield-mate!"

"No," I said, my gaze focusing on her. "You're not."

Her body stiffened. "What?"

"You're a woman," I said. I folded up my mother's letter. "You're not a soldier. This isn't your place."

Helena's hand slipped from my arm. Shock rippled across her features. Disbelief. Her breath caught as her expression deepened into one of pain.

I saw my words stab into her like a knife plunging through the barest chink in her armor.

Nausea twisted through me.

Her eyes were so wide, raw with the depths of her hurt. But I clamped down on my feelings. I turned away, pulled from her by a weight that was so much heavier than my mother's letter.

These past few months had been a lie. Happiness? Love? Comfort? I didn't have a right to any of it. Not until I repaid everything that I owed my parents. I was *stratiotai*, like my father and his father before him. I was the soldier my mother had wept to see me become. As I moved back towards my place amongst the blood and bodies, I felt myself walk back along the path of my life. Back to that fork where I'd once chosen a new direction.

My mother was right; it was time I returned home.

Chapter Twenty-Three

Free the Empress

I HADN'T EVEN TAKEN a step, however, when something jerked me around. It was Helena, her face alive with fury.

"Is this who you are, then?" she spat. "Was everything a lie?"

I tried to hold her gaze but couldn't. "This is who I've always been."

"What a crock of horseshit. I know you, Leo. You're choosing this, and all it took was two fucking words from your mother."

I didn't answer, trying to draw away. But Helena wouldn't let go.

"Look at me."

"Helena, I—"

"Look at me! Look me in the fucking eyes and tell me it was all a lie."

I forced myself to look up. I took in her wide, cypress eyes, her auburn hair, and the warm bronze of her skin. I saw the feelings of betrayal, anger, and pain that streamed as tears down the lines of her face.

"Say it. Tell me that you don't want me, that I have no place beside you."

I was trapped there, at the fork of my life. My foot was raised, ready to step along the path that I'd always been meant to follow. But I couldn't move, not while Helena held me back.

"Let me go," I said.

"Say it."

"Let go of me!"

"Then fucking say it! Say it and I'll let you go."

Our voices echoed through the passage. I opened my mouth to speak, but the words wouldn't come. Instead, I tried to yank my arm free, but Helena's grip was iron.

"Let me go, Helena. Please."

She screwed her eyes shut as tears still spilled from behind her eyelids. A sob gathered within her; she inhaled deeply, and it seemed to be on the edge of breaking through her. But it didn't, held back by the strength and will that had pushed her from the brothel.

"No," she said, exhaling. She opened eyes that no longer cried. "I'm not going to."

"Helena—"

"Side by side against the future," she said. "That's what we swore. I don't know what you're going through, Leo, but I'm not letting you face this alone."

"There's nothing to face!" I shouted. "Let go of me!"

"No! I'm holding you to your fucking oath, shield-mate!"

She tried to haul me back towards her, but I resisted. For a few moments, we just pulled back and forth against each other, neither willing to give ground, neither able to let go.

"Grat!" Helena yelled. "Sergius! Get over here!"

The men had been listening to us, of course. It would have been impossible not to. Sergius's voice, when it came, was hesitant.

"Lass, I don't know if we should—"

"Shut up!" Helena snarled, still fighting me. "Your *centenarius's* head is so deep in his own ass that he can't see past his shit!" I growled, wrenching my arm to the side. But Helena didn't let go. She didn't even turn to me, still speaking to my friends. "You told me that you owe him your life. Well, I'm telling you, as the one who fought beside him, that he's about to throw his life away. Help me with him!"

Sergius didn't speak for a few heartbeats. His eyes flicked to me, searching my face. When he spoke again, his voice was firm. "Alright. What do you need?"

"Come grab his arm," Helena said. "We're bringing him to the Empress. Grat!?"

"Lovers' quarrel?" My other friend said, sauntering over.

"Shut your fucking hole," Helena barked. "Come on."

"Let go of me!" I shouted, struggling against their grip.

"Can't do that, *Centenarius*," Sergius said. "This will be good for you."

"Yeah," Gratian said gripping my other side. "And maybe the Empress will give me a kiss this time."

We found the Empress in her salon, not far from the door I was pulled in through. She was still in her torn and bloodied dress, though she'd kicked off her ruined sandals. She paced back and forth while two of her maids filled a tub with heated water. The curving metal bathtub had been dragged here from deeper within her quarters.

"What's wrong?" the Empress demanded, moving towards us. "Are we under attack?"

I saw in her the same sort of tension that I'd seen before. She was still clamped around herself, always moving, unwilling—or unable—to relax.

"No," Helena said. "It's Leo."

"His wounds?" the Empress asked, checking my bandages. "Is he hurt?"

"I'm fine," I said.

"He's hurt in his head," Helena said, speaking over me. "It's like some lever was flipped. He's changed completely, saying a bunch of things ... Here." So saying, she plucked the folded letter from my hand.

"It's from his mother," she said, handing it over. "He read it, and it's like ... I don't know."

"I'm fine!" I said again, trying to free myself. "Let me go!"

"Be silent, Leontius," the Empress ordered, taking the papyrus from Helena. She scanned its contents, raising her eyes to consider me. She stared at me for a long time, recognizing something, I thought, within my gaze. Finally, she let out a long breath and folded the letter back up.

"I don't know if there's anything wrong with him, Helena. It seems to me like he's simply made a choice."

"He hasn't!" Helena exclaimed. "Not yet. Or, not really. I don't know, but it doesn't— Can you just try talking to him?"

"This is his choice to make," she said, as gently as she could.

"Please," Helena said. "Just ... please."

The Empress looked between us for another few moments, before nodding slowly. "Very well, I will stay with him a while. But, Helena, you might not like—"

"I don't care," she interrupted. "I don't care what you do. I just ... I need ..."

Helena's own emotions cut her off. I tried to ignore the twist within me at seeing her in such pain. The Empress moved to her, touching her arm and murmuring a few words into her ear.

Sergius growled something, and on my other side, I felt Gratian's grip tighten. "Leo, you prick."

"Very well," Theodora said, stepping back towards me. "Gentlemen, thank you for bringing our Leontius to me. You may release him."

"Err, your pardon, *Augusta*," Sergius said. "Won't he just run off?"

"He will not. Isn't that right, my soldier?"

"*Augusta*," I said. "My place is outside."

She arched an eyebrow. "Your place is wherever I say it is."

"Empress—"

"No!" Theodora snapped. "Enough! I am your Empress and I will have your obedience."

I stiffened, my spine pulled to attention by the whip crack of her voice.

"Good," she said. "Thank you, gentlemen."

Sergius and Gratian released me, bowed as smoothly as they were able, and retreated. Helena lingered a moment, her eyes on me. "Fix him," she said. "Bring him back to me."

The Empress smiled softly, and soon, it was just us and the maids standing by the ready bath.

She drifted over to it, leaving me where I stood, stiff and silent. She trailed a hand through the steaming water, making a small sound of appreciation.

"Thank you," she said to the servants. "You may leave us."

Both women bowed, retreating deeper into the Empress's suite of rooms and leaving us truly alone. Theodora stared into the ripples of water for several long heartbeats before turning back to me.

"Come here," she ordered.

I obeyed, though somewhat hesitatingly. As I approached, the Empress reached up and freed her hair from the sweat and blood-crusted strip of purple that had held it back. She shook loose walnut and gold tresses, watching me all the while.

"Give me your arm," she said when I was before her.

Again, I obeyed.

I thought she wanted to check my bandages, but to my surprise, her fingers worked at the straps of my armored bracer. She had it off within moments, letting it drop to the floor before reaching for the other.

I was determined not to speak, staring ahead woodenly. I could still hear the screaming of the mob from out beyond the Empress's wide balcony. I thought I could hear the distant sound of fighting as well, though I couldn't be sure. I tried to focus on it, but Theodora moved nearer to me, her fingers tugging on the straps of my breastplate.

I was breathing in her scent, her sweat, and the smell of her hair. Her odor was sharp, thick, and powerfully feminine, a heady, lavender-tinged cloud that smothered any sort of concentration I tried to muster. But I was determined not to speak.

That determination lasted until she pulled my breastplate free from my body with a grunt. "*Augusta*," I said. "Forgive me, but I don't understand."

She tottered a few steps away, setting my bloody armor down on the stone floor. I was in my sweat-soaked *tunica* now, my heated skin crying out in relief at the cooler air of Theodora's salon.

She turned back to me, still too tightly wound, moving with a bare shadow of her usual dancer's grace. "It's very simple, Leontius."

I waited, but she didn't elaborate. Instead, she surprised me again by kneeling at my feet and reaching for the straps of my greaves.

"*Augusta*," I shifted to step away but was brought up short by the lightning crack of her voice.

"Stay still!"

I once again stiffened into obedience. I was confused, distracted by the feel of her hands on my calves. She set my greaves down one at a time and then unlaced my heavy boots and pulled them off my feet.

"Your *tunica*," she said. She'd settled back onto her heels, her eyes calm, expectant. I hesitated, then obeyed when I saw them start to harden.

"Aren't we going to talk?" I asked, now naked save for my loincloth.

She didn't immediately answer, still looking up at me, her face, a bare arm's length from the bulge between my legs.

My face was burning. I was naked, defenseless, and completely off-balance. In this unexpected silence, I felt myself once again begin to unravel. I was swamped by a flood of emotions, losing my way, searching for my earlier certainty.

But it was fading away, eroded by her touch and the sharp scent of her sweat.

"No," she said, and I nearly leaped out of my skin when she raised both hands to touch my hips. "We're not going to talk."

She held my gaze with hers, hooking her fingers into my final layer of clothing. I felt my crotch stiffen. My mother sobbed into my head, another note roaring through me.

It was all too much.

A storm raged within me, a thousand doubts, fears, hopes, and emotions crashing into each other. I couldn't think, couldn't feel, couldn't do more than stare into the eyes of the woman at my feet.

And those brown eyes gazed back at me, endless in their depth.

I was frozen at the crossroads of my life. I tried to come down on myself, to force myself to step away from her and put an end to whatever this was about to be. That was all I had to do, my mother urged me, nothing was holding me back.

The Empress waited, eternal in her patience.

Refusing her now would put me back on the path my parents had made for me. I'd be gone from here, from her, from Helena. I just had to take this first, irrevocable step, and I'd be on my way home.

Move, my mother screamed.

But I couldn't.

Something shifted in the Empress's eyes, a ghost of a smile playing on her lips. She pulled my wrapping away, freeing me.

Fire tore through my body, staining my flesh. Theodora made a sound low in her throat, breathing in the naked stink of my growing erection.

"Neither of us are in a place to talk," she said.

Her eyes finally left my face, tracing the lines of my chest and stomach on their way down to my cock. Her lips parted.

"I'm all locked up," she said. "I keep thinking about the battle, and it's like I'm still there."

I groaned, as the Empress's palm wrapped around my twitching shaft. She slowly worked her hand up and down my cock, gently stroking.

"In my head," she continued, "there's this sea of boiling emotion: fear, anger, doubt. It's tearing through me, and I can't seem to move past it."

She rolled the skin down from around my tip, leaning in and inhaling deeply. She moaned, and I saw her eyelids flutter. Heat curled beneath her dark skin. "God ... Nina was right."

My blood roared in my ears, loud enough that I could barely hear as she continued to speak.

"I see that same storm in you, my Leontius." Her voice was low, edged with something desperate. "And so, you're going to fuck me."

Her tongue darted out, flicking over my swollen head and taking the barest taste of me back into her. I jolted as her tongue, cool and wet, sent lightning through me.

"You're going to fuck me so we both forget," she murmured, her breath ticking me. "You're going to pump that storm into me, and smother the ocean boiling within me."

Her tongue slithered once more from between her lips, wrapping around the burning tip of my spear. Then, she bobbed forward, taking all of me into her mouth. My entire body went rigid as I lost myself in her damp heat. I grabbed her hair, my fist closing around strands of golden wire, holding on like a man lost at sea.

The Empress worked my cock with her tongue and throat, taking the time to taste every inch of me. After a few more moments, she pulled away. She spat onto the floor, working in the saliva she'd left on my manhood with her hand.

Augus—" I started, but swallowed my words just as she plunged back onto me. She swallowed me, pressing her nose into my pubic hair. Her throat flexed around my tip, her tongue, a pillow of silken moisture. My hand was limp in her hair, but she held herself there for one heartbeat and then another.

Finally, she gagged, sliding back, hacking up spit and my fluids with tears streaming down her face.

Her lips, however, were curled into a contented smile. "What a taste."

Theodora pushed herself to her feet, smoother this time, though it was hard to tell through the slitted blur of my vision.

"You're going to fuck me, my Leontius." She lifted the ruined hem of her dress, revealing a flash of pale silk that was wrapped snuggly around her sex. "You're going to fuck me with none of the gentleness you show Helena."

She pulled that slip of silk down, stepping out of it an instant later and pressing the sliver of fabric into one of my hands. It was soaked through.

Without thinking, I brought the Empress's loincloth up towards my face. She watched me sniff the wetness-stained fabric, her eyes burning.

I groaned, my knees buckling. Her scent stabbed into me; a powerfully feminine blend of her sex and sweat, it burned down to the tip of my manhood like a river of fire. I inhaled more deeply, losing myself in a fog of her liquid arousal. Then, I felt her hand reach up and pull my arm down. I blinked, and it was all I could do to focus my eyes on her.

"You're going to fuck me, my soldier."

Theodora stepped into me, tilting her face up to mine. Her arms snaked around my neck, the swell of her chest pressing into mine.

"You're going to break me free," her voice, a breath through parted lips. "Then, we can talk."

I surged into her.

Our lips met, crushing into each other. It was a hard, desperate kiss, our tongues bursting out to attack the other. My arms wrapped around her body, hers tight around my neck. We kissed, and after a few pounding beats of my heart, I threw her loincloth away, looped my hands beneath her ass, and lifted.

The Empress gasped as her feet left the ground, and moaned into my mouth when I spun us around and pressed her into a nearby column. Our lips parted as she wrapped her bare legs around me, her breath scalding my throat.

She reached down below where I held onto her hips, grasping my cock and pumping me furiously. I growled into the cloud of her breath, pushing her hard against the pillar. I let go of her hips, shoving the ragged layers of her dress up past her waist.

My hands slapped down to grip her naked ass. Theodora gasped and bucked against me, forcing her body lower. She guided my manhood to the nectar-drenched petals of her center, parting her lush heat with the aching tip of my cock.

I groaned, pressing harder into her. I longed to plunge wholly into her, but the Empress held herself there. She kept pumping my shaft, sliding my head along the ready wetness of her silken slit.

I pulled her ass cheeks apart, unfurling her, letting more of her spill from that divine font.

We breathed raggedly into the space we shared, the heat from our flesh like waves between us.

"Leontius," the Empress panted. "Fuck me. Fuck me like this."

I growled, wordlessly. Then, I jerked her down and impaled her on my burning spear.

The Empress mewled, arching her back. I thrust into her dew-soaked depths, my head skipping along her silken shape. She ground her wetness into me, shoving her shoulders back against the stone column.

I slipped my hands up to her waist, gripping the bones of her hips, keeping my cock buried in her liquid pussy. I shifted her up and down, slowly at first, grinding her navel into mine. My already-abused muscles screamed, but they were easy to ignore, as were my bandaged wounds. The storm in my mind faded as well, evaporating beneath the fire this woman had ignited in me. There was only her: the slide of her moisture-slick triangle of pubic hair, the smotheringly warm tightness of her insides, and the frantic need I saw burning within her lust-slitted eyes.

I shoved her back against the pillar, her sweat-reddened legs shifting their grip on me. Her hands clawed at my shoulders, and I used mine to pin her hips against the stone. Then, I flexed my hips back and thrust into her. She moaned, wrapping her arms around my neck, holding on as I crashed into her again and again.

I moved faster, pounding her, burying my cock into her again and again. I pulled her hips towards me with every thrust, and soon, the slap of our meeting flesh filled the room.

"Harder," she panted in my ear. "Harder!"

I growled low in my throat, redoubling my effort. But her fucking dress was in the way, the fabric coarse against my naked chest. So, I ground Theodora into the pillar, pinned her with my hips, and used my hands to rip the dress from her body.

I tore through most of it in that first, savage pull, ripping it from her neckline to where the purple fabric bunched at her waist.

"Oh fuck," she gasped, undulating her hips. "Oh yes."

I took a beat to watch the flex of her now naked stomach, the way her muscles rippled and played. The heavy, golden cross was stuck to the sweat of her abdomen, glinting at the end of its long chain. She arched her body, pushing her exposed breasts high. They were perfect, as lithe and dark as the rest of her. I watched them quiver, her deep-rose, lust-stiffened nipples pointing to heaven.

I slid my hands along the smooth flesh of her side, closing around her hips. The Empress moaned low in her throat, grinding harder into me, her eyes fever-bright through her sweat-darkened locks of walnut and gold hair.

I pulled back, driving my cock into her wet-heat. I watched her tits bounce with every thundering thrust, the golden chain skipping about her sweat-slickened flesh.

She pushed herself off the column, clinging to me, sinking her teeth into my shoulder as I hammered my body into hers.

Then, after a few endless moments, she let go of me, unwrapping her legs and sliding off my manhood. It gleamed, coated with the nectar of her arousal, red from the fire that still coursed through me.

"Lie down," she said, her breath ragged. "On the floor."

I obeyed, hardly feeling the cool stone on my naked back. My eyes never left the Empress, watching the quiver of her limbs and the sweat dripping down her body. She stood beside my feet, taking a moment to stretch, feline in her grace. Her lips curled in pleasure as my eyes roved her body.

"Do you remember the day we met, my soldier?" My heart was the crash of a chariot's wheel in my chest, my mouth flooding with anticipation. "Because I remember it very well."

She swept her hair back from her face, her breasts shifting with the motion. She took the first languid step towards my head. "I remember how you tasted me. The hunger in your eyes when you looked at me."

A growl rumbled through my chest. I wanted to look at her now, to gaze upon her every luscious fold and curve. But I'd only managed to rip the dress down to about her belly button, leaving the rest of her covered by the hem that fluttered around her knees.

"Mmm," she purred through a bitten lip. "Just like that." She was level with my waist now and stepped over to straddle me. She paused, her eyes on me, as she slowly tied a knot in her hair. "Don't look away," she said. Then, she brought her hands down to the end of the tear I'd made, and with a flex of her muscles, ripped the purple silk away.

My breath caught, somehow unprepared for the glory of her naked, heat-flushed body. The dress still hung like a cloak from where it looped around her shoulders, though it no longer hid anything from me. I jerked upward, reaching for her. She laughed, planting a naked foot into my chest, and pressing me back. "Not yet."

When she was sure I'd submitted, she flowed forward, liquid in her grace. Within moments, she stood above my head. My eyes were locked on her flesh, the air furnace-hot in my lungs.

"That hunger," she said, her voice an airy little breath swirling down the length of her body. "Keep it leashed for me, my Leontius." Then, as she had on the day we met, she folded her legs and lowered herself towards my face. I groaned, afire with the sight of her.

Her hole was already soaked through, stretched by the shape of my cock. Her inner folds were stained red, swollen into lush ripeness. Her pussy was a liquid garden, crowned by a triangle of pubic hair matted with her own wetness. "Keep watching me," she said, holding herself just above my wide eyes. She wove the fingers of one hand into my hair, holding me down. "Fuck ... breathe me in."

Her scent washed over me. Her heat, sweat, and arousal thickened the air around me. She moaned a soft, breathy little sound. My eyes flicked up, past the dangling, golden cross and the heaving curve of her naked breasts to meet her gaze. And there, I found a hunger, a fiery *need* that matched my own.

One that was far from sated.

"Not yet," she murmured. "Keep watching me."

With her free hand, she traced a line down the slope of her stomach and over the mound of her navel. One finger drifted through her trail of steaming pubic hair to ghost along the edge of her silken seam.

"Do you remember how I taste?" My blood thundered through me, my entire being focused on the playful caresses of that single finger. She explored herself with agonizing slowness, running that finger through every over-ripe fold and dew-soaked petal.

And when she slipped that digit into herself with a throaty gasp, I thought I'd burst.

"I remember how you lapped at me. How you worshiped me."

Her breath was coming faster. She dug that finger into herself, letting out another soft moan as she started to roll her hips. I groaned, watching her ready pussy sway back and forth a few fingerbreadths from my thirst-maddened tongue.

"You lost yourself in me," she said, as she slid in a second finger beside the first. She reached deep into herself, her hips rolling and fingers dancing. "And I see it ... fuck. Mmm, oh yes. You want another taste, don't you, my Leontius?"

My breath was the foundry's roar of heat. I ran my hands up the naked muscles of her legs, moments from pulling her into me, burning beyond the ability to continue relinquishing control.

"Helena told me what she calls you. A lion. Her lion." She suddenly ceased her hypnotic sway, drawing her fingers out from herself. Her swollen folds didn't want to let go, clinging to the warm flesh of her digits. They emerged gleaming with her arousal, coated in her silken nectar.

Another growl rumbled from my chest, my muscles bunching.

"But perhaps," she said, her eyes wickedly hot. "A part of you is mine as well."

Then, she lowered her fingers to my lips. "Drink from me, my lion."

I exploded into motion, whipping my tongue along her soaked fingers, lapping at her wetness. Her taste burst through me, making me burn hotter. I was desperate for more. And so, barely a heartbeat later, I pulled her down onto me.

I felt her gasp thrum through her body, her tongue-cleaned fingers curling into my hair with her other hand. I drank deeply of the Empress as she ground herself into my face, smothering me in her luscious flesh. She slid herself along me, back and forth, riding my whole face.

I pressed down on her hips, keeping her tight against me, taking all I could from her. Her taste was sweet, different from the sour flavor of the woman I truly longed for.

Theodora rode me until I shoved her away. I sucked in huge lungs full of air, watching as stood, stepped back, and squatted above my aching cock. She dug her hands into my chest, steadying herself while she lowered her hips to impale herself on my stiffness. My cock was swallowed by her silken heat. She got on her knees and I lifted my hands to grip her waist as she started riding me.

I let her take me like that for several moments, pushing my torso against her palms. She gazed down at me through slitted eyes as she rode me, her tits shivering with every undulating stir of her stomach and hips.

But I couldn't hold back for long. I wrapped that golden chain in one fist, yanking her down towards me. I devoured her lips with mine, taking in more of her taste while my hips started to pound into her.

She mewled, held in place by the chain at her throat, my cock spearing into her again and again. She sunk her teeth into one shoulder once again, writhing atop me, screaming into me as I hammered my body into hers.

Our flesh was slick with sweat. I dug the fingers of my other hand into the gold and walnut strands of her hair, keeping her head tight against me. She gnawed and licked at the length of my neck. I felt her pussy clench tightly around me, an orgasm ripping through her as she cried out to God in my ear. She went limp against me, but I didn't stop venting all of me into the willing wetness of her body.

When she started to react again, I once more shoved her off of me. I leaped to my feet, hauling her up after me. I drove her towards the stone column, still holding onto the golden links at her throat. Her back was to me, and she leaned forward to grip the pillar.

I ripped what was left of the purple dress from her back, drawing a moan from her. She was panting with hunger, her pleasure-glazed eyes peering back at me through falling strands of hair. "Please," she begged. She reached back, pulling aside one ass cheek, stretching her dripping hole for me. She held it open while I positioned myself behind her. "Fuck me ..." A gasp of desperate need. "Please."

I thrust into her in one quick lunge, her ass rippling from the force. She threw her head back and screamed. She rammed back into me, clinging to the stone lest she be swept away. I drove back into her, again and again, lost in the rippling bounce of her ass.

She was so tight against my cock, her pussy gripping me, pulling me into her no matter how far back I drew myself. I felt the fire within me rage even hotter, an inferno of gathering fury. I pounded into her faster and faster, holding tightly onto the chain, knowing I was close.

Theodora's back arched. Her moans and cries of ecstasy became low and raspy as the golden links dug into her throat. I shoved her face and chest into the stone pillar, and her body loosened as another orgasm screamed through her. I leaned my head down towards hers as my hips slammed my final few blows into the cushion of her ass.

I bit down on her shoulder. My entire frame shook when my own orgasm exploded out of me and I emptied myself in the silken slit of the Empress.

Afterward, as I staggered backward, thick, milky globs of my seed spilled from her. She slid down to the floor, her legs quivering, her flesh red and breath ragged.

I collapsed as well, suddenly drained, a raw void within me. And then, I wept.

My body shook with great, heaving gasps. Everything was too much: the battle, the blood, the letter, Helena ... It was all too, too much.

There I was, frozen at that same damned crossroads, weeping, with no idea how to go on.

Not far from me, I felt the Empress move. Through the haze of my tears, I saw her body tremble. She crawled towards me, but I could do nothing but curl up around myself and sob. Theodora lay her warm hands upon me, lowering herself onto the stone floor at my side. I wept, and she gathered me to her naked chest.

"Thank you," she said, choking on her own tears. "Thank you for fighting. Thank you for saving my life."

Chapter Twenty-Four

The Empress's Name

I don't remember the last time I had cried so, though the tears felt good, in a way.

If the sex had stripped me bare, then the tears helped soothe what was now raw and exposed. Like winter rain after a sun-scorched summer, the water readied me for what was to come: for the growth that was the mark of spring.

Eventually, the Empress and I fell silent. Neither of us had anything left to give.

I was the first to move, rolling onto my back. Theodora shifted with me, our flesh stinking and sticky with sweat. She lay her head on my chest, slid a palm onto my shoulder, and entwined her legs with mine.

I hugged her close, too beyond everything to worry about propriety. My breath slowed to match hers, or perhaps hers was the one that adjusted to mine; it didn't matter. We breathed together, trusting each other with our vulnerability and taking comfort in the simple presence of each other's bodies.

After what felt like an eternity, though was probably only a few minutes, the Empress shifted her head. She slid her palm from my shoulder to the strip of purple cloth she'd tied above my bicep. She picked at it with her fingers, while I wondered how I'd been able to forget its existence so completely.

"Purple is a heavy color is it not?"

I cleared my throat. "You wear it well, *Augusta*."

"No," she shifted against me. "Not here. Until we get off this floor we're just Dora and Leo."

"Alright."

"Say it," she said.

"What?"

"My name, Leo, say it."

"Theodora," I said, after a moment's hesitation. "Dora."

"Good."

She let out a breath, relaxing back into me. I loosened my grip on her, tracing patterns on her flesh that made her skin prickle.

"I knew death before I met my husband," she said. "I knew poverty, I knew pain and hopelessness. But it was only after wearing purple that I learned to kill." She paused, but I didn't speak. I kept my chest rising and falling beneath Dora's head, still tracing soft circles along her back.

"My husband and I have sent the legions out to war. We've changed laws and have punished those who break them. Millions of lives are affected by my every decision, Leo. God only knows how many have died because of me."

Dora's fingers stroked the ragged strip of purple silk, a few strands of gold still gleaming in her hair. "I don't know whether or not the good I try to put into the world will be enough to balance the weight of all that death. But I've made my peace with that, and when it is my turn before God, I won't hide from what I've done. And yet, for all that, for all that I've clawed and fought to get here, today was the first time I killed with my own hands."

My hand fell still on Dora's back. I closed my eyes, hesitating a moment before speaking into the darkness that now surrounded me. "It's easy, isn't it?"

She let out another long breath. "Easier than I ever imagined."

"I hate it," I said. "I hate everything about it."

"And yet you became a soldier."

I laughed, low and bitter. "I did."

"Tell me," Dora said, her voice as warm as the feel of her beside me. "Start from the beginning."

And so, opening my eyes once more to the light of day, I did. I began with the moment I'd tottered into my home to find my mother weeping over the news of my father's death. I told her about my childhood, how we'd worked and suffered, and how brittle my mother's smile looked set within hunger-hollowed cheeks. I'd been pushed to train, I told Dora, molded in my father's image.

Unburdened, the words flowed out of me. I was not a very good storyteller, though she was a great listener. She stayed silent, her cheek not leaving my chest, urging me on with gentle squeezes of her fingers.

I spoke to her of my time in the legions, of the horrors of war, and the first time I stained my hands with another's blood. Then, I told her about my time here. I spoke of her and of Antonina, of the doubts and prejudices I'd had, and how I'd grown to admire their strength and wisdom. But most of all, I spoke of Helena, of everything she meant to me and inspired within me.

Lastly, I spoke about the fork in my path, my paralysis, and the hope for my future that I feared was undoing me.

"You're changing, Leo," Dora said. "Not coming apart."

"But I can't let myself change. Not in this."

"Why not? To change is to be alive."

"Not in this," I insisted. "My parents—"

"Your parents," she interrupted, "did a lot for you."

For the first time since we lay down together, Dora raised her head. She held herself up with a forearm against my chest, her eyes firm. Her cheek was red, I noticed, lined from the time it had been pressed against me.

"You owe your mother a lot," she said, reaching to cup my bearded cheek. "You owe her your love and support. But your happiness, my Leontius, and the direction of your life—those things are yours. You are your own man, and you have to choose." Then she leaned down and kissed my lips. It was a soft, lingering kiss, one that took nothing but promised to give all that was asked for.

"And whatever you decide," she said with a smile. "You'll have the weight of an Empress behind you."

She pushed herself to her feet, groaning at the quiver of her muscles. I got up as well, my body stiff enough to be near debilitating. Theodora took my hand, pulling me to a table beside the bath that held fresh linen and a bucket of water. There, she washed my chest, back, and arms, checking my bandages and changing the ones I'd bled through.

We didn't speak while she tended to me. Her hands were soft, touching me with gentle care, like a gardener coaxing their charges into bloom.

Finally, she tightened the purple around my arm before pressing a palm to my cheek and turning to slip into the warm water of her bath with a happy sigh.

I pulled on my *tunica*, feeling new. My mind returned to the crossroads I faced.

At that moment, a scream tore through the Empress's door. I whipped my head towards it, hearing a sudden storm of screaming, cursing, and the crashing of iron. We were under attack.

I heard the splashing of water and looked back to find the Empress sitting up, her eyes on me.

"Stay there," I told her, scooping up my sword.

I sprinted to the entrance, running without knowing towards which path I would step: duty, obligation, or a chance at something different. And though this certainly wasn't the time, I was determined to finally take that step.

And so, when I burst into the hallway, I did.

Chapter Twenty-Five

The Empress Fights

I burst into the hallway in time to watch the last of my friends die. It was Gratian, of all of them. Stupid, crude, loyal Gratian, slumping to the ground a dozen paces away, cut down by warriors armored in gold.

"Look at this, boys," a man said. "The last of the bitch's pets."

"Doukas, you dumb bastard," I heard myself say. "What have you done?"

I swept my eyes over the scene, almost whimpering in relief to see that Helena was alive. Doukas, his pretty mouth curled into a sneer, held her with his sword to her throat. Four other Excubitors stood between us, their grins as bloody as the swords in their hands.

"You charge in without armor, or even any God damned boots, and I'm the stupid one?" Doukas snickered, and his companions laughed with him.

I ignored them for now, reading the story of what occurred in the butchered bodies of my friends.

They'd been ambushed, surprised by those they'd no doubt welcomed as allies. I saw Maurice and two other *stratiotai* lying at the passage's far entrance, dead without having drawn their swords.

Niketas and Suda had died a few paces further into the room. Niketas's sword was still in its sheath, but Suda's was buried to the hilt in the throat of a dead *Excubitor*. And though this was the first dead Imperial guardsman, he wasn't the last.

Sergius, Gratian, and one other had held out the longest, killing a handful of the traitors before being cut down themselves.

Doukas said something else, but I couldn't hear him over the blood roaring in my ears. My friends were dead; they were all dead. Grief tore through me for a heartbeat before I clamped down on it and shoved it away, along with my pain, exhaustion, and emptiness, packing it all deep within me.

I was *stratiotai*, and though my friends were gone, Helena was not.

"She's not so tough now, is she?" Doukas grinned, seeing the direction of my eyes. "Eh, Copper? You've got to feel like the dumbest whore in the city."

"Helena," I called out, ignoring him. "Are you okay?"

She'd been disarmed and her helmet was gone. I could see fear within her wide, cypress eyes, and dark blood matting her copper-colored hair.

She started to answer, but Doukas cut her off by tightening the blade at her throat.

"I'm the one doing the talking here, dog," he said. "Pull that slut from her den, or this one dies."

"You opened the gate, didn't you?" I said, my voice steady. "You let in the rioters."

"Obviously." He kicked the legs out from beneath Helena, forcing her to her knees. "Now, get the fucking Empress!"

I met Helena's eyes, opening myself to her, hoping she could see into me.

I'd chosen my life's path. I was running along it now, propelled by the oath that was etched upon my very soul.

I swear myself to you. I vow to stand beside you and face what comes with your shield locked onto mine.

There was no future without her by my side. Whatever happened next, I wanted her to see that I was there with her. We were together.

Because she was my shield-mate, and I loved her more than I had breath in my soul.

"Get. The fucking. Whore!" Doukas shouted.

"I presume you mean me?" the Empress said, calmly stepping through her door.

She was a sight to boggle the mind. She bore my shield and little else; her legs and stomach were bare and still gleamed with bath water. Her chest and waist were wrapped in what was left of her soiled, purple silk dress. Yet, despite her near nakedness, she stood as an eagle of Rome: an Empress, straight-backed and proud.

"You show even less wisdom than your father, oath-breaker," she said. Her hard eyes swept over the scene. "To think my home crawled with such treasonous vermin."

"You're the traitor," Doukas said, leering at her body. "We've taken the palace. Now, surrender. The people have won."

The Empress snorted. "There'd be a lot more of you here if my palace had truly fallen. Run back to your father, fool, before the rest of my husband's men find you."

Doukas sneered. "Justinian's a spineless worm. He'll give himself up once we have you. And then the three of us can go see my father. You'll be the guests of honor at his coronation tomorrow."

"Where we'll both be executed, no doubt."

Doukas's laugh was the cackle of a carrion eater. "Not before we have a bit of fun with you."

The other *Excubitors* laughed along with him. I recognized them as Doukas's cronies, men who owed their position to their father's wealth and power rather than any skill with the sword. There wasn't a real soldier among them.

Yet, they were five and we were three. They were armored in metal, armed with swords, shields, and daggers at their belt, while we had one sword, shield, and set of armor amongst the three of us.

This was not a fight we could win.

"Get on your knees and beg like the good little slut you are," Doukas said. He twisted his fist into Helena's hair, jerking her head around. "And if you please me, I'll even let your pets go." Doukas was lying, and a glance at the Empress told me that she saw it too.

"You won't run?" I asked her.

"No."

"Give up!" Doukas barked.

"Then keep the shield," I said, turning to Helena.

I couldn't save her, and the knowledge was an icy fist around my heart. I hoped she could see the love in my eyes, the love that I wished I'd been able to say aloud.

"Last chance," Doukas said.

"I promise to believe in you," I said, not looking away from Helena, "to trust that you'll hold that place beside me, and face what comes with your shield locked onto mine."

For a moment, her eyes shone, and the fear within her faded. She was my shield-mate and would be until the end.

"What the fuck was that?" Doukas said. "Was that a surrender?"

"No," I said, readying my sword. "The first two of you that attack will die with us."

I saw nervousness flicker across a few faces. Doukas gritted his teeth, pulling Helena's head back to the edge of his sword.

"Fine," he said. "Kill—"

"Wait!" Helena shrieked. "Wait, wait, wait!"

Nobody moved, everyone's eyes flicking down to her in surprise. "That's it?!" Terror twisted her features. "You're just going to let me die?"

I blinked. "Helena—"

"Fuck you!" she screamed. Her breathing was rapid, her cheeks flushed. "You leave me out here to go stick your cock in the Empress and now you're just going to let them kill me?!"

"That's not it!"

"You talk about trust and then you stab me in the fucking back! You limp-dicked fucking bastard!"

The *Excubitors* guffawed.

"Nothing yaps like an angry bitch, eh?" Doukas said, grinning in delight at my wide-eyed stare. "But I guess that you weren't ever man enough to tame her."

"You have no idea," Helena said, latching onto his words like they were her lifeline. "I had to work for hours just to get his pathetic little worm stiff enough to stick in me."

Doukas cackled, the sound filling the narrow hallway. "Ah, Copper, you were always a needy little slut. I'm almost sad I have to kill you."

"Don't," Helena begged. "Doukas, please. Don't kill me. I can help you!"

"I don't need your help," he sneered.

"Come on," she said. "Please! I'll ... I'll attack them first!"

"Do you think I'm stupid," Doukas said, drawing a thin line of blood from her neck. "I can't trust you."

"You can!" she exclaimed. "Doukas, please. There are five of you here against only two. You outsmarted us, Doukas, you won. Why would I want to go back to their side?"

"Helena," the Empress said. "What are you—"

"Shut up!" Helena said. "Can't you see it's over? He beat us, you dumb whore! We never had a chance."

Doukas's smile was all oily smugness. He shifted the blade a fingerbreadth away from her throat. "You're a whore too, Copper. Even if you're a bit smarter than this one."

"I am," Helena said. She licked her lips. "But I can be your whore."

Doukas smirked. "What?"

"I can be yours," she said. "Do you remember the night you fucked me? Do you remember how I loved it?"

"You're such a fucking slut, Copper," he said, laughing from low in his throat. "Whores like you never change."

"I was a good little whore," she said. "Remember?"

Helena shifted on her knees, and Doukas loosened his grip on her hair enough so she could turn to face him.

"Leo wasn't enough for me," she said. She reached up slowly, placing her palms on Doukas's armored skirt. "But you know how to take me. You know what I need."

"And what do you need?" he said, resting his sword against her shoulder.

"Please," Helena murmured. Her hands were sliding up the bare flesh of his legs between his skirt and greaves. "I'll be so good. I'll do anything."

Her fingers slipped beneath his armor, running up his naked thigh. Doukas laughed, letting go of her hair to push back on his sheathed knife and adjust his belt.

"Fuck, you really need it, Copper. Why'd you run away that night at the gate?"

A couple of the other *Excubitors* laughed, leering down at her.

"I'll do anything you want," she said. Doukas grinned as Helena's fingers unwrapped something beneath his armor. She started stroking him, jingling the metal that protected his waist and legs. "You won, Doukas. I'll be so good."

"Doukas," one of the unsmiling *Excubitors* said. "We have to hurry. I think I heard something."

Hypatius's son started to shift his focus up, but Helena's voice kept his eyes on her. "He told me that he loved me," she said, still stroking him. "After we fucked one night, he told me I was the woman of his dreams. I laughed in his face."

"Copper, you wicked bitch," Doukas said, his voice deepening. "No wonder he's leaving you."

"I couldn't help it," Helena purred, rolling her wrist. "He's not strong like you. He's not powerful."

"Doukas—" The other guard tried, but Helena spoke right over him.

"Show him. He loves me, but you've won. Take me right here, Doukas. Show him what a real man is."

"I've won," Doukas said, with another low laugh. "Fuck, yes. I've won. Take them, boys."

The other *Excubitors* started advancing towards us. Doukas, however, stayed behind. He lifted a flap of his armored skirt, exposing Helena's hand sliding up and down his swollen member.

She stroked him faster, her eyes never leaving his face. "Is he watching?" she breathed. "Can he see how happy I am with a man like this?"

The advancing warriors were halfway to us. At my side, the Empress tensed, lifting my shield. I felt Doukas's burning eyes fall on me. But my gaze was still on Helena.

And so, I saw the exact moment she plucked the knife from Doukas's belt and ripped it through his cock.

He screamed, blood spraying, body spasming. Helena jammed the knife into his thigh next, jerking down on the handle so that he collapsed into a shrieking tangle of blood and iron.

The advancing men whipped around, locked into place by shock and surprise.

I, however, had been ready to move.

I charged forward, seeing Helena surge to her feet and scoop up Doukas's fallen sword. I drove my own blade through the back of one *Excubitor*, crashing into him a moment later.

His scream joined Doukas's shrieking agony. The three others turned towards me, and off-balance, I wasn't able to block the nearest one's panicked slash.

His sword bit into me, and I saw my death in his snarling face.

But then, Helena was there. She rammed Doukas's sword into my attacker's side, the tip of the blade punching through his armor. She pulled me up with her next motion, and I felt something rip deep within my shoulder.

But I didn't care. I moved into my place beside her, my sword ready and my face twisted into something like a grin. My shield-mate was with me.

We faced the final two men, wounded and only half-armed. But we did so together, and I felt the oath between us sing. I'd believed in her, trusting that she'd find her way back to me. And now that she was holding that place by my side, I felt the last slivers of doubt fall away.

Helena was my shield-mate. She was the woman I loved, and with her here, I felt myself become whole.

The Empress slammed into the flank of the two men, knocking them off-balance with her weight tucked behind my shield. Helena and I moved as one, lunging forward and thrusting into whatever gaps we saw in their armor. Both *Excubitors* went down, Helena's sword through one's neck, while mine had plunged into the space between the other guard's breastplate and armored skirt.

Helena roared in triumph, laughing over the sound of Doukas's mewling sobs. The Empress threw down my shield and wrapped her in a tight hug, tears streaming down her face.

I grinned at the two women's joy, my heart beating wildly. I turned to pull my sword from the *Excubitor's* gut, but my hand slipped from the hilt. I tried again, flexing my fingers, but my limb wouldn't obey. Then, I noticed the dark blood pouring from the wound in my shoulder.

Agony seared through me, and I collapsed.

Darkness was closing around me, and I heard Helena scream. Her bright, copper-colored hair blazed in my fading vision. Her mouth was moving, but I couldn't hear her words. Within heartbeats, all I could see was the cypress of her eyes and the vast glory of her love shifting within her. It was so beautiful, I thought.

"I love you," I croaked.

And in the next moment, I knew no more.

Chapter Twenty-Six

An Empress's Legacy

The Blues and Greens wrote their legacy into the annals of Rome with the blood of thirty thousand. Though their entry was but a footnote, that blood may have bought more than a chapter if not for *Augusta* Theodora.

The halls of her home, they said, were not yet clear when she burst into the Emperor's chamber. She interrupted a meeting of lords, wearing nothing but shreds of purple and the blood of her fallen guardsman.

Her husband rushed to comfort her, but she stepped away, voicing her scorn at the nobility's plan to abandon the capital.

"*My lords, though it is not tradition for a council of men to hear a woman speak, you will listen to me nonetheless. We are all of us born to die, and for those of us who rule, that death cannot find us as exiles. My husband, to flee across the sea with our riches may preserve our lives, but that is a security I will not take.*

"*Because I will die before I let them take the purple that robes me. I will fight, for never will I see the day when those I meet do not call me Empress. Death comes for us, my husband, no matter our choices. You must simply decide on the color of your shroud.*"

So inspired by his wife's words, the Emperor of all of Rome decided to remain seated upon his throne. He called his generals to him, biding the great Belisarius to summon his legions.

"*March them into my capital,*" he proclaimed. "*Have them point their swords at the traitor Hypatius and all who would follow him.*"

The general obeyed, leading his soldiers to surround the venerable Hippodrome where the mob gathered for a coronation. And no sooner had a false crowned touched Hypatius's head, did those soldiers' swords spill the blood that would ink that page of history.

"It's a good story," Helena said. "Especially when you learn that Hypatius, Alexius, and Diocles all got their heads lopped off."

"Sad to have ... missed it," I panted, forcing my trembling limbs forward. "Although, the only mention we get is as a stain on the Empress's skin."

"That's you," she said. "I didn't bleed enough to be talked about."

We rounded a corner, moving through the halls of the Imperial Palace. Summer had faded into fall, but still, my body was sheathed in sweat. It had been more than two weeks since the attack on the palace, and days since my fever had broken, but I was still so damned weak.

"You're the one who saved us," I managed. "They should be singing your name at Kostas's."

"Yeah, well," she said, her face twisting into a grimace. "I'm happy to keep my part a secret. *Lena Cock-Taker* doesn't have a good ring to it."

I wheezed something like a laugh. "Is that how Doukas died, then?"

Helena nodded, grimly. "He bled out right there on the palace floor. We tossed his body into the same pit as the rest of those traitors."

Lady Irene and Lord Arethas appeared before I could say anything else. We exchanged a few pleasantries, Irene informing me that they were on their way to bid farewell to the Empress. They were returning to Samos, she said.

Lord Arethas, meanwhile, had the poleaxed gaze of one whose life had changed dramatically. And though he still appeared conflicted about his young wife's choice of dress, his eyes softened considerably when she looped her arm around his. They would be ok in the end, I thought.

Once they were gone, I lowered myself onto a nearby bench, needing a rest. Helena sat down beside me. This particular bench was before a columned window that looked out over the glittering expanse of the Marmara Sea. We breathed in air that smelled of salt and bathed in the golden light of the setting sun. We were silent for a while, my good hand finding one of hers.

And as they often had in the time since I'd regained real consciousness, my thoughts turned to the friends I'd lost. Sergius, Gratian, Niketas, Maurice, and Suda; dead so that we might live. They hadn't been the only soldiers to die in the defense of the palace, and though all who'd fallen had received the Emperor's thanks, only their squad had received that of the Empress.

She'd buried them with full honors, speaking at each one of their interments. Those widows and children who had been left behind would be cared for, their every need seen to by coin from the Empress's own purse.

I'd been to their graves yesterday, my first outing since leaving my sick bed. I had wept until my strength had left me. And though I'd mourn them for years to come, the edge was already fading from my grief.

I shifted my grip on Helena's hand, running my thumb along her callused palms. "I came so close to losing you."

She shifted closer to me. "You're the one that almost died."

"Before that," I said. "My mother's letter ... I almost threw it all away. But you didn't give up on me."

I squeezed her hand tightly. She lifted her head, and I gazed into the wonder of her features. "You saved my life," I told her, the words getting caught in the lump in my throat. "I love you, Helena. I love every part of you."

Her cypress eyes shone. She reached a hand up to cup my shaggy cheek, her lips curling into a soft smile. "And I love you, my shield-mate, more than you will ever know."

Our lips touched in a slow, tender sort of kiss. Once we parted, I pressed my forehead against hers, breathing in her warmth and scent.

Helena was here. She was beside me, and I was whole.

"Leo," she said, after a while. "You really stink."

I laughed, pulling away and meeting her grin with a quick smile. "Well, bathing is hard when you spend more than two weeks fighting off a fever and a near-mortal wound."

"Hmm, the rest of us just called it 'resting while there's work.'"

I laughed again and made to push myself to my feet, but Helena held me back.

"Let me check your bandage first," she said, getting up.

"Helena, we've barely left the Empress's wing. You don't need—"

"Hush," she said, moving to fuss over my shoulder.

I settled back down, trying not to wince as she prodded the wound with gentle fingers. Despite my somewhat cavalier attitude, I knew that it had been a near thing. The wound had been deep, cracking bone and severing muscle. Even now, a couple of weeks later, I had to keep my arm in a sling. The weight of it pulling on my shoulder was a constant ache, and any sort of movement beyond the twitch of my fingers sent pain throbbing far into me.

Yet it had been the fever that had nearly killed me. Infection had burned through my too-wounded body, barely kept at bay by the care of the expensive healers brought in by the Empress.

"We'll put some more of the salve on it after you bathe," Helena said. "Do you need help standing?"

I was about to answer her when the sound of chatter washed over us. A large group had turned into our hallway, and they came within sight of us a few moments later.

"Leontius," Antonina said from the head of the group. "I'm so pleased to see you on your feet."

The Empress's best friend swayed towards us, her curves crammed into a brightly colored gown. Her blonde hair was loosely braided, a few stray locks tumbling around her face.

"Or, at least, out of your bed," she said, quirking her lips at me.

"Thank you, Mistress," I said. I shifted to push myself to my feet, but Helena once again held me back.

"He needs to rest," she told her.

Behind Belisarius's wife, the group of men and women tittered. They were nobles, each of them sporting the frilly clothes and up-turned noses that I'd come to associate with that class.

"Oh, come now," Antonina said. "Surely he has the strength to greet an old friend?"

"He can speak to you from the bench," Helena said. "He's still very hurt."

"Perhaps we should let him decide?"

"He can decide all he wants," my shield-mate said. "But he's not getting off that bench."

Antonina's eyes glittered, her smile, curling up to reveal bright teeth. Helena remained in her place, holding the blonde woman's draconic stare.

I tried to swallow past my suddenly dry throat, shrinking back from the air that crackled between the two women.

"How dare you," a man said, stepping out from the herd of nobility. He jabbed a finger at Helena. "We know who you are, whore. You have no right to speak to your betters in such a way."

I saw my shield-mate struggle against the urge to roll her eyes.

Antonina, for her part, turned her glare onto the frilly noble. "You're an idiot, Davos," she snapped. "Keep your nose out of this."

I heard him gulp. "But, but ... Antonina!"

"Shut up! If I wanted to hear a dog bark, I'd throw meat onto the street."

The noble shrank back, to the snickers of his compatriots. But Antonina wasn't done. She swept her eyes over the gaggle of honking nobility, silencing them.

"Move on to the party," she ordered. "I'll catch up."

Nobody objected. The group scurried away, leaving the three of us alone in the palace hall.

"Interesting company you keep," Helena said, once they were out of earshot.

"Fools," Antonina said, shaking her head. "I swear, the only reason none of them sided with Hypatius is because they were too thick-headed to realize what was happening." Then, she let out a breath and surprised us with a warm smile. "I really am happy to see the both of you."

Helena narrowed her eyes. "Why?"

"Why shouldn't I be thankful to those who saved my life?" Antonina said. "We'd all have been doomed if Doukas had taken the Empress. And I know what you had to do to protect her."

The blonde woman surprised us again by wrapping Helena in a tight hug and kissing her on the cheek. "Thank you, Lena," she said. "Thank you."

"Yeah," Helena said, taken aback. "You're welcome."

"Hmm," Antonina said, drawing back. "And didn't I say that you were better on your knees than with a sword?" She laughed as my shield-mate flushed and sputtered. She turned to me next, wearing that same warm smile. "My thanks to you as well, Leontius."

Then, with a palm set on my good shoulder, she leaned in to kiss my cheek.

She moved with exaggerated slowness, granting me all the time I needed to take in the pendulum sway of her approaching cleavage and the golden chain that disappeared into that endless canyon.

"You did a lot for our Empress," she said, her voice low, smoldering with something deeper. She was still near enough to me that her scent, rich and spiced, was all I breathed. The soft valley of her breasts filled my vision. "And I hope that you'll soon be able to do the same for me."

I choked out a response, ripping my eyes away to give Helena a pleading look.

"Don't you have a party to go to?" she growled.

Antonina laughed, straightening as slowly as she'd leaned in. "Indeed, I do. If you're on your way to the baths, make sure you don't wash our Leontius too thoroughly. I quite like his smell."

"I will wash *my* shield-mate as much as *I* see fit," Helena said. "Aren't you going to be late?"

"Yes, yes," Antonina said, waving her hand. "I'm leaving. I also quite like your look today, Lena. It suits you."

"That damned woman," Helena muttered, her eyes following Antonina's vanishing form. "What the hell is she talking about?"

I knew, but for now, I simply let myself take in the sight of her. She was in her familiar green *tunica*, standing before the window, framed by the sea and the light of the setting sun. The sunset glowed on the bronze of her skin, setting the waves of her auburn hair alight.

"What?" she said, noticing my gaze on her.

I smiled and tried to put my thoughts into words. But how could I? How could I possibly describe the confidence that now shone within her? Or the new brightness in her eyes, or the strength of purpose that had settled onto her war-scarred body?

All of her—it was so wondrous, so *right*.

The woman standing before me was so much more than she'd been, and the glory of her shone bright enough to blind me.

"Shield-mate," I said. "You're so beautiful."

Helena flushed to the roots of her hair. She ducked her head, bashful in a way I wouldn't have thought possible. I blinked away tears, relieved that she'd caught something of the depth beneath my words. She moved to me, and I saw that beautiful vastness shift within her cypress eyes.

"My lion," she breathed, brushing her lips against mine. "Never look away from me."

"I love you," was my answer.

Then, after another gentle kiss, she pulled me to my feet. We continued down the hall, her arm attached to mine.

☧

I groaned as the hot water enveloped me, taking the weight of my arm off of my wounded shoulder.

"Don't get your bandages wet," Helena warned.

I grunted my response, leaning back into my seat in the steaming pool. We were in the Empress's bathing room, alone now that the servants had been dismissed. I relaxed, closed my eyes, and listened to the sound of Helena preparing something at the table behind me.

Eventually, I felt her palm on the nape of my neck. "Lean forward."

I obeyed, allowing her to sit behind me on the pool's edge. She slipped her bare legs into the water, pulling me back into the space between them.

She scooped out some of the water with her hand, wetting the flesh of my good shoulder, and washing away the grime of weeks with a soft, soap-lathered rag.

"This is the only sort of bath I ever want," I said, sinking into her touch. "I need to get injured more often."

Helena laughed softly, pushing me forward so she could wash my back. "I should let you bathe yourself, then. I don't want to encourage you."

I opened my eyes. "Well, it'll be harder now. I'm done with war."

"You're going to retire?"

Her voice, I thought, sounded much too casual. I smiled, though she couldn't see. "As soon as I'm healed enough to use my arm."

Helena's fingers kept working, gently scrubbing at my back. "What will you do?"

"I'd like to go back to Rhodos," I said. "I'm thinking of buying a boat, sailing it over, and building a little tavern by the sea."

Her hands paused, and it was several long moments before she spoke. "Back to your mother?"

I made to shrug and then decided against it. "Just long enough to answer her letter. She lives too far from the coast for me."

Helena hummed an answer, pulling me backward once again. She reached down over my shoulder, starting on my chest and neck.

It was several more moments before she said, "You're probably not a very good sailor."

"I'm terrible," I acknowledged. "And I'm not much of a builder, to tell you the truth."

She snorted, though I heard the smile in her voice. "Those are some definite flaws in your plan."

"Maybe," I said, sure that she could hear my grin. "But I'm hoping to find someone who'll come along and help. Know anyone who might be willing to be my partner?"

"I'm not sure," she said, drawing out the words.

There was a splash of water as she stood and stepped from the bath. I heard the rustle of cloth and the sound of wet feet walking over tile. Helena stepped into the pool across from me, naked save for her smile and dancing eyes.

She glided towards me, moving slowly enough that I might drink in the wonder of her shifting muscles and rippling curves. Water lapped against me as she set her knees on either side of me on the bench, her legs straddling and sliding against my own.

"I know a woman," she said. Her smile shifted into an exaggerated frown of consideration. "But she might not be a good fit. Your mother would hate her."

"I'd be happy to assure her that my mother has absolutely no say in this."

Helena made an approving sound in her throat. She looped her arms around my neck, keeping her back straight so that her face was above mine. Her large, naked breasts filled my view, and I could feel her smirk as my eyes devoured her.

"Well, partners might stand one behind the other," she said. She let herself sink atop me. "And this woman wouldn't be interested in that."

"Hmm," I said, resting my good hand on her hip. "What about something more? I could swear an oath."

"Maybe." She leaned closer to me, her nipples brushing my chest. "Although it would depend on what you swear."

I slid my palm along her curving shape, amazed that my fingers could ever be this clean. "I'd swear myself to her, vowing to continue to stand by her side."

I looked up into her cypress eyes, seeing the whole, wondrous, uncovered vastness of her love. "I'd promise to keep believing in her, knowing that she'll hold that place beside me. We'd face what comes, together, her shield locked onto mine. Do you think that's enough?"

"I think she'd accept those terms," Helena murmured. Her face drifted towards me, her copper-colored hair ticking my flesh. "But it takes a kiss to seal an oath."

"What sort of kiss?" I wondered.

Her laughter was a swirl of warmth on my skin.

"My lion," she breathed, pressing her lips to mine. "Always hungry."

The Patriarch's Indulgence

Epilogue

I SHUT THE DOOR on the newest pair of the Empress's Guards, moving through the corridor towards her salon. My eyes drifted to the spots where my friends had died, searching the cracks between the stones for any trace of them.

But summer had faded into fall, which had withered into winter to then bloom into spring; what blood Sergius, Gratian, Niketas, Maurice, and Suda had left behind had long since been washed away. It was better this way, I thought. It was hard to move on if you left too much of yourself behind.

I entered the Empress's open and airy salon, setting my shield down against the wall. I rolled my armored shoulders, feeling a low throb of pain where I'd been wounded. It didn't bother me much anymore, though some days were worse than others.

A slow breeze drifted through the empty room and, on a whim, I decided to follow its source. Despite the weight of my thoughts and armor, I felt myself grow lighter with every step. By the time I emerged onto the open balcony, I thought that I might float up into the sky.

As of this moment, I was officially retired.

I leaned out over the balustrade, staring out over Constantinople for what might very well be the last time.

It had changed much in the months since the Blues and Greens had nearly torn it apart. The Emperor had poured money into repairing his capital, employing thousands to clear the streets of debris and rebuild what so much fire and fury had destroyed.

The Hippodrome's new seating gleamed in the evening sun, and beyond it, I could see the framework of the Hagia Sofia rising from the ashes of its predecessor. The construction would take years, for the Emperor had declared that this new cathedral would be unlike any the world had ever seen. It would be a symbol of the Empire's faith, of its strength and resilience.

Peace with the Sassanid Persians was also going well. News had just reached of old King Kavadh's death, and the new Persian ruler was already proving to be much more amenable. There was real hope now, or so I was told, for there to be an eternal peace between our two empires.

Of course, Helena and I would be long gone by the time all this was settled. Then, as if she'd stepped from my very mind, I heard my shield-mate's voice behind me. "How's the view?"

I turned, finding Helena gliding towards me with a small smile curling her lips. The sight of her melted whatever thoughts I'd had in my head.

Her body was sheathed in layers of tight silk, the thin, emerald fabric doing little to mask her curving shape. The hem of her *stola* swirled down around her feet, the neckline cut deliciously low. The exposed slice of her chest quivered with each of her swaying steps, the whole of it pinned in a way that left much of her shoulders and arms bare.

Her waves of auburn hair had been tamed, made to shine with oil, and piled elegantly atop her head. I didn't even try to speak, delighting in the vision of her, mesmerized in the glow of her bronzed flesh and the sparkle deep within her cypress eyes.

"I always have to repeat myself around you," she teased, leaning a palm against my chest to kiss my lips.

"The view?" I breathed deeply. Her scent filled my nose: a warm swirl of cedar and oil layered over her familiar blend of sweat, salt, and sun. "The view is much better here."

She smiled, a faint curl of heat traveling up her bare neck. "Do you like it? It's been a long time since I've worn a *stola* and ... I feel a bit ridiculous, honestly."

"You look amazing," I said, reaching out to slide my palms along the cool silk hugging her hips and ribs. "Although, it doesn't look very practical for the shield wall."

Her smile widened into a grin. "Good thing I'm retired."

I laughed, pulling her closer. "Well, you've also got to sail us to Rhodes tomorrow. Can you manage that?"

"Oh, my lion," she breathed, looping her arms around my neck. "There's a lot that I can do in this dress."

Then, she kissed me, deeply enough that I could taste the tide rising within her. My heart was pounding by the time we parted, sending sparks of heat rising through me.

"Hmm," she said, pink staining her cheeks. "Maybe, I'll wear this more often."

I jerked my head up and down, taking the time to peek into the shadowed depths of her cleavage. She laughed. "Happy retirement, love."

"Thanks," I said. "I feel so ... good."

Helena's gaze softened, she made to speak but I cut her off with a grin. "I got you something."

"Oh?" she said, taking the pouch that I drew out from beneath my armor. "Honeyed figs?"

"Are they squished?" I asked. "I tried to be careful ..."

"They're perfect," she said, popping one in her mouth. She chewed blissfully for a few moments, kissing my cheek. "Thank you. But shouldn't I be the one getting you a gift?"

"You retired this morning, as well," I reminded her. I made a show of looking her up and down. "Besides, I already have my gift."

Helena rolled her eyes, looped her arm around mine, and pulled me forward. "Save your hunger, my lion. We have a dinner to attend."

"I still don't understand why I have to wear my armor," I said, letting her guide me deeper into the Empress's quarters. "It's not comfortable to sit in."

"Antonina insisted," Helena answered. "And the Empress didn't object. Is your shoulder okay?"

I grumbled out a few words before letting out a breath. "It's fine. I'll just suffer while you all lounge about in comfort."

"My poor shield-mate," she said. "Forced to spend an evening with three beautiful women."

I laughed, squeezing her arm. "Aye, fair enough. It'll just be the three of us then?"

Helena made an affirmative sound.

"And, uh ..." I cleared my throat. "Do the Emperor and General know we're eating together?"

"Oh yes," she said.

Then, instead of turning towards the Empress's private dining room, Helena led me onward.

"Helena," I said, slowing down. "This is the way to ..."

"Don't worry," she said, pulling me into Theodora's bed chamber. "Everyone knows exactly what we're having for dinner."

This was a room I'd seen before, though no more than a handful of times.

The Empress's sleeping quarters were large and opened to the outside through a couple of windows and a balcony. Her large bed lay beneath one such window. The mattress stretched into the room, cornered by tall posts and shrouded in muslin curtains.

Dozens of paintings, tapestries, sculptures, and crosses decorated the walls. There was a little seating area of thickly upholstered chairs and divans by the ocean-facing balcony.

And it was from these divans that the two women rose.

"Finally," Antonina exclaimed, setting down a goblet of wine. "You took your sweet time with him, Lena."

"As is my right," Helena said.

She squeezed my arm once before releasing me. She moved towards Antonina and the Empress, the two women resplendent in their own ensembles of layered silk.

"Remember our deal," the blonde woman said. "I get to go first."

"Yes, yes, Nina," Helena said, draping herself over one of the divans. "Don't worry."

"What is ..." I started, swallowing my words when the attention of the three women fell upon me. "Uh ... food?"

Helena laughed, while Antonina's smile turned wicked. "Oh, I'm going to enjoy this."

"Why don't you come sit with us," the Empress said, finally speaking up. "Let's relax a little."

Her smile was warm, though topped with the extra curl of one who knew a secret you did not. My body jerked into motion, pulled forward by the crook of her beckoning fingers.

I was off-balance, knocked off-kilter by the heat I saw blooming within three pairs of eyes. I didn't know what was happening, and my face burned scarlet.

God help me, these women were perfect.

They were more than beautiful, especially with all the effort they had put into dressing themselves this evening.

My Helena was all muscled limbs over areas of remarkable softness, a contrast of strength and sensuous femininity. She shone in her green dress, the color lovely against her bronze skin, auburn hair, and bright, cypress eyes.

Antonina was lusciously curved, a sultry package of blonde hair and milky flesh wrapped in blue silk. I could see a dragon's hunger smoldering within the depths of her eyes, and a predator's fangs veiled in the shadows of her smile.

The Empress was in pale lavender. The soft fabric seemed to flow along her body, clinging to her lithe, dancer's frame. Her dress had slits along both legs, exposing an endless length of smooth, dark flesh. Gold glinted around her arms and ankles, bands of it visible in the complicated, braided chevrons of her walnut hair.

"I think our Leontius approves of our preparation, ladies," the Empress said, her smile curling even higher.

She reached for my arm, pulling me over to a divan, where I was made to sit in the middle. My armored bulk didn't leave much space, but Theodora and her best friend squeezed themselves in on either side of me.

"I should hope so," Antonina said, trailing her fingers along my bracers. Her huge breasts pushed against my bicep. "It took long enough."

I stiffened, trying to shift away, but the Empress was pressed against my other side. She had an arm thrown over my shoulder, her other hand picking at the edge of my armored skirt.

"It did," she said. "But I think that it'll all be worth it."

"What?!" I coughed. "Preparations?"

Helena was seated alone, on a divan across from us. I met her eyes with all the desperation of a drowning man, but I found no succor in her reddened cheeks and satisfied smirk.

"Of course," she said, fingers reaching up to play with the edge of her neckline. "These *stola*, washing, grooming, oiling ... A proper Patriarch's Indulgence takes a lot of work."

"I still don't know what that is."

My voice was a bit ragged, frayed by the cloud of heat my pounding heart sent billowing through me. Sparks shot down to my crotch, bringing it to life.

"It's very simple, my Leontius," the Empress said, her fingers tugging at the straps of my bracers. "When we used to work at the brothel, the Patriarch himself was one of our more frequent clients."

"'*To forgive you wicked women the sins of your flesh'*, he always used to say." Antonina's fingers worked the straps of my breastplate loose as she spoke. "Although that just seemed to mean sticking his cock into as many of us as he could afford."

"Well," the Empress said, "for a sin to be forgiven, it must first be committed."

The others laughed, but I was rapidly losing awareness of anything that wasn't the silk-wrapped flesh of the two women beside me.

Flames rose inside me, fanned by their touch and the spiced, floral blend of their perfumes.

"So," I managed. "This is ..."

"The meal I promised you, my lion," Helena said, her chest flushed and her smile pleased. "Happy retirement."

I searched her face, glancing at both other women in turn. I couldn't quite believe what was happening, no matter how much my stiffening cock screamed it was true.

Antonina shifted against me."Although, you're not the only one who's going to eat."

I coughed, drawing out another tinkle of laughter from the three women.

"My poor Leontius," the Empress said, her smile warm and eyes hot. "I apologize for just springing this on you, but Lena said it would be better as a surprise."

"*Augusta* ... I—"

"Oh, no," Theodora interrupted. "You're with Dora again. And for tonight ..."

She leaned into me, my hand instinctively reaching for the cool silk at her hip. Her nose brushed against mine, her breath swirling over my lips.

"Indulge in us."

Then, she kissed me. Her lips were soft, yet moved with firm insistence. She explored me, eager, without the frantic need of our last encounter.

"Ah," Antonina said, pulling me away from the Empress. "That's not how this is going to be."

"What?" I asked, my head spinning.

"We promised Nina that we'd obey her in this first part," Helena explained. "It was the only way to get her to agree to this."

"That's to be expected," Antonina said, tilting my face towards her with a finger. "I'm the only one he hasn't fucked yet."

She pressed her lips into mine, opening herself to me. She was the dragon I remembered, and I could taste the heat of her hunger. That fire was fuel to the one within me; I kissed her back, letting her taste my own burning desire.

When we parted, Antonina's eyes were bright with predatory delight. "Ah, there's that lion." She pushed herself to her feet, clapping her hands loudly. "Right, stand up. We need to get this armor off. Dora, get his boots. Lena, help me with the breastplate."

I stood and watched as Rome's Empress slid down to the floor and untied my boots, an amused expression on her face. Helena made her way over as well, working with Antonina on the straps of my armor.

"Are you sure about this?" I asked her, knowing that I wouldn't be able to stop if we went any further.

Helena smiled. "Everyone here knows where their heart belongs, my shield-mate. Yours is mine, and nothing that happens here will change that."

I nodded because every word she'd said was true.

"Besides," the Empress said, pulling off my second boot. "Lena has you for the rest of her life. But this might be our last chance."

"Stay on your knees, Dora," Antonina ordered, once I was in nothing but my *tunica* and loincloth. She gestured impatiently for me to remove my outer garment, taking it with her as she moved back to her goblet of wine. "Lena, you get down there as well."

Helena smirked but obeyed.

Both women knelt just an arm's length from the noticeable bulge between my legs, copper and green beside purple and gold.

"Good," Nina purred, bringing the wine to her lips. "Now take out your cock."

I hesitated a moment, looking down to meet Helena's gaze, checking one last time for any hint of doubt or discomfort. But I saw none. There was only the vastness of her love behind her cypress eyes. And the rising ocean of her desire.

"I love you," I told her, making that vastness shine.

Then, with a final thanks to God for the blessing of these women, I undid my loincloth. My erection sprang out, and all three women gazed upon it with hungry, heavy-lidded eyes.

"Nobody touch!" Antonina said, still a few paces away.

I looked towards her, just in time to see her blue, silken dress puddle at her feet.

My heart pounded as my gaze moved down from her wicked smile. Her naked breasts were milk-pale and heavy. Her stomach was surprisingly flat, her hips and thighs wide and decadent. She sauntered over to where the other two women knelt, her flesh jiggling with every swaying step.

"The first taste is mine," she said, kneeling between Helena and the Empress.

They laughed from low in their throats. Antonina wrapped her hand around my cock, stroking me slowly and leaning towards the tip. "God," she said. "I remember that stink."

Her hand moved faster, heat blooming beneath her naked pallor. Helena and the Empress leaned in as well, inhaling deeply. Theodora quietly moaned, her fingers digging into my thigh for balance. Helena's lips had parted, her breath coming faster.

"Mmm," Antonina said, still breathing me in. "And you fools wanted him to bathe."

"Not me," the Empress said.

"Nina," Helena breathed. "Hurry."

She laughed, rolled my foreskin back, and tasted me. I groaned as her silken tongue caressed the tip of my spear. She coated me in her spit, licking every burning inch of my cock.

Then, she pulled me into her mouth, her tongue swirling, her eyes on mine. She bobbed her head, not once looking away from me. She took me to the back of her throat, letting me see the hunger that raged in her. Then, she came off me with a pop, stood, and shoved me back to the divan.

I sat down heavily, in time to wrap one arm around the swell of her waist as she slid in beside me. I grabbed a fistful of her ass, marveling at the weight of it. She wrenched my face towards her, locking her lips to mine.

The kiss was ferocious, her breath sour with wine and the stink of my cock. I pulled her into my lap, mashing her heavy tits against my chest and grinding my mouth into hers. Her hips started to roll, rubbing herself against my hardness.

Suddenly, her fingers gripped my hair and she jerked my head away. She started at me with slitted eyes, the space between us filled with the fire of our panting breaths. We were lion and dragon, each of us recognizing the hunger within the other. We would glut ourselves on the other's body, taking all we could while being taken from in turn.

She bared her teeth into a savage smile, and within me, that same primal thrill surged.

"Ah," she rasped. "What a mess we'll make of each other."

I squeezed her naked hips, and her smile curled into something pleased. She arched back, granting me a full view of her breasts. They were two mounds of pale cream, her nipples the cherries on top.

"But not yet," she sighed, sliding back onto the couch.

I growled something, turning to glare at her, but she just laughed. She was on her knees on the cushions beside me, her back straight.

She kept me still by squashing her naked breasts against my face and wrapping a hand around my manhood. She started to stroke me, and with the arm that was still around her waist, I slapped my palm against her ass.

Antonina laughed, crooking a finger at the two women that I'd nearly forgotten were there.

"Come," she ordered. "You can have your taste."

I watched with fever-hot eyes as Helena and the Empress moved towards us. But they didn't get up to walk. No, they crawled towards my cock, two, eager little kittens desperate for their treat.

"Look how good they are," Antonina purred. She kept stroking me. "So hungry for a taste."

I groaned my agreement, turning to pull one of her cherry-stiff nipples into my mouth. I flicked my tongue over it, causing her to shiver. She pumped me faster, releasing my cock only when the other two women arrived.

"Let's give him something special," Helena said.

I peered down at her from where my face was still buried in Antonina's flesh. I sucked on one breast, watching as Helena kissed my inner thigh, running her tongue along its sensitive flesh. The Empress's hand, meanwhile, took the place of her best friend's. She stroked me, taking a moment to breathe me in.

"From the tip?" she asked.

Helena, her body still wrapped in green silk, made a sound of approval. Then, the two women wrapped their lips around my bulbous head. A growl rumbled from me. I gripped Antonina's ass, scoring one of her nipples with my teeth and making her gasp.

But still, I watched both kneeling women. It was like they were trying to reach around my manhood to kiss each other. The sensation was otherworldly; the only thing better than the feeling of one moist tongue and mouth on me was the feeling of two.

"Good," Antonina breathed, watching with me as both women worked their lips down my shaft. "So good."

Then she pulled away from me, her breast popping out of my mouth. She pushed herself upright, standing on the couch, my hand sliding down the smooth flesh of her leg.

I looked up, past Antonina's reddened tits and into her burning eyes. She gave me a draconic grin, stepping across to straddle me. I ran both my hands up and down her silken legs, while she wove the fingers of one hand into my hair.

Her thick waist was level with my eyes. I lost sight of the two women sucking my cock as Antonina shifted closer. She lifted a foot to place it on the sofa's backrest, filling my vision with the glory of her unfurling sex

My fingers tightened around each of her legs. Everything within me roared, but the sound emerged as a low moan.

Her pussy was shaved bald, her folds tight and neatly packed away within her. I heard her breath catch, one finger from her free hand coming down to slide along her silken crease.

"Fuck," she said. Her voice was an airy little gasp that deepened with every word. "Fuck ... Dora, Lena ... look how he wants it." Her finger emerged shiny with her own wetness. She curled it right back into herself.

"Then give it to him," I heard Helena say.

I felt the Empress take me completely into her mouth. I shifted my hips up, going deeper into her. But I still held on to Antonina, my gaze fixed on her razed wetness.

"Mmm," she said, sliding her finger free. "Come eat then, my lion."

I moved slowly, wanting to savor my first taste of her. I took a moment to inhale her thick, decadent scent. I ran the tip of my tongue along the skin just to the side of her ready seam, tasting her sweat and the perfumed oil she'd rubbed into herself.

"Don't tease me," she growled. I felt her fingers flex in my hair, but I wouldn't be rushed.

Between my legs, I was still wrapped in someone's mouth, while another mouth sucked on one of my testicles. Antonina was spread wide before me, and I took a moment to gaze into her pink, glistening lushness.

I brought my face to her, first tasting her outer folds. She moaned, pushing her hips against me, grinding her pussy into my mouth. So, I dove deeper, lapping at her wetness, taking all I could of her. Her taste was layered, luxurious in its richness. It was overindulgence, a taste that bade you to wallow in it. She was dessert after a feast, the sweetness that led to rot.

I glutted myself with her, but my hunger was not so easily sated.

It wasn't long before I scooted back, freeing my cock from the two eager mouths, and surged upward into Nina. I got my feet under me, my shoulder driving into her waist. She folded over me with a squawk, so that when I stood, she was slung over one shoulder.

"What are you—"

I carried her to the bed, throwing her onto the mattress so that she landed on her back. She made a sound between a laugh and growl, her eyes burning and flesh red with heat. She spread her legs, opening herself to me.

The bed was tall. My hips were level with hers though I still stood on the floor. I yanked her to the edge.

"Fuck," she panted. "Put it in!"

I lined my member up with one hand. Nina raised her hips to meet me, her delectable body spread out before me.

"Helena, Dora," I growled. "Come."

"No," Nina snarled. "You're mine! Me—"

I thrust into her. She stiffened, clawing at the sheets, her cloying sex slick enough to swallow me whole. I shifted my hands to grip both of her ankles. I stretched her wide and stabbed into her again and again. Her face contorted, a canyon-deep moan emerging from her lips.

Her pussy was tight around me, her inner ridges drawing me deeper. Her massive tits rebounded as I fucked her, the room filling with the wet slap of our flesh.

Then, Theodora was there. She trailed her fingers across my back, pressing her silk-wrapped body against my side. I let go of one of Nina's legs, hugging Dora's waist. I turned to kiss her, still thrusting into the mewling blonde.

Her scent washed over me: a floral-wrapped sharpness that swirled into the rich cloud of Antonina's arousal.

I pulled Dora tighter against me, kissing her harder. She moaned into my lips, her tongue as desperately hungry as my own.

Another form slid in beside me, and this time I smelled cedar and sun-kissed skin. It was Helena. I turned towards her, growling when I saw that she'd left her dress behind. I used my other arm to pull her to me, her body naked and warm.

Her breasts pressed against my side, and when our lips met, I tasted the ocean of her desire.

Dora and Lena's mouths were hot, their breaths sour with the heat from my cock. But I loved the taste of me on them, and so I kissed them both again and again.

A clench of Nina's pussy brought my attention back to her. She'd propped herself onto her elbows, the golden links of her chain sticking to her lust-reddened body.

"Fuck me!" She growled up to where I still stood on the floor. "Leave them alone and keep fucking me! I go first! You're *mine*!

I had slowed my thrusting, distracted by the taste of other bodies. But now I picked up speed, hammering my cock into her and matching her snarl with one of my own.

Lena and Theodora were still wrapped around me, my arms around their waists and fingers squeezing their hips and asses. They each held onto one of Antonina's ankles stretching her bald, little slit wide for me.

"Fuck her," Dora moaned in my ear. "Break her."

"My lion," Helena breathed into my other, "oh, my lion."

Lena was the rising storm, the tide that lapped at the shore. She rolled her naked body against me, grinding her dripping sex up and down my thigh.

Nina's breath was coming into ragged bursts. She sunk back into the sheets, my hips pounding into her again and again.

"It's coming," Dora said, her fingers gripping my hair. "Oh, fuck."

"Make her scream," Lena purred, my leg slick with her moisture.

A few more thrusts into the blonde, and I saw it too. Her gasps were getting louder, and deeper. She arched her hips into me, her eyes rolling back. She grabbed one of her flopping tits, clawing at the nipple.

Then, her body went rigid and she screamed, as her orgasm tore through her.

I grinned, hearing the two other women purr in pleasure. I kept thrusting into her until I felt her go limp, slowing but never stopping as I watched her come back to herself. She met my eyes with a heavy-lidded gaze and a curl of her lips.

I finally stopped but stayed inside her as Lena wrenched my head to the side. Her cock-sour breath washed over me as she mashed her lips into mine. She ground herself harder against my leg, her hips rolling with the ocean of her need.

I felt Dora slip out of my grip, but paid her no mind.

I slid my arm from around Lena's waist, working my fingers into the soaked snarl of her pubic hair. She moaned, her toes curling on the stone floor. She kissed me harder, shifting her hips back to let me dig a pair of my fingers into her steaming center.

Our lips parted. We were still pressed together, my sweat coating Helena's flesh. We panted into the space between us, gazing into each other's flushed faces.

"I love you," I grated.

"My lion." She let out a breathy little gasp, grinding herself harder onto my penetrating fingers. "Show me."

I turned fully towards her, my cock finally slipping from Nina's stretched pussy. I knelt on the floor between Lena's legs, bringing my tongue to her lust-swollen folds. I kept my fingers inside her, stroking her inner layers while I drank from her sour heat.

She moaned, her hips rolling against my face. I felt her pussy flex around my tongue and fingers. The ocean was churning within her, the storm gathering higher and higher.

I pulled myself from her before it broke, standing and turning both of us towards the bed.

That's when I noticed that Nina hadn't moved; her legs were still spread at the edge of the high mattress. She was pinned, I saw, by the smothering wetness of Theodora's sex over her face.

The darker-skinned woman's knees were on either side of Antonina's head, her back straight. She ground her pussy over Nina's features, her eyes glassy, facing Helena and me from the other end of Antonina's body.

Dora hadn't bothered to remove the purple that hugged her body. The slits along each side of her dress let her simply hold the central flap of cloth with her teeth, exposing everything below her rippling stomach.

The blonde woman shifted, wrapping her arms around Theodora's thighs. Her throat flexed, her tongue working deep within the rolling Empress.

Lena was the first of us to move.

She pulled away from me, crawling atop Nina's body. Her back was to me, her tits hanging over Antonina's. She dropped her hips, shifting so that her pussy met Nina's.

Helena's back arched upward; her hands planted on the bed on either side of the blonde woman's body. She started to rock her hips, smearing her wetness against Nina's reddened slit.

Theodora's face steamed with red heat. She reached up, yanking on her dress's neckline until she freed her chest. Her rosewood nipples were stiff in the open air, her breasts shivering with every grinding flex of her hips. Then she leaned forward towards Helena, letting the saliva-soaked flap of her dress slip from between her lips so that she could press them into Lena's.

My shield-mate responded with an eager growl. She planted a hand on Thedora's hip, pushing her harder onto Nina's face, and returned her kiss with abandon. Dora mewled into Helena's mouth, reaching with a hand to tug and squeeze at Lena's large, swaying tits. Antonina, her face now hidden by a tent of cloth, moaned into Dora's liquid seam. She shifted her hips, angling her stomach to better rub her swollen hole against Helena's silken pussy.

The three of them had made a triangle of their bodies. I watched them coat each other in their wetness, my hand stroking my cock. Blooded roared in my ears, my chest heaving. It was hard to breathe. The air was thick with their arousal: a sharp scent of decadent sweetness and sour sweat.

My hand worked faster.

The liquid slither of Nina and Lena's grinding pussies was hypnotic. My eyes were drawn to the strands of shining moisture that stretched between them and snapped whenever they shifted. Helena broke from Dora and peered back at me over her shoulder, her lips parted by the fog of her breath. Strands of her sweat-darkened fell over her eyes, slowly unraveling the once elegant pile atop her head.

Finally, I could bear it no longer. With my feet still on the floor, I lifted Lena's hips, angled them, and drove my cock into her.

She gasped, taking all of me into her lush sex. I didn't waste time with any slow thrusts, grasping two great handfuls of her ass and hammering into her.

"Fuck," she panted. "Leo, oh fuck—"

Her body churned like the ocean, her tits swinging above Nina's. Her ass rippled with the thunder of my every thrust. She stiffened into numb surrender, her head flopping limply with every slap of our hips. Dora pulled Lena's face to her chest, their sweat and heat mingling.

I knew Helena's body, and after a minute, when I knew that she was close, I pulled my cock from her and thrust down into Nina's still-waiting pussy.

Her hole was hot and eager, welcoming me easily into her liquid depths. I heard the blonde woman moaned into Theodora's slit, her legs shivering on either side of me as I speared into her again and again. Lena whimpered her dismay, shoving her hips and reddened ass back. She rolled against me, a wave on the edge of breaking.

Dora silenced her by weaving her fingers into her auburn hair and pulling her up into another ferocious kiss. Then, while their lips were still locked together, I pulled out of Nina and jammed my cock back into Lena's desperate slit.

She gasped into Dora's mouth, her ass rippling with each one of my thrusts. I pounded into her, bringing her to the edge before once again slipping out of her and into Antonina. I switched between the two women for the next several minutes, my hands alternating between gripping Lena's hips to Nina's legs.

At some point, Theodora had slipped off of Antonina. The blonde woman's eyes were slitted in pleasure, her chin and lips slick with Dora's juices. She clawed at Lena's body and sucked on her tits every time I fucked her, stretching back on the sheets to watch Helena's flesh quiver above her whenever I moved to thrust into Lena.

My breath was ragged, my vision hazy from the heat of my flesh and muscles. Sweat coated my chest and back, dripping from my forehead to splatter against Helena's naked back. I was fucking her now, my hands clamped around her hips.

Directly across from me was Theodora. She was on the bed just behind Antonina's skull, leaning back against one hand, her legs spread open. The central flap of cloth was back in her mouth, her tits heaving and her eyes fever-bright. She watched me fuck both women, pumping two fingers in and out of her spit-matted pussy.

Helena's body clenched around my cock, the ocean within her a roiling maelstrom of built-up pleasure and desperate need.

"Leo," she panted, her face just about Nina's. "I can't—Fuck ..." That last word was a deep, toe-curling moan.

Helena's hands dug into the sheets, strands of her copper hair glued to the sweat of her back. I felt the moment that the tide broke and pulled out of her as she screamed her storm.

Rain burst from her, spattering Nina's nakedness.

She whimpered, her body flexing as another deluge sprayed from between her legs. She drenched Nina in her body's liquid, squirting once more before collapsing onto the blonde woman.

Antonina bared eager fangs, grabbed a fistful of Lena's hair, and pulled the woman's lips to hers. Their tongues writhed around each other's, their tits and lust-reddened flesh slipping in the sweat and spray that coated them.

I left them there, grinding atop each other, and got onto the bed, moving towards where Dora waited for me.

"Break me," she said, pulling her fingers from her pussy.

I shoved her onto her back, thrusting into her with a groan. Dora's dew-drenched sex welcomed me within its silken folds, her hips bucking with my every motion. I held myself atop her, breathing in the hot stink from her every gasp and whimper.

I lowered myself down onto my elbows, carpeting myself over her and wrapping her head and shoulders in my arms. I thrust into her faster, feeling her naked tits slide against my sweat-drenched chest. Dora's nails tore into my back. I gripped her walnut and gold hair, holding her tight.

She moaned in my ear, wrapping her legs around me and rolling her hips. I stirred her depths with my cock, staying within her while her orgasm built.

At some point, I reared up and stretched my arms out to clamp my hands around the underside of her knees to lift her legs up high. Then, I leaned my weight into her, folding her flexible, dancer's body partly over itself and driving my cock into her with all the power I could bring to bear.

Theodora cried out, throwing her head back, her rosewood nipples pointing to the ceiling. "Fuck! I'm almost there! Oh God! Fuck—"

I fucked her hard, though it only took a handful more pounding thrusts until, with another scream to heaven, she finished.

Her orgasm left her weak and trembling. But I wasn't done, pulling her towards where the other two women still played.

Nina was still on her back, stretched out, undulating her hips. Lena was now upright, leaning into one of the blonde's legs. She mashed her hairy pussy into Nina's, her cypress eyes fogged with pleasure. Her hair dripped with sweat, and her naked, spray-soaked tits heaved with every gasp of hot air that she pulled in between her parted lips.

I pushed Dora onto all fours so she straddled Nina's face. The blonde woman growled her eager approval, tilting her head back to meet my eyes from beneath Dora's slit. That same, draconic hunger burned within her, and she opened her mouth to receive me.

I grinned as I slipped my cock between her lips. I didn't pump into her, however, merely held myself there while she licked me clean.

When I was ready, I pulled myself away and thrust back into Dora.

The woman whimpered, collapsing into the mess of fluid that was Nina's pale body. Dora kept her ass arched up, however, holding her pussy just above the blonde's face.

"I want it," Antonina begged. Dora's juices splattered her waiting features, her nose and chin tickling my swinging testicles. "Come for me. I want it."

I was so close, fire raging through all of me. I hammered into Theodora as hard as I could, watching her gasp and squirm. My eyes met Helena's and some instinct must have pierced the haze of her mind because she threw herself at me.

She pushed Dora down, crawled over her, and kissed me just as I erupted into the Empress.

Distantly, past the raging heat of my orgasm, and the feel of Lena's lips on mine; I felt Nina's tongue lap at the bit of my milky fluid that leaked from Dora's sex. So, I shifted my hips back, pulling out and letting thick gobs of it fall into her eager mouth.

When my orgasm abated, I fell backward onto the bed.

The three women crumpled into a pile of sweat-soaked limbs. They untangled themselves, rolling apart to lie panting on the Empress's wide bed.

Heat vented off of me, my heart thundering like the hooves of chariot team. For several long moments, the four of us did nothing b breathe. Then, one by one, the women pushed themselves up and moved towards me.

First, there was Helena, her jungle of pubic hair matted and muscles taut beneath her sticky flesh.

Antonina was second, her luscious body crusted with sex and stinking of all of us. Her tongue flicked out, swallowing the last little bit of my seed from around her lips.

Finally, there was the Empress. A mix of our juices dribbled down her leg, her hair a mess of hanging locks and gold.

I looked into the faces of all three and I laughed low in my throat. For within each, I saw a hunger that, like my own, had yet to be sated.

"It's not even dark yet," Antonina said, her breasts swinging as she crawled forward.

"And we don't leave until morning," Helena added. She was upright against me, her skin hot, my arm wrapped around her thighs.

"Mmm," the Empress said. She stood on her mattress and finally shimmied her tight body out of her lust-soiled dress. "A dinner party can't end without dessert."

"Perfect," I said. "Because I'm still hungry."

"My lion," Helena purred, pulling my face into her naked chest. "Of course you are."

Historical Note

Following the events of the Nika Riots, and the subsequent "Eternal Peace" with the Sassanid Persians that lasted a bare eight years, Justinian and Theodora would go on to oversee a period of great legal reform and territorial expansion.

Laws were changed and codified, corruption was stamped out, and Belisarius (often accompanied by Antonina) led their armies in the recapture of many old Imperial provinces in places like North Africa, Spain, and even the Italian Peninsula and Rome itself.

It was a time of great upheaval and change. Central to some of the era's most interesting (in my opinion) changes was the Empress Theodora.

Theodora was a woman born into poverty, an alleged prostitute and actress whose rise to Empress would have shocked her contemporaries. She is today a canonized saint of the Orthodox Church, and is remembered as a ferocious champion of women's rights, a devout early Christian, and a supporter of her society's most downtrodden.

The laws she put in place for the protection of young women were seen as particularly radical.

Much is unknown about her early life. Procopius's *Secret History* is our foremost source on the matter, and in his record, he describes Theodora (and Antonina) as former prostitutes of shameless sexual appetites. Yet, as is the case for many powerful women whose stories were written by men, their sexual promiscuity was likely greatly exaggerated. Today, much of Procopius's works are highly criticized and are seen as inaccurate and overly slanderous.

So, while *The Silken Empress* leans into this aspect of Theodora, the truth about the woman is likely different. To write her this way was my own narrative choice, as it lends itself well to the story I wished to tell.

What cannot be debated is that Theodora was a truly remarkable woman in a time when women were not permitted to be remarkable. I encourage you to read more about her, for while I touched briefly on some of her achievements within this book, there were many more that I left out.

Rate and Review

Thank you so much for taking a chance on *The Silken Empress*. This story was a labor of love, and I truly hope that you enjoyed reading it as much as I did writing it.

If you've made it this far and would like to see more of my writing, please take the time to rate and review this book. This is my debut novel, and as an indie author, your feedback is the literal lifeblood of my career.

Once again, thank you so much for reading. I hope to see you soon, within the pages of a new story.

About the author

Robyn Bee is a writer who bumbles through life with all the grace of a honey-drunk bear. He is a lover of forest meadows, fantasy, history, and any sort of books that feature beautiful women and furious sword fights.

Expect stories of action, love, magic, and adventure; each one liberally sprinkled with spice.

Printed in Great Britain
by Amazon

55908844R00148